THE SHELTERING STONES SERIES

5

GOLDEN GIFT
FROM THE MEADOW

A NOVEL OF HISTORICAL FICTION

JOANN KLUSMEYER

Published by Innovo Publishing, LLC
www.innovopublishing.com
1-888-546-2111

Providing Full-Service Publishing Services for Christian Authors, Artists &
Ministries: Books, eBooks, Audiobooks, Music, Screenplays, Film & Curricula

THE SHELTERING STONES HISTORICAL FICTION SERIES

Book 5

GOLDEN GIFT FROM THE MEADOW:
A Novel of Historical Fiction

ISBN: 978-1-61314-735-1

Cover Design & Interior Layout: Innovo Publishing, LLC

Printed in the United States of America
U.S. Printing History
First Edition: 2021

Has God called you to create a Christian book, ebook, audiobook, music album,
screenplay, film, or curricula? If so, visit the ChristianPublishingPortal.com to
learn how to accomplish your calling with excellence. Learn to do everything
yourself, or hire trusted Christian Experts from our Marketplace to help.

CONTENTS

CHAPTER 1

THE HAYSTACK

She had gone as far as she could go. Not even one step more. It was late in September that the first cutting of hay had been piled in the sheep pasture, and it had now turned golden in the early fall sunshine. The second cutting of the rich prairie grass would be soon, and then the present stacks would be hauled to the barn for storage, or tarp-covered in the field. It happened that way on the prairie.

The young woman had traveled as far as her strength permitted. Total exhaustion had teamed with the infected gunshot wound in her leg and she knew she could go no farther, even though the church steeple she saw before her was within what should be easy walking distance. The sight of the cross on its tip had pulled her along for the last mile.

Beside her was the haystack. Tempting. She stopped and rested beside it, for the small protection it gave, and she tucked the basket of her most precious possession under the edge of the hay. She must shut her eyes and rest, and if she awoke, she might be able to reach the steeple and certain help.

Easing back against the fragrant hay, she heard the music.

The melody seemed to fill her entire being. So relaxing. Her exhaustion, hunger, pain and fright just floated away. She was no longer uneasy about the baby's future. There, in the warm sunshine on the sheep pasture, she sighed her final breath and permitted herself to be pulled upward toward the voices. Toward the music that seemed so close it had become a part of her.

So loving and enticing were those angel voices…and then she was among them. They were all around her…seeking ways to comfort her. She sighed, and drifted…floating….

The little dog was sniffing bushes and grass clumps for messages from other four-footed residents of the area, and he sniffed a message he could not read. Best he call for help, so he barked. And barked and barked.

The woman at the piano heard the bark and when it seemed to continue, she called the dog to the house. "Biskit! Come on, Biskit!" But Biskit did not come.

Eventually she realized she would have to go after him or listen to his yips and barks for who knew how long. Pressing a bonnet down on her hair, she walked out to the haystack.

Seeing the woman before she reached her, she called back to the house, "Daniel! Come please. Looks like trouble."

It was when Biskit finally hushed and bounded toward her that she heard the baby cry. What terrible thing had occurred to cause a baby to be under their haystack?

Momentarily ignoring the body of the young woman, she pushed aside the hay and was greeted with a red face and open mouth. And a lot of screaming from a set of healthy lungs.

Baby well clothed but soaking wet. Also obviously hungry…and for how long?

It was a known fact that babies were occasionally found on doorsteps of homes and churches, but under a haystack? And what had happened with the mother?

The field from which the hay had been cut was a large one. It was currently rented to a sheep farmer who grew special sheep for a certain kind of long fibered wool…merino, it was called. Great demand for it, actually.

There were at least two cuttings of the rich, prairie hay to be harvested each year in the sheep pasture, and sometimes three. These golden piles fed the sheep during the winter.

The field was also the playground of the community's children. Backing up, as it did, to the tract of land owned by Miss Josie, the originator of the Prairie Academy, groups of children tended to spill over into the sheep meadow with their games.

It bothered the sheep not one bit, and if they were occasionally hit by a flying ball, their luxuriant wool absorbed the blow. They continued their nibble and chew, and the production of small ones to carry on their work of producing wool.

The wool was highly prized, even before the government began to buy it up for uniforms. There was always a war to be expected, and nothing was better than wool for the clothing that got such hard use.

This sheep meadow was a favorite with the children. The fluid and intermingled ages of groups lent interest as they laughed and played their way through the summer. Any child who could slip away from duties at home could be sure of a welcome. Miss Josie's children had been among them.

Summers on the prairie of the Oklahoma Territory were a happy interlude of sun, fun and games tucked in between the beginning of fall, the inclement winter and the budding spring days that were filled with work. Everybody had a job.

What these children could look forward to were bowed heads over books, cramped fingers from chalk and slate, and hours with bent elbows, lesson books and lamplight on their family supper tables.

Miss Josie had been firm about schoolwork and home work, and her successors at the Prairie Academy were even harder, if possible.

Miss Carmelita and Miss Rosalie were indeed firm task masters, having been taught by the best. The two ladies might be Mellie and Rosie during parties or in family gatherings, but they were properly addressed when present at the school. Respect for teachers and other elders was one of the lessons taught.

There was one summer that stood out above the rest during times when memories were reviewed. There was Daniel, age almost fourteen, and the oldest of that particular group…also the acknowledged leader on this special summer.

Then there were Aaron and Adam, age almost twelve. Then came the second set of Miss Josie's twins, John and James, age ten. Next was Josie's daughter, Mutt, who had just cleared eight. Daniel's younger sister, Prissy, came in at six and a half and was followed quickly by Sunny and Rainey Day, a year younger.

These last two were grandchildren of Nettie Wilson, the aunt who took in Josie when her parents were killed. The twin girls were actually Catherine and Carolyn, daughters of Esther Wilson Day, who gave up her life when her daughters were born. She just found no strength to go on.

There were these nine children, ten when Miss Josie's youngest son, Barney (actually Barnabas, after Miss Josie's beloved tutor) could slip away from his mother. With ten players, there was no end of the games to be invented. The wide sheep pasture welcomed all others who could slip away and join in.

Most of the games began with a few trips sliding down the haystacks. Dust, grass seeds and injuries from splintering hay stems were a small price to pay for exuberant squeals and heels-over-head tumbles.

Then came the struggle through the loose hay to climb to the top…and the shrieks and screams and unsuccessful ducks in avoidance of someone bigger who was determined to push you back.

Finally, there would be the ultimate joy of standing on top of the wobbly center of the pile deciding when to slide. Or waiting for someone to give a shove.

Miss Francine Canfield, the teacher of the school in the nearby town of Shady Ridge had made a rhyme about the haystack. Of course, Miss Francine had rhymes about a lot of subjects, many of which the students in Prairie Academy were required to learn to read with correct emphasis.

Miss Carmelita demanded perfection and Miss Rosalie was the enforcer. Hard task masters, though they were, some of Miss Francine's rhymes were fun. The one about "Under the Haystack" was one of those.

It had come about when she was collecting her own pony from being shod at the blacksmith's that she had overheard a group of gray-haired loungers recounting the fun they had as boys on a haystack. Miss Francine, herself, had enjoyed her share of the screaming fun, the hay straw down her neck and bruises when someone behind her was sliding faster. Tumbling and rolling together, landing finally on the soft grass and scattered hay.

Miss Francine always saw things from all sides, Miss Rosalie had explained, and she wanted the students to learn to see everything from many angles. It was the only way good decisions could be made...she explained. Miss Josie had insisted the two teachers learn the rhyme when they were the students, so it was therefore worthy to be taught to the next generation.

UNDER THE HAYSTACK

Green prairie grass cut with the scythe
Waves of emerald, scattered on the field.
Insects, wildflowers, seed pods, all
The sharp scythe slays the prairie's yield.

Turned and raked and left in rows,
Moisture pulled by summer sun.
The hay is stacked with pitchforks high
For boys...a playground full of fun.

At this very moment, she could hear the shrieks and squeals from a nearby field. The sight and sounds of the fun tugged her back into her memory.

Climbing high and sliding fast
With grass straws ripping into backs.
King of the Hill, and other games,
Of Hide and Seek and Sneak Attacks.

And then, of course, there were treasures to be found on the ground when the hay was finally taken to the barn...or when it was consumed by the sheep.

And tunnels under...with whoop and holler
A fortress. Treasures on the ground.
Upon the earth and hid in stubble
A pen knife, long lost...now is found.

The torn end of a handkerchief
A button from a bygone shirt.
Foil that wrapped a stick of gum,
A watch chain pried up from the dirt.

It was true that summer fun must be enjoyed fast because there was always the looming specter of the eight months of school. Months of heads down at the slate and chalk and late-night work by lamplight.

However, fun must happen fast.
A haystack does not last forever.
It's not for dark and stormy nights,
Or cold and rainy winter weather.

Nodding at the mental picture it gave her, Miss Francine's pencil traveled on amid the jiggle of the buggy pulled by the shaggy, brown pony. She sighed for that summer fun, stored in the memory, so now it would provide a pleasure that could not go away.

Not just a joyful summer day
Of climbing, sliding fun begun.

They're making memories when they play,
And memories last when youth is done.

Memories…decades later…bring a smile
Sharp ends of hay won't itch and prick.
The speed in sliding down is greater,
The burs and dried out pods won't stick.

The wonderful thing about memory is that it conveniently sorts out the best pleasures to retain and often tosses out others that were disagreeable. A whole new picture can be painted.

The fields are now just sunny warm,
The swarm of hungry flies at bay.
Small moments on their golden slide
Become long summer days of play.

Through the magic of the years
Unpleasant memories? There are none!

Moments in the stacks of hay
Become—
Bright pictures in a youthful book.
Become—
A summer packed with fun.
Become—
The dreams of old, gray men.
As they now sit—
And doze and dream in summer sun.

This rhyme had been a difficult assignment in Miss Rosalie's class. Every inflection and hesitation must be just right. Especially that last part. Miss Rosalie would have it no other way. For what did these children know about "old, gray men" and what they would dream of? And why would this rhyme mean anything to them?

That year of 1907 was a magical one, and it became the last one before this particular group began to dissolve.

Daniel, the oldest, was the first to go, and he was to go far away. He was sent to a seminary up north where he would learn a lot of things, and many of them would be from his Bible. His very special Book.

There had been a story about that particular Bible. Ordinarily a boy of his age would not personally own such an expensive book, but his third great grandfather, who he had never heard of, had left this one to him. The Book had been many years finding its way to this particular child.

The old great grandfather, his long-ago relative, was named Daniel Ledbetter. He had been conscripted into the War of 1812, the war in which the fledgling United States would cut the last vestiges of force and the many ties that had bound it to other countries. The "cord" so to speak, had been severed from the motherland, and the new country now breathed on its own. All because of the War of 1812.

The first Daniel had donned the uniform and sword… picked up his firearm and beloved Bible…and had gone to war when called upon. It was the right thing to do.

The old sword now had a few rust spots near the hilt, the firearm had been cleaned and oiled, though the residue of the whale oil had disintegrated long ago. The leaves of the Book had a few rips and some smudges of dirt that indicated strong usage. It had evidently gone with him into battle.

It would have been so wonderful if there had been more information about him. Evidently he was just one of so many. When a person is living in the midst of the fear and the danger, there is often no thought of leaving words to the future for who might wonder about it.

However, when the old man left his earthly life behind, he had instructed that the Book and the weapons be handed down to his first grandson.

The firm of solicitors at that time had tried for years to do this, but it seemed that only girls were being born into that family and after a marriage name change, they were impossible to locate. Or at least very time consuming.

Also, it was a time of national transition and whole families were on the move toward the west. Following the call of the sun, they said.

Young Daniel's own great grandparents had been victims of a sudden disaster, but the grandsons of the first legal solicitors persevered and had eventually found his grandmother, Carlotta Owens, "somewhere out on the prairie." Clearly the next nearest relative.

Challenged by the difficulty, and with the persistence of many solicitors, they had managed to find her and congratulated themselves on their success.

This had happened shortly after Carlotta's son, also named Daniel, had been born. It was then that the inheritance had finally reached its rightful heir. The old Kiowa doctor, Miz Gray Owl, attending young Daniel's birth, had said there would be a surprise about their young Daniel. As it turned out, there had been a number of them.

The boy attended school at the Prairie Academy under the above-mentioned taskmasters named Miss Carmelita and Miss Rosalie. At age twelve he had completed all requirements offered for Certification to Teach.

There was a summer of fun during which he turned thirteen. Shortly after, the boy was sent north to the boarding seminary for higher education. With that move, the "group personality" of the neighborhood children changed.

It was the next year that Miss Josie's twins, Aaron and Adam, were placed with Uncle Jefferson to help with his special Conamara horses. Pioneer life demanded that all men become acquainted with the current most reliable method of travel, and the two boys spent the summer there, learning to break young animals to the rigors of a saddle and the restriction of being harnessed.

That same year, Mutt Cullen, Miss Josie's only daughter, and Priscilla Carpenter, Daniel's sister, had been reined in by their mothers and sent to learn the art of sock darning, patching and adjusting the size of dresses to match growth.

Girls aged eight and nine were deemed to be the perfect age for these lessons, as set forth by Miz O'Grady, who had been "trained by the best." Those lessons consumed a lot of each summer afternoon.

By the end of the summer, the girls were introduced to the mystery of paper patterns and how to create them. Also how to use them to cut new dress fabric.

Sunny and Rainy Day teamed up with Barney Cullen and several of the younger set. The haystacks were still their prime center of interest.

The next summer, Adam and Aaron were moved on to their father's blacksmith shop and introduced to the hammer and anvil, and the art of keeping the coals blazing hot.

Their vacated places in the corral of Uncle Jefferson were filled by James and John, Miss Josie's second set of twins.

By then, Mutt and Prissy were making simple items of clothing for themselves. Skirts, aprons and underwear…and were taught the fancy work of making hankies and scarves. With a sigh, Miz O'Grady agreed to take on the Day twins.

The wonderful summer of 1907 became a fond memory to be tucked away and there, within their memory, the stolen moments of fun became a whole, uninterrupted summer of joy. The mind can do wonderful things with a few pleasant afternoons.

Daniel Carpenter, now boarding at the seminary and accustomed to taking schoolwork seriously, bent his mind toward every subject he could manage. His marks were so high that the professors smiled together and agreed that he could very well be the new nation's next great preacher, and couldn't the country use one?

The boy had a month of vacation each summer for the next three years, and that was hardly enough time even to find his place within the fabric of his hometown.

So much happened so quickly at that period of time that by the time he was filled in on local events, it was time to leave again, so his interest naturally felt more at home at the seminary than at the Corners. There was no way to help that.

The year Mutt was eleven, she was steered by her mother to learn to play the organ. Her mom, Josie, had firmly insisted. Here was Violette, Miss Francine's stepdaughter, who was a bonified music teacher. Giving lessons and all. So why not learn?

The girl loved Violette, and that was what made the lessons bearable. She learned adequately, if not artistically.

For the next years, the large stone house of her parents rang with hymns and popular songs when she could manage to find sheet music written for the organ. A redeeming factor of having to take lessons was that a girl's skill at the organ, however limited, was an important social asset and group singing was one of the most used sources of entertainment among young people.

It was when Mutt was fourteen and Prissy twelve that the magic thing happened. It was then that Gwinnie and Kristie MacLaughlin had other things to do and needed help. Though the owners of the Cookie Jar managed the business fairly well during this period, there were a lot of times that they brought the two younger girls in to fill in the gaps. Mid-afternoons, for instance, when trade was light.

Also for an hour in the morning if one or the other of the owners was occupied. The breakfast rush could hardly be handled by one person. Someone cooked and someone served. The younger girls were delighted to be permitted to do either.

They earned a few coins, but that was next to nothing compared to the fun of it all. The prestige of wearing the little white cap and the frilly apron that hardly covered their tummies. Handing out food, counting up the charge and making change. Like school, only a lot more fun.

Daniel, not yet out of his teens, dropped by and was served by his former playmate. He looked more than twice at Mutt, now a glowing barely fourteen. *Hmmm. Made good use of her growing up time, she did.*

He might not have noticed the gradualness of it if he had been continuously at the Corners, but absence gives new eyesight. Did her golden (hazel?) eyes always have that twinkle, and those flecks of brown? That chin dimple? Was it always there, and the tanned complexion setting off the wave-of-wheat-colored hair?

Somehow she had managed to acquire these attributes in his absence, and his mind could project how she would look in a couple more years. Here she was, hair pulled back and tied with a ribbon. Frilly white cap on top!

When there were no customers, she came to sit with him at the tiny ice cream table on the chairs made of curly wire that looked fragile…but weren't.

Chin in hands, elbows on the table, she begged for stories about how it was at his school, so far away. She seemed so interested, it was difficult to resist telling her of this and that. Then it was time to leave again and return to school.

This was just after the time that the officials at the school decided that, along with their other studies, the advanced divinity students could be offered a rudimentary medical training. Daniel was among those chosen as the test cases.

Along with other duties, a bit of medical training could only be a plus in the ministry which would, of course, be their eventual duties. Especially for those whose grades were high enough to allow for the extra subject load.

Daniel was fascinated by it all. Then a student position opened up with one of the medical professors, and Daniel was first choice to fill it. That year, his summer vacation was reduced to three separate long weekends. Hardly time enough to say "Hi" and "Goodbye."

And now there was talk of war. He had brought home his inherited Bible, sword and firearm and handed them to his mother for safe keeping. Miss Carlotta, his mom, had said nothing, but sighed for what was not told her. Leaving her his relics told her a lot more than she wanted to know.

Something different was surely afoot, and his mother was certain she would not be in favor, nor would she be able to prevent it. So she put away her son's treasures and smiled. And asked no questions.

Her son knew his mother would not be in favor, nor would she be able to prevent it, so he did not burden her with the knowledge. He had, however, on a tiny scrap of paper, sketched the three items of his inheritance from that other "Daniel" and he tucked the paper into the pages of the new Bible he had been issued at school.

He nodded with satisfaction. It would be a bookmark, and a tether…or perhaps a lifeline that would connect him back to the Corners whenever he saw it.

He did, however, tell his mother that he was being transferred for further study, and that he would now be in Kentucky. He would send her his new address when he got there. His mother took a deep breath and put a smile upon her face. She knew, of course. Mothers can be very wise.

The clickety-grind of the drivers on the metal track lulled the young man into sorting his thoughts. It was late at night, and the engine pulling his railcar now passed through the rolling, knobby hills of central Missouri, though none would know it.

The train windows were black with a reflection of the interior of the train, lighted by the tiny gas lights along the inside of the car.

Daniel sat in the comfortable seat reviewing the few hours he had spent at the Corners, and the face that had peered up at him from the ice cream table in the Cookie Jar. It was truly amazing what little girls could do with a couple of years and a ruffled apron. They hovered delicately between little girls, squealing in their play and young ladies, with hair pinned up and dresses lengthened.

Remembering the latest rhymes of Miss Francine that often decorated the Cookie Jar, he smiled and thought of a butterfly, hovering between the cocoons they had just exited and the float to earth after their final eggs were deposited for the next generation.

Then he chided himself. *Come on, now, Daniel. Thinking like that will do you no good.*

So he shook himself and turned his face toward the black windows with a reflection of the train's interior. His own face looked back, momentarily startling him. Rounded chin was now chiseled around his jawbone. Nose lengthened. Hair darker and hairline more pronounced. What had happened while he had buried his head in the books at the seminary?

Such a change in such a short time. He hardly recognized his own appearance. He would soon be eighteen.

His new position as professor's assistant had drawn attention to him, as well as others in his class. He remembered the gist of a recent lecture given by a visiting professor. "When you climb, remember and expect that he who stands taller than the rest, draws the most fire from the enemy." And the lecturer had continued, "But remember that someone will always be taller than the rest, and every time it will be someone who is brave."

The old man's eyes had pierced each member of his class as he had made certain they understood. "Will it be you who stands taller, or will you be always looking up to the one who does?"

That was when the war rumblings that had started in Europe had become in earnest. Year 1914, and the restlessness of Germany caused small skirmishes in France. There were those Americans living abroad who had seen their resident doctors pulled from their midst to care for the casualties of the skirmishes. The answer was simple. America must send them some doctors of their own.

A number of prominent medical men were conscripted to go, and along with them would be the top tier of medical students. Daniel, of course, was among them.

The young men bent their heads together and discuss the happenings. Was this assignment to be a plus or a minus? A plum or a lemon? Hard to say, but it was only to be a three-month rotation, and he was a young, eager student, as the others were. Also, how bad could three months be?

How could he help but be excited, but he did not tell his mother. Miss Carlotta was left to wonder, also knowing there would be a reason why she had not been told. It had been arranged that she would write to him at the station in Kentucky with letters to be forwarded on, and his answering letters would be from there. Three months was not a long time. Was it?

To France. The trip would take fifteen days, maybe more if the weather "kicked up" along the way. What would he find there? As the driver wheels of the train ground their way forward, his thoughts continued. He was again amazed at how he had gone to school to be a preacher and had ended up in the army in the field of medicine.

Clever, actually, the way it had all happened. And there was the old riddle as to which came first, the chicken or the egg. As a class assignment, he and his classmates had discussed, at length, which should be foremost, the saving of a soul or the saving of a life. Obviously, there had to be life, in order to be considering the saving of a soul…but then, if life was lost, the saving of the soul should have already been accomplished. Back and forth it went but it was never settled.

This was the year that Mutt Cullen taught school. Not that she intended to, it was more like it was just the way it happened.

Neecie Bramwall, one of the students who had done well at the Prairie Academy, had been encouraged by Miss Carmelita to teach in her own school, due to her excellent Certification testing score. She and a friend had teamed up, and for several years had conducted Midway Academy, two miles north of the Corners.

The friend had suffered a run of bad luck, health wise, and would be obliged to miss a year. Neecie was in a bad state. Handling a classroom of twenty students was possible if nothing went wrong, but something always went wrong. At least there was always the potential for it.

Finally, Neecie's younger sister had reluctantly volunteered, but would have had to miss her own final year at Miss Carmelita's school. It was Miss Carmelita, herself, who had suggested that Neecie check with Mutt who had qualified but preferred operating the Cookie Jar and other pursuits.

Mutt had thought it over. Age fourteen. Barely. The exact age that Miss Carmelita had started teaching, also Miss Francine. Eve Adams had started at fourteen when the community of Enterprise had become desperate. So now it was her turn. Fourteen must be a good year.

Fortunately, a lesson plan had already been established, so she took her place with the toddlers of the Territory, teaching the five- to seven-year-olds. Neecie Bramwell was so pathetically grateful for her help that Mutt (who then became Miss Mery) had actually enjoyed periods of pleasure and self-righteousness over helping a fellow human in a time of "trouble."

When not otherwise occupied, Prissy, Daniel's little sister, tagged along with her and found a way to make herself useful to the young students.

In due time, the ship carrying the emergency medical staff had docked. First port was Liverpool, England. A sorting out happened, with some personnel being left and others picked up, and they moved on to the English Channel and the French port.

France, at last. Even Daniel was appalled at the conditions at the makeshift hospitals. Lack of medication. No actual ambulances. They used only the donated motor cars of some of the wealthier residents.

Besides being inadequate to transport the injured, these private cars were of such varying models and makes, and had suffered such hard usage, they were in constant need of repair.

Lack of special parts unique to each model, along with no skilled mechanics, the donated cars were less than useful, though they filled the paperwork requirement space on the roster of availability. They were counted as operable but were not actually usable. Poor record keeping.

That was the sort of thing to be noted in the records that would be kept by the medical students such as Daniel. If (actually, when) a full-scale war broke out and if (actually, when) America was pulled in, some great changes would be made. And they would be made in a hurry. Therefore, it would be well to have advance knowledge of at least some of them.

It was decided that there must be only one uniform type of vehicle that would accommodate the injured, and it was crucial to have a stock of interchangeable parts. This vehicle should be made to carry at least six of the injured as well as a medic and a driver.

Sanitation must be upgraded. Utility personnel such as cooks and laundry help must be provided for relief of the overworked medical staff. These small details of living must be handled by others in order to free the doctor's time and ease the effort of the nurses. No skill could afford to be wasted.

The students made lists and drew grafts and they figured costs of acquisition. These specially picked young men must set their minds to producing more efficient ways of operation, for certainly the surgeons had no time to do it.

Daniel had been taught, in some part, by his mother who had been in Miss Josie's first class. She had been one of the "Blossoms in the Grass" that Miss Josie had been so proud of. Her son, Daniel, had often been Miss Carlotta's student in her class of one, as well as attending the Prairie Academy. Now he competently figured requirements for the war that was for certain coming at them. Full speed.

At the end of the prescribed three months, replacements arrived and Daniel's group was sent back to Kentucky. The young men who had left the halls of the training center returned much smarter. The three-month stint had aged them about three years in the knowledge of the world around them. Also, in the evil that humans could inflict upon other humans.

Newspapers came to the Corners, and were, with luck, sometimes dated as recently as a week ago. And there was always that grumbling that happened in Europe over something or other. It was read about but it was hardly a concern of theirs. Hadn't it always been that way?

And do you think we'll get any rain? It was next to impossible to concentrate on something so far away…when the growing crops were just outside the window.

Closer to home, there was speculation in the blacksmith shop. "Can you believe the price of that fancy wool on the backs of them sheep over back'a the church yard? Looks like the government is intent on buying it all! Whatever for? Wouldn't you think the big wigs back east would have enough other things to be concerned over? Buying up sheep wool…I tell you!

"Besides…what are those Germans doing messing around over in Poland…or whatever it was that the name of the place…? France, too. Don't them German folks have enough to do, making them fancy cars that cost so much? Daimler, the name of it was, wasn't it…? Wonder how it'd be to drive one of those babies?

"And have you noticed how them boys of Brad Cullen's have took to the blacksmithing? Especially them two oldest twins. Brad'll have 'im a good crew if he don't let 'em wander off like young men seem to do."

Those in the blacksmith shop found a lot to talk about and covered most subjects every day. The wool on the back of the sheep was a lot easier to understand than the problem of using private cars for ambulances in France.

Adam and Aaron, the twins who were making such good blacksmiths, studied the week-old newspapers. "How long, do you think it'll be? For a fact, there'll be a call-up for soldiers. Wouldn't be chance of that war comin' on and bein' over before we get a chance at it, would you?"

They and other groups of young men in their teens gathered and talked. What'd a body have to do to get in the army? They get paid good money, too! For marching and shooting. Imagine that!

Mutt Cullen was barely over fourteen and a half when the Midway Academy let out for the summer. During the time she had been helping Neecie at the school, she had been offered three different areas if she'd just come and bring her "New York" education along with her. "Just name your price, Miss…uh… what was it that your name is?"

"Miss Mery" just smiled and shook her head. "Other plans," she told them. Actually, it had been a fun year and she was glad to know she could do it if the need arose. But now she actually did have other plans.

The music that had been forced into her head and hands had actually seeded and grown, and melodies now whirled around in her mind that she must pick out by ear on the organ keys. Only for her own fun, of course.

Another thing that intrigued her was the continued writings of Miss Carmelita, actually her cousin. Any little thing that happened around town, her former teacher could convert into words and let it sail through the mail to Aunt Sharon in New York. Aunt Sharon made a very good literary agent.

Sometimes she sent things straight to the newspaper to feed their column, "Voice from the Prairie." This column was salted with any happening that she thought might interest someone who had not been there, and it was worded in a cozy, neighborly way.

In due time, a check would come flying back.

If Miss Carmelita's reporting was the "salt," then Miss Francine's poems were certainly the "pepper," but they were never sent in by Miss Francine, herself. They were only given to Miss Josie, and the former teacher did the sending on.

Miss Josie, amazed at Francine's skill with rhymes, sent them on as fast as one came to her that she thought the New Yorkers would like. Checks came back, and the practical Miss Francine turned them into writing paper and new library books for her school in Shady Ridge.

So Mutt, who read everything that came into her hands, read her cousin's stories with interest...sometimes saying to herself, "Now, if I had written that I would have added...." whatever it was that was in her mind.

Then her agile mind reminded her of what she knew to be true. She admitted to herself, "Of course, I could have written the whole thing if I'd tried. Haven't I done it enough times in school? I know all the rules for stories, narrations and lists."

Then a thought! *Hey, there are papers in other big towns in the east. New York isn't the only place. I could create my own market. I'm older than Carmelita was when Miss Josie first sent away her stories. I wonder....*

But for a long time, it was just a continued "wondering," as the girl found other things to do. Growing up on the prairie could be a complicated and consuming activity.

The newspapers had almost nothing to say about England's unfortunate alliance with some little place in Europe... was it Belgium or something or other? There were not many who would have read about it, or cared if they had. It was not like if it had happened in Kansas. Say now, that would be something to talk about.

It was nearer 1915 that a few readers had noticed England's precarious position. It was noticed by a Medical group called "Washington 21," or something, and there were a few other places...Kentucky?...that the matters were discussed.

Miss Carlotta commented to Daniel's father, Ralph, that...wasn't that where Daniel was? And what, exactly, is he doing there? The parents just shook their heads in silence. They could only guess and none of the guesses seemed good. Then England was pulled into the skirmishes.

CHAPTER 2

Volunteers to the British army became more sparse by the month, until in 1916, forced conscriptions had begun. No able bodied person was passed over just because of what he did for a living. Surgeons and doctors were called up to man the guns right along with farmers and sheepherders. Consequently, the medical personnel shortages were becoming precarious…and dangerous.

Long before that, however, the American Red Cross had begun to assemble just about anything an army medical corps would need except the actual personnel. There was no government funding, so the tireless Red Cross began to amass private funds on its own.

It was patently OBVIOUS to them that America WOULD BE a part of the next conflict, and it was the nature of the Red Cross to be READY. So, when England had placed their trained medical personnel in the trenches along with everyone else, the doctor shortage reached an unsustainable peak, and it came as no surprise to the far-sighted American Red Cross.

The messages came to America, (hat in hand, so to speak), begging for doctors.

"How many?" they were asked.

"A thousand," was the reply.

The generous American response came back, "Two thousand will be there in a week." It was a bit more than a week for some, but it included many more than the two thousand promised.

A full-page ad in a St. Louis paper for anybody who could do something, filled up the quota for support personnel. Ditch diggers who could sign their name stood beside weapons-research personnel, cooks and hunter-trappers. Daniel and his fellows were enlisted without being given a choice or even having to sign their names.

Of course they would be the first to go. They had BEEN there, and they KNEW the problems. They had even created ANSWERS to some of the expected problems.

The first increment of support personnel to go had been literally scraped from the edges of the nation and molded into working groups within days of time. Training sessions were held during the days of the sailing of the ship. Classes were held on the rolling decks when the sun shone.

The private civilian doctors practiced standing for hours to toughen soft leg muscles. Cooks practiced cooking, producing massive quantities of SOMETHING with the most available ingredients in the least time at the least cost. The end result was often edible, depending on the extent of the hunger.

The fledgling British war personnel descended *en masse* upon France, where there was absolutely no system or structure… but that was where the casualties were. It became Britain's war, using American personnel, on France's soil and it produced its own tug of war of responsibility for duties and operating turf. It took time to get itself sorted out and rolling.

Bottom line fact was that the injured were paying the price.

With pure British logic, the local racetrack in Rouen, France, was selected as the operational hub of medical service because it was roomy, flat and had certain usable buildings already in place.

No matter that the terrain was low and sandy and enjoyed the heavy rainy season of that part of the Seine valley climate. The area grew wonderful grapes and very soggy inhabitants. Damp and musty living quarters and eternally wet feet. There were jokes about their toes becoming webbed together.

Daniel and his fellows were stationed in the barns that surrounded a fringe of muddy paddock. Exhausted personnel slept on any flat surface they could find that was reasonably dry, and they were too done-in from work to complain. Wind coming off the river water flowed freely through the inadequate walls originally built for animals.

Tents were erected on the parade ground for the female personnel and were equipped with a wood-burning potbellied stove. The first increment of nurses arrived and they were the "specially chosen." They were older and more seasoned than those who would come later.

Upon arrival, these angels of mercy were issued uniform attire in the form of long dresses made of heavy blue serge fabric, the better to provide cover for the layers of flannel under-drawers and wool stockings they would need to keep their feet and legs from petrifying from the cold. Not to say the loss of toes from frostbite.

When possible, shoes and stockings were changed midway of their working shift. Damp ones were hung in the tents with stoves to dry them out for the next day.

The nurses' first duty of the morning was to thaw out the medicine that had frozen solid in the night, even though the ineffective stove had been kept burning. The bottom-line fact was that canvas tents were notoriously hard to heat.

The injured came in by train, on flatbed barges, and in ambulances, though many of the vehicles that were still used were the donated private cars. Daniel and other seminary students wore the chaplain's cross as well as the medical insignia, the better for both staff and personnel to know who was who and was therefore qualified to do what, and for how long.

His first night of that duty followed a long day. He was stationed at "incoming" and charged with making the decision as what was to be done first. His first patient, a young girl, was carried in and placed on his table. First glance told him that one leg was gone from above the knee, and the stump had been hastily wrapped with muddy rags to staunch the bleeding.

His second glance saw an oval, lightly tanned face and hazel eyes that stared up at him…wonderingly. Obviously in total shock, which was often the first anesthetic. She was maybe twelve years old.

He had been on his feet for fourteen hours. His weary eyes saw what seemed to be an expression mirroring one that had stared up at him, chin in hands, elbows on the tiny ice cream table beside the wire chairs that looked fragile...but weren't.

He shivered violently and uncontrollably from head to foot, and leaned forward, bracing his hands on the board where the girl lay. He had at least two hours of his shift yet to go...at best. Those medical personnel on "incoming" triage could not afford wayward thoughts. *Square up, man*...he chided himself.

A concerned voice beside him inquired, "Doctor...?"

He stiffened his shoulders and answered, "I'm fine. Really."

A sympathetic response came, "It's these long hours, friend. Takes some getting used to. Mind gets to playing tricks after the first ten hours."

His reply, "I imagine so." With that, he squared his feet flat on the floor to brace his courage, and began with cold, stiff fingers to remove the putrid dressing that had staunched the bleeding and had perhaps saved her life. So far.

The experienced nurse was wielding her needle that would bring comfort to the girl. Then she began to wash the young face, and the beautiful hazel eyes slowly closed. Maybe they would open. Maybe not. One could hope.

Muddy garments were cut away and a gown wrapped around her, and the nurse worked with him to clean mud away from the stump without causing the bleeding to re-start, and then she was moved into surgery for the other doctors to do...what? The act of moving her made her no longer his concern. He would be open for the next...well...whoever it was.

Thoughts were hard to shake. She was just a girl, living where she had been born. None of this war was of her making and certainly not all casualties wore uniforms.

At midnight, Daniel was relieved by another student, still rubbing the sleep from his eyes. And trying not to gag at the putrid smell that hung over the room. Daniel no longer noticed the stench. He had not realized that he had become used to it and didn't even realize the smell was there.

He walked out of the room shaking his head. There are some things that the human race just should not get used to. But he and the others needed to get used to it quickly.

The barn where he was to sleep was dimly lit by candle lanterns, most of which had been extinguished by the wind blowing through the walls. Deciding against undressing, he wrapped himself into the thick robe that had been furnished and crawled onto the shelf that had been assigned to him.

His shelf was middle way of three, with one below and one above. He was grateful. How could he possibly have climbed up one step, and if he must lower himself to reach his bed, he would surely fall to the floor from exhaustion.

He stretched himself out onto the shelf, melting onto it in his total exhaustion, and he pulled up the meager cover. After that, he knew nothing until he was standing on the unstable top of a very large haystack.

He noted that he was totally exhausted from the climb to the top of the haystack, but he had made it…though still a bit shaky. It would be better if his footing were more stable, but, no matter. He was there, now.

Before he was ready to slide down, his feet began to slip. He relaxed, because he knew there would be no way to stop on the slippery golden straw, and the landing was always soft, or if not, at least not sudden.

But this time it was sudden. This landing was accompanied by a screech of metal against wood, followed by crashes and scrapes. Then a force pitched him forward and rolled him out onto the ground (floor…?).

His hands felt a surface of rough boards instead of hay stubble. The screeching, splintering sound was still happening, and the person who had landed on top of him, was attempting to remove himself from a combined tangle of blankets and legs.

A rushing gale of wind blew out the candle lanterns, but the light around him was replaced by a much brighter one. The medical students who had been so abruptly aroused, as he had been, stood aghast, staring at the blazing flames consuming the end of their sleeping barn.

A gaping hole had appeared at the northeast corner nearest to the river and the shelling action. The single-wall construction had given away and portions of it were leaning in multiple directions. Stray rocket?

Had they really been that close to the front? Apparently so. Shells were now crackling like popcorn in a pan as the "home guard," who had been assigned to the protect the medical compound, moved into action.

Screaming rockets sailed across the water, reflecting a fiery strip of brightness on the surface of the river. A series of blasts and an interlude of nerve-wracking silence, then a heavily laden barge appeared through a pause in the firing. The barge was loaded with wounded and moved across the river under the protecting barrage of the home guard rockets.

Then the popping of shells and the scream of rockets began again with a vengeance.

Daniel and his associates were moved, stumbling from exhaustion, into another building and told they were free to find themselves a place to sleep on the floor, if they could. They could.

Amazingly, their young, sleep-starved bodies were now asleep in minutes, lying practically on top of one another. Weary and aching legs were sometimes arched over their neighbor's weary and aching arms, and neither of them knew or cared.

Things had to get better. The Americans began to make changes.

The British, in their logical efficiency, took in the wounded as they came, signed them in and attended to their needs in the order they were received. It had seemed to them to be the fair way, and no one had an exceptionally long wait.

It worked, except for those who would have likely survived, with a bit of help given more quickly. These often paid for the "fairness" with their remaining shreds of their lives.

The Americans instituted the simple triage. The wounded were sorted into three groups, those likely to survive, those who might survive, and those who were practically hopeless. In this order, they were treated. The percentage of survival went up with marked speed.

Another problem was the vermin. Animals in the woodland that were killed in crossfire, had shed their hungry fleas and lice, and the insects merely transferred themselves to the human injured and dying who were lying tossed conveniently about. Consequently, the whole medical compound became infested.

One of the medical students, an engineering major, designed a "bathhouse" with heated water in barrels. When there was sunshine, the warmth helped to heat the water. Otherwise, precious fossil heat was used.

Every victim was first funneled through the bathhouse and was stripped and washed. If he was unable to do it for himself, there was help. Then he was given a hospital-issue gown and a blanket covering. These were furnished, incidentally, from the inventory of the American Red Cross and had been purchased primarily with private funds. In America.

Stripped off clothing was all piled in a vat of insecticide treated water, to be sorted out later. All vermin died in the vat. Any garment usable was retained as there was a need for every item of clothing of any size, and if the garment was too far gone, there was always a need for cleaning rags.

The medical personnel were pathetically and intensely grateful for no more lice and fleas.

What gave the students the most pleasure, however, and created more than one satisfied grin, was the fact that the whole bathhouse was built with German prisoner labor. The same labor later repaired the sleeping barn where Daniel had been sleeping, and the walls were reinforced and weatherproofed before the group was moved back into it.

After sleeping on pallets on the floor, the warmer sleeping barn and the off-the-floor shelf-beds seemed almost luxurious. No longer did a sleeping body turned over in your face, and a movement of your leg did not bring on a startled yell from an awakened bed partner.

Another thing happened. The Americans took over the mail service for their own personnel. The ships that docked with supplies brought bags of letters that had been sorted en route.

The rapid receipt of letters could revive the whole medical compound. Daniel's mother wrote several times a week, and the letters had piled up into heaps waiting to be delivered. Now he could count on SOMETHING reaching him two or three times a week.

Granted, there were the occasions when he was too exhausted to read them, but they made such a comforting pouch under his pillow, and such a welcome greeting in the morning.

Back at the corners, Mutt decided, finally, to put action to her words. She had gathered newspapers, the age didn't matter for this purpose, and looked for the addresses. She had listed these in the order she thought she would contact them.

This sort of routine research was a chore she had always liked while in Miss Carmelita's class. Her cousin was always organized and she expected the rest of the world to be the same. Maybe it was a family trait, but Mutt found she worked better in orderly surroundings.

The girl had also composed a letter that would, she hoped, insure that whoever opened it first would not trash it, but send it on to someone who could make a decision. She had been clear in her quest for information and now she had only to prepare the requests and mail them.

Armed with paper, a sharpened pencil and her list of addresses, she settled herself on the bench attached to the outside table under the cottonwoods. The Cookie Jar was close by, should she need a snack.

The cottonwood trees, planted by Mr. Digby who had been such a help to Miss Josie, whispered through their leaves in the south breeze and dancing dapples of sunshine peeked through them, making moving patterns on the tables.

Pencil poised, she began to write. "Dear Daniel...."

Startled, she looked at the words under her pencil lead. Like a carved statue, she sat...staring...pencil still poised. It was more than somewhat disconcerting when the pencil took over on its own. The wooden stick with the lead filling was usually obedient and waited for orders, but not always.

As she stared at her own hand...at the impatient pencil with a mind of its own...and at the sheets of paper before her... pictures moved through her mind. Colorful pictures of that wonderful summer of 1907.

...Struggling to keep up with games, and Daniel's strong hand lifting her into position.

...Standing at the foot of the haystack beside Daniel, who stood with Prissy on one side and herself on the other.... The boy climbing slowly and holding the two smaller girls steady until their feet found footing in the slippery straw.

...Pictures of him reaching in his pocket and taking out a brightly colored snail shell he had found while fishing in the stream.

...Or, breaking his cookie and giving her half because the dog had taken her cookie from her hand.

He could be pushing the two swings that still hung in the cottonwoods beside her. Herself in one and Prissy in the other. Four older brothers she had, but it was Daniel who saw when she could use some help. Or maybe some fun.

Games.... Dropping the handkerchief behind her in the circle game, and then running slow enough that she could catch him. And in later years, listening patiently to the whole song when she had learned a new one on the organ.... And insisting he had enjoyed it.

And then, most of all, sitting on the wire chair in the Cookie Jar and telling stories to her while she watched the black, black eyes light up with this or that thought. He could have been somewhere else, doing something fun with her brothers or his other friends, but he sat there with her. She could see him now with his wide smile, tiny patch of whiskers trying to grow on the outside of his jawbone. She could admire the way his eyebrows formed along the ridge above his eyes, and his black, black lashes just fitting within the arch of brow when he looked at her.

And then the pencil began to move again. After all, this was something she had intended to do for sometime, and just did not realize it until now. The pencil knew that now was a good time to start and it had encouraged her in the best way it could.

She had known subconsciously that there would come a time that she would hold the pencil and think of others who would see her words. She had known she would write words for them to read for information and pleasure.

They would be words that interested the people...or maybe they would be words the reader needed to hear...and they would be the words that only she could write. When that time came, she would know what to write. Perhaps that time had come.

So she watched as her pencil flowed along on the lines of the paper, reminiscing on happy times with Daniel. He had listened carefully to her that day in the Cookie Jar, so he would still listen to her now, even though she didn't even know where he was...or what he was doing.

Inside, he was still just...Daniel.

When she had finished three pages, she signed off, folded it and slipped it in an envelope. She would see Miss Carlotta in a day or so and get his address.

She gathered up her newspaper addresses and stationary and put them in her writing bag. Today was clearly not a day for writing to New York. Or Pennsylvania. Or wherever. That would be later.

She had just taken a mental tour through the most pleasant parts of her life, and that was enough. It was a starting place for the rest of her life.

Besides, she had to walk down the mile and a quarter to Miss Carlotta's house and get that address. And she had it do it now. She could not wait a day or so. She ran most of the way.

Miss Carlotta wrote the needed words on a slip of paper and handed it to her.

"Just so you'll have it for later, dear," she had whispered. Her mouth had smiled, but her eyes were filled. She slipped her arm around Mutt's shoulders in a quick and gentle hug and the girl knew that she had done the right thing. Or maybe it was just the pencil that had done it.

She felt her face lift up toward the woman's smiling face and plant a light, quick kiss on the side of her chin, the way she sometimes did to her mom when something special had gone between them. Without looking back, she slipped through the door and ran the whole mile and a quarter back home.

What's gotten into me? she asked herself. Both her hand and her mouth seemed to have taken on a life of their own. Imagine! Writing Daniel's name when she hadn't even been thinking of him, and then kissing his mom on her chin. She had never, ever, kissed another woman than Miss Josie, her mom, and Miz Nettie, her great aunt who seemed like a grandma. Since she didn't have one.

But the feeling she had all day was so soft and comfortable inside her that she began thinking of things to tell Daniel next time…for there would certainly be a next time. How his mom must miss him!

There were many things to write…incidents while teaching school, things overheard in the Cookie Jar, some of the funny hats the Irish girls made, and that ladies actually bought. And wore.

There was the hat that was covered with buttons, big and little and sewed to every scrap of the felt, and they were not all new buttons. Some of them were even chipped, and they were in all colors. But that hat wasn't actually as bad as the one that had a brim but no top in the crown. Across the top was a spider web made of crocheted thread and it looked very real.

"And that Bridie, you remember how funny she is? She made the little black spider from thread and put a red dot of a bead on its back. A black widow!"

One letter regaled him with her own difficulty with knitting. His sister, Prissy, was funneled into Mrs. O'Grady's tutelage with her…to learn knitting and crocheting. She described her battle with the crazy shaped needle and the scratchy wool thread, and how difficult it was to "turn the heel" of the sock.

She even told him how his sister was being punished because she sassed her mother about learning. But now she crochets such beautiful things.

About two weeks after that letter, Daniel received a soft, lumpy package that spilled out two gray wool socks with a red strip knitted around the top. They were a perfect fit. And very, very warm on feet that stood for ten to twelve hours at a time… on a floor that was perpetually cold and damp.

His first answering letter was addressed to Miss Merytaten Cullen, but on the inside it said, "Dear Angel." He explained that he had always known that angels bring good messages, and that her message was so perfect for his awful days, he knew it was from an angel.

He also shared that just because she didn't get an answer to every letter, it wasn't that he didn't like them. It was just that at the end of some work shifts, there wasn't enough of him left to write a coherent word. "But," he had added, "That doesn't mean I can't read and re-read them, whether I am coherent or otherwise."

Once there came in the mail a square, tightly tied package for him. Packed with cookies. Inside was the note from Kristie, the Cookie Jar owner.

"Mutt ordered these for you. She said they must be molasses cookies so they wouldn't dry out and be sandwiched with marshmallow so they wouldn't break in transit. So if you don't like them, your fight is with her."

With the first bite of the cookie, he was back in the Cookie Jar. There was something unmistakable about the taste of the "Corners." Treats were usually shared among the overworked and lonely, but these cookies he hid in his locker. He needed them for times when there wasn't much left of himself. The special cookies seemed to bring back some of what was missing.

It was on her fifteenth birthday that it was time to move a step farther. She took up her first letter to him and also the second one, (she was taught that a copy of a personal letter must always be retained to be certain of what she had written and whether questions had been answered).

She read these two letters with a critical eye. After the second reading, she determined that, by a subtle changing of the wording and the actual names, she could make them less personally meant for a certain person. She could make them more chatty, stressing more graphically and colorfully the good times she'd had when they were younger.

Picking at random a paper in Pennsylvania, she enclosed the two re-written letters, stating that she wondered if the paper had a place for them as encouragement for everyone to write to their own particular soldier.

Back came a letter with a check for twenty dollars. The accompanying letter stated that they would be glad to use them, and by accepting the check, she gave permission to do so. Could she, if she had others, send them along as she had the first two? They thought the letters would add interest and flavor at this particular time.

She kept this act a secret as long as she could, and finally began to "create" letters especially for the newspaper audience, and not one that had been written for Daniel, as his were special and he might not want to share them with the world.

When the secret was out, she began to slant the letters toward local interest using actual local names. She began to post the printed copy on the Cookie Jar walls, along with Miss Francine's rhymes and Miss Carmelita's stories.

One nice thing about the letters, even better than the money, actually, was the fun way the words just tumbled into her head when she needed them. Just flowed into her head...and then out from the lead of the pencil.

She could watch the words flowing from under the point of her own pencil, sometimes giggling at what they wrote. When asked how she thought of so many things to say, she said she didn't. It was the pencil's idea. Her pencil wrote what it wanted to write. They laughed at her good joke...the joke that wasn't a joke...but the truth.

It became 1917 and England was begging for help. The homeland island was now drawing fire, and they had no more men to send to stop it. Their aircraft was no match for the Kaiser's birds, and the German boats were holding supply ships at bay. Help had to come now or it would be too late.

A full page ad in America about the viciousness of the ocean-going enemy brought a flood of volunteers. Miss Josie's oldest twins were as restless as a pair of prairie dirt devils, their thoughts spinning themselves into a tizzy wanting to go help save the country.

Miss Josie walked about with downcast eyes and lips in a firm line. She had no way to stop them.

Their father, Brad Cullen, wore slumped shoulders and a fresh-grown beard for his fears to hide behind. He knew, though, that when the older boys went, there would be no stopping them and the younger ones would not be far behind.

He could remember being young and wanting to change the world. He knew what his sons felt, but that didn't mean he liked it. Young men thought they could save the world, but the mean old world refused to be saved.

And they went. The younger twins would have gone as well, but they were much too young. There was a farewell party for the pair of handsome fellows, but Miss Josie pled a headache and didn't attend the farewell.

Mutt received a letter along with one of her checks and it must have been meant as an encouragement. They were right... it was.

They told her that the newspaper sales had increased largely because her "letters" were being clipped from the papers and enclosed within their own letters when family members wrote to their soldiers. Imagine that, her "letters" were being re-sent! Good news and thanks...but life moves on.

The best cure for a strange restlessness within her was the planning of the next letter...the constant watching for a happening that would be of interest...thinking of what other soldiers would like to hear from home.

It would have been interesting to know how many of her letters were now in France. How many were resting in shirt pockets for future, multiple readings.

Then, back in France, the worn and hollowed-out triage nurses were sent away for rest, usually just across the channel to England. At the south most point of the island is an area called Land's End, and the sound of the rockets was too far away to hear. The overworked women could have a whole night's rest with no emergency routing out of bed, to hurriedly step into shoes and button dresses on the way.

It was at this time that more younger nurses were acquired, filling in where the first had burned out. The preference was for strong farm girls, able to lift and push. Girls who were accustomed to doing what had to be done, whether they could or not. Failure was not an option, and these nurses did not fail. It was not permitted.

Nurses who only fluffed pillows and brought tea...? These chosen ladies certainly were not!

With sober faces these young, strong girls disembarked their ship and accepted the gift of the long, blue, heavy serge dresses along with thick flannel knickers and the no-nonsense shoes. Shoes with firm, lace up tops and arch-fitting insoles. Built for comfort and serviceability regardless of style.

The wheels of the medical personnel system seemed to grind slowly, but eventually came out with a finely ground product. Practically and durability became the word, and the nurses for the facility at Rouen, France were specially hand-picked as much as possible.

Most of the girls had lost a brother, cousin, friend...and now they thankfully accepted the remains of those who had left parts of themselves out on the battlefield field. Clean them and put them back together as much as was possible.

These ladies could smile and bring food, but they could also pick bone slivers from living flesh or excise a putrid swelling with the point of a scalpel. They could inject morphine, and they could hold the arm as frostbitten fingers, now gangrenous, were amputated to save a life.

And then they would assist with the removal of metal shards from a belly full of blood and intestines. A small, sterilized magnet was often helpful in locating the smaller slivers, shards and metal filings.

Daniel saw them...these girls...and felt a knot of admiration form in his throat. He thought of Gwinnie and Kristie McLaughlin. Cheerful and friendly, and who chose to arise before the rooster so they would be ready to feed those who were headed out for a hard and long day. Their day was also long, with popcorn being shelled late at night, and peanuts being ground into butter. Tired eyes watched as their tired hands wielded the sharp knife to shave the dried venison for an early breakfast favorite.

He pictured the Irish girls, laughing and dimpled, but they created new designs, worked with sore fingers, knitted with cramped wrists and worked by lamplight so Miz Someone would have what she needed for an occasion. They thoughtfully turned pages of fashion magazines, studying what they could do to make a design more attractive and more artfully their own. They did the job that was put before them.

Any one of these girls would walk off that ship, pick up their warm dress and help pull bone slivers from living flesh. They would be cheerfully chatting as their morphine needle assisted a mangled mass of injured humanity to pass painlessly on to their reward and then they could walk away with square shoulders to do the next thing that absolutely must be done. Immediately.

And there was Carmelita and Rosalie, Francine and America Forrester. Also Neecie Bramwell Forrester and Eve Adams. Different jobs, but each one gave her all. If it had been one of them who stepped off the ship, they would continue to do their all. Because it had to be done.

His homeland produced strong women to work beside and hold up their men. With a smile he thought of the "letters" that were being clipped from Eastern newspapers and re-sent to be a moment of relief to those on the fighting front. A link with home and sanity.

Such a wit had Miss Josie's only daughter, and who could know the future she would have? Everyone was good at something and didn't the wisest man, Solomon, note in the Good Book that "laughter doeth good...like medicine?"

And was there a chance that one of her letters, modeled especially for him, would be waiting for him at the end of his shift? Whenever that would be! It was a thing to be thought of with pleasure. It could happen!

Back at the Corners, it was a gray day with a dark and lowering sky. A steady patter of rain had kept Mutt indoors. Prissy was otherwise occupied with food processing at her home. Peas to shell, beans to snap and tomatoes to scald and peel.

The slow patter of rain was a blessing in the territory, the weather being so often dry and blowing, and everyone had plenty of duties to occupy them indoors.

Mutt, however, had spent a number of studious minutes contemplating her pencil. Strange thing, it was. It looked just like any other pencil and was exactly like its predecessors as well as those that would be its successors.

Yellow paint, a stick of lead enclosed in wood and topped with a pill shaped dot of rubber. It did, however, have the ability to pull words from her deepest thoughts, sort them and fit them together and then commit them to paper...totally bypassing her mind.

When faced with a sheet of paper, the pencil could transform its lead center into words. It had the ability to write down thoughts and phrases that she did not consider as hers until after a bit of thought.

She and Miss Francine had experienced some interesting exchanges of words. Miss Francine saw a scene or had a thought, and it transformed itself into rhymes with virtually no assistance on her part. She did not, however, have reason to blame her pencil. She had needed the pencil to download the rhymes to paper and it obeyed her. But other than that, the pencil had no particular part to play.

Mutt, on the other hand, had a pencil with a mind of its own. It seemed to produce words that had no relationship to what she saw or thought. Or possibly intended.

Miss Francine was one of the girl's favorite people and they smiled together over their various unusual traits, but the teacher softly reminded the girl, "Remember, Miss Mutt, that it is YOUR hand that holds the pencil and you are in control. It will be up to you to harness that pencil and drive it into the direction you want to go. It must not be allowed to run away with your thoughts."

"What if I don't yet know the direction?"

But the teacher was not to be drawn aside. "Of course, you know. You may not realize it, yet, and you may not really want to realize it, but you know. As soon as you take control, it will become clearer. In the meantime, write your model "letters".

That's something that Carmelita or Rosalie would have told you to do if you had asked them instead of me."

So here she sat…on this rainy afternoon…alone with her thoughts. And her pencil. *What would I be if I could choose? What do I like?*

Well, I like thoughts that have a lot of parts. I like finding out something I didn't know…that I didn't know. A surprise, maybe. I like research.

The trouble was that the Corners was so small. Not many surprises. Including Enterprise to the south and Shady Ridge to the west…and even pulling in Sentinel Rock, there were about twelve square miles. *All right, if that's all I have, that's where I will start with my research assignment.*

Surely there are many stories within twelve square miles.

And Daniel had a circumstance that produced a grin. The whole group of medical students based at Rouen received a notification that they had been graduated, in absentia, and were now fully accredited physicians. It had been determined that the knowledge they had gained in France had equaled at least year-for-year at the school, and possibly more. They'd had greater access to more illnesses and injuries than they might have seen in ten years in America.

In addition, they were encouraged to try for surgeon, their experience as assistants being considered in the requirements. Daniel nodded to himself; it was a thought…but not for today. This was his turn in the rotation to work in the triage.

Incoming wounded. Hardly any two exactly alike. The young, quick minds of the students, who were now accredited physicians, were able to swiftly determine the probable future of the victims. Those likely to recover were still treated first. Next likely injuries, they would be later.

And then the third group were consigned to receiving pain alleviation, with a comfortable bed and morphine. But even then, some of the third group were finally treated, and lived. Perhaps they would have lived even without help. The human body was a machine wonderfully made. Even David, Jeremiah and other Biblical figures had recognized that (Psalm 139:14).

This particular night was exceptionally discouraging. Perhaps it was the continued rain in the Seine River valley that thoroughly soaked the countryside and the men. Rain, and more rain. Rain that created accidents through slipperiness. Rain that encouraged dangerous varmints to sniff around the wounded victims and occasionally attack them.

Rain and dampness that caused misfires of weapons and injuries to hands. It was a soaked world that created chills from inadequate food and wet clothing as well as there being no way to rest.

More than one sturdy young man, ragged of uniform, was brought in with vacant eyes, unable to state his name. Another one who had sat down, stating that he could not move, even though his company had been ordered to retreat. Punished muscles had refused to accept yet another strange message from his brain.

He had been dragged to triage by the arms between two of his caring comrades. And there had been three, at different times, who had dissolved into tears and seemed not to hear anything that was said. Amongst these were sprinkled the wounded who were fully aware and conscious of every searing pain, and those who were bleeding…with limbs hanging at unnatural angles.

It was the nurses who met the barges and the ambulances. Their aching arms carried the stretchers and administered emergency anesthetic. This heart-rending activity was made to be the duty of the nurses simply because they were better at it.

Maybe it was because that the wounded themselves reacted to a feminine face and voice, or, more likely, that the hardened nurses had seen so much, they could turn it from their mind and quickly do what they needed to do…what they MUST do.

There was the ambulance driver who brought in his wounded, while driving with a compound leg fracture, two burned hands and several broken fingers on both hands. He had been the only driver who was available, and there was no way he could do it…but he did.

CHAPTER 3

It was impossible to think and act under such pain…but he did. His burns were caused by protecting a wounded man from a log that fell from a burning rocket-damaged tree, and the award of a purple heart did not reduce the painful stretch of the scar tissue on both palms. Every morning. The scar tissue did not change.

Daniel had reason to see this driver in his own capacity as chaplain and discovered him to be a resident of his own hometown.

Phillip Armstrong, son of Rev Armstrong from Carlile Corners, stayed in Rouen for four days, his fractured leg suspended, then he was transferred to a convalescent hospital for therapy. Daniel did not get to see him after he was transferred, and in three weeks the driver was back behind the wheel of the ambulance, broken leg in a cast. Of men like Philip was the army made.

Due to its success on the front line, the Rouen facility became the most important triage hub, and for reasons of space, the wounded were moved as soon as they were able to withstand the trip. Room must be made for the incoming.

Daniel spent his week and was rotated. It was decided that no matter how well they did their job, the young doctors must not be wasted by risking a mental burnout from "incoming." Rotate them and move them on. Let their minds heal so they could serve again. Daniel was glad to go back to pulling shards from young muscles.

His table received a head wound, bare and bloody to the bone. With a sigh, he took the scissors to trim back the hair, and a feminine hand reached for the instrument…and looked meaningfully into his eyes. Her plain, strong face was ringed with tight curls of red hair. Irish.

She whispered, "I'll do this, doctor. He needs you in other places."

She was right. But side-glances noted that she placed wet cloths gently on the wound to soften it, then snipped the scissors closely into the long battle-filthy hair, leaving a clean field for antiseptic fluid and future stitches. The white of the skull did not detract her from her skillful snipping and wiping.

When next he saw that soldier, the young man managed a smile under his huge bandages as he was moved to a convalescent hospital. "Thanks, doc. I was afraid I'd had it, but you fixed me up."

There was not time to explain that it was as much his nurse as his doctor. *Dear Lord*, his mind begged, *how long can this go on?*

There had been discussion about the quarter section just south of Miss Josie's and across the street from old Gaither Cullen, her father-in-law. Good place. Why hadn't it been settled? It had gone to cottonwood sprouts, clumps of bluestem grass and Scottish thistles.

And then it turned out that it had been settled. Seems to have been tangled up in legalities when the homesteader who had first staked it out and registered, had disappeared. He was not the first to have that happen, of course. Thieves and robbers plied the territory for lone persons who seemed to have something of value. Like horses. Maybe coins or firearms.

The pull of a trigger left no witnesses to the crime and coyotes cleaned up the evidence. That could be what happened, but the man left paperwork that had precipitated a search for heirs. In the same way that the government could lose paperwork forever in their own abyss of rules and regulations, they could also hold a discrepancy open for decades looking for a reason to close it.

In this way the quarter section just south of Miss Josie's found closure in the form of George Mead who resided in Tennessee. What had actually helped was that Mr. Mead had been named "George" after his uncle so he MUST be the one. Nephew George had known enough of the right answers to prove that he was, indeed, a nephew, and likely the only heir who existed.

The government was happy to hand over the land so that they could finally, at some future time, receive taxes from it. Immediately, however, the second George must agree that, within five years, he could fence, cross-fence and cultivate twenty percent of the land. He must build a habitable dwelling and create a well, either hand-dug or punched. It looked like a good deal for George (the second) and he happily signed his name and moved his family from their St. Louis rented home.

George Mead had a daughter, age sixteen, and boys, ages thirteen and nine. That is how Marchella Mead came into the life of Josie's only daughter. They became close neighbors, less than a mile apart.

There are people of all types. Lighthearted and sober, laughing and quiet. Those to have fun with, and those to call on for help. There are those of whom nothing is good enough, and those who give of themselves until nothing is left.

Miss Merytaten Cullen, Miss Josie's daughter, was like a tugboat. She was a force in whichever direction she chose to go, though she was seldom totally sure she was going in the right direction.

Miss Prissy Carpenter was a happy-hearted friend and follower. A good-natured addition to any group and much in demand for parties.

Miss Marchella Mead, on the other hand, was a "strong tower, and a very present friend in time of trouble" (Proverbs 18:10). There were those who would describe her as having a rainy day personality, a person to cry with…when one had to cry. Basically, though, hers was a natural ability to empathize.

Such a threesome these young ladies made. Summer evenings so often found them at the Cookie Jar, occupying the benches at the tables under the cottonwoods. They might be the ones to light the oil lanterns to hang in the trees at dark. They were right there handy to serve lemonade if needed, or to pop the next popper of corn. They could grab a mop to sop up a spilled drink, and they were an attractive magnet to draw in whatever male person who had still not enlisted in the army.

Adam Cullen, Mutt's oldest brother, was quick to notice Miss Marchella and her lovely English complexion that stayed pink and white regardless of the prevailing sunshine. He also noticed her hair that spiraled softly in shades of cream and gold around her face but trailed down her back like flowing butter and honey, straight and smooth. Or it might be braided in shades of gold to honey and formed in a crown over her head. Yes, he saw everything, and it was tormenting to him that she had appeared just as he had made up his mind firmly to join the army.

Adam and Aaron had reached the age of "doing what they wanted to do without parental consent." The pair of young men had even gone so far as to talk with the recruiter and had almost signed but decided to wait one more month.

This was now the time of summer fun, and when fall rains set in, that would be soon enough to go to France…as that was seemingly where everyone went at first.

Marchella readily accepted the attention of the handsome neighbor. Such an attractive addition she made to the tables under the cottonwood trees! She seemed not to mind the move from the center of social life in St. Louis to the far fringe of population out in the territory.

Marchella's family had always lived in St. Louis, and she had been able to attend a good school. Such an asset to the Corners. And so had her two brothers. Everyone agreed that it was so good to see that quarter section of land settled. With very desirable people.

Before the twins left to enlist, the far thinking Adam had secured what he considered a promise from Marchella that she would write to him. Lots of letters, he had insisted. She had smiled and filled his lemonade glass, and he took that for a "yes."

Because of perfect health and high test scores, the boys had both gone in as officers. The infantry in France went through a lot of officers in a short time, and they were reluctant to promote exceptionally good sergeants, as exceptional sergeants were even harder than officers to keep.

In October were the final farewell parties. Pathetic efforts to be cheerful. Friends gathering around…attempting to avoid brooding silences. Looking for something to say. Consuming a lot of lemonade.

Their parents excused themselves from the party early. Mutt stayed, her mind twisting one way and the other, but she owed it to her brothers. Marchella stayed close, sensing the pain of her new friend. She had smiles and friendly words for the handsome, excited Adam, and a watchful closeness for Merytaten.

Promises to write. Yes, she could. Marchella could do that for a friend. Though she had the feeling of being forced into professing affection for the young man she hardly knew. She could, however, write to him. Letters were important, she understood, and she could surely do that much for one brave enough to volunteer himself.

And they were gone. It was as though another piece of the Corners went with them, but life would go on. Somehow, it always had.

And life went on…in a manner speaking…for their parents. Father, Brad, continued to fire the blacksmith furnace and bend the iron. But the coals were allowed to cool as he gazed, unseeing, at the work before him. He stood in the shop doorway and panned his vision from south to north. The O'Day's across the street. Plume of smoke indicated where Matt Wilson lived. The Cookie Jar and its FAREWELL sign undulating in the breeze under the whispering leaves of the cottonwoods. Beyond was the building of Hats and Hankies. Next came Canfield Grading with its usual movement of people and horses, pulling massive, dirt-moving machinery.

None of this, however, was actually seen by the father of the twins.

A nudge at his elbow, and there was old Gaither Cullen with a steaming cup of what was called coffee. He had no words for his son, but he offered what he could. After all, he also felt the pain...as the twins were his own grandsons. Brad nodded thanks and took the cup...and the mug of black liquid cooled in his hand.

Miss Josie wandered the house like a bird waiting for migration, but there was no migration for her. No escape. She had wept for others who left, but for her own sons she had no tears. Only heaviness and dread. Only the horrible awareness that this must be lived through.

Gone. The words of Miss Francine's poem of agony ground itself into her mind.

"Gone, just little boys. Left behind are boyhood toys. It can't be true, they'd gone away. Just little boys, called from their play."

The words of the poem tore themselves apart and fitted themselves together again. Just little boys...with different toys.

Carlile Corner's first twins were actually gone. Sitting at a table under the cottonwoods was their sister. Sadness for her parents and a bit of guilt as she had contemplated the safe and defended activity of her pencil while her brothers had decided to defend their country with their lives.

At her elbow was Marchella, making no attempt at words. Knowing instinctively that there were no words that could fill the hole in her friend's heart. The rainy day friend. The friend to be sad with, who made no attempt to take her from her sadness. Hadn't a learned writer said "...weep with those who weep..." (Romans 12: 15)?

Marchella's parents had excused her from duties knowing she had a mission. The girl's mission was to wait until her friend could speak, and then she would know her next move.

It was four days later that Mutt picked up her pencil and tapped her cheek with the eraser end. A normal action.

Words came, and Mutt said, "…Ella, let's find an empty buggy somewhere and ride over to Argyle."

A crisis had passed. The girls spent an hour looking at the Montgomery Ward Catalog. Commenting on the wonders offered therein for those with coins. Spooning ice cream at the Sweet Shoppe. Life goes on and there were letters to write.

It was a few days later, when Marchella had other things to do, that Mutt laced up her solid shoes and headed west, down the path made by sledding stones from the ridge. She walked past the berry patch and the woodlot crowded with growing Blackjack oaks. There was the windbreak of persimmon trees that broke up the strength of the north wind. Windbreak…planted by Mr. Digby.

The cemetery. Now a restful place, but a place that had seen many tears. Would see a lot more.

She climbed over the stone ridge that still had a lot of building stone to offer…if someone wanted to build. On, she went, and paused to look at the stony markers and give thought to the old crippled man who had been such a help to her mother. Digby. He was crippled no more. For walking the "streets of gold" he would now have two good feet.

Then her thoughts moved on to Miz Carlile who furnished the name for the Corners. Important person she had been. Mutt had no personal memory of her.

There was the headstone of her cousin Esther, mother of the twins, Sunny and Rainy Day. There was a lot of room for the many more who would need a place of final rest.

She walked on and could see the church building in the distance. Between the cemetery and the church was the sheep pasture. Those long-haired animals with the expensive wool. They grazed here and there, and lambs romped among then.

And haystacks. A favorite childhood play yard.

Haystacks. And here was the place where one of the stacks had been hauled to the barn. The place where it had been was now littered with clumps and wads of the rich prairie grass mixed with the new plant called alfalfa.

She remembered tunneling under the hay, the itchy straw down her neck that was ignored because the fun of it had consumed all her energy. And there were the items that accumulated under a haystack. The gathering rake pulled together with the hay, and anything else in its path. Anything that had been dropped, carried in, blown by or tumbled under...there it was, spread out in a curious array where the haystack had been.

Slipping between the wires of the sheep fence, she strolled over to the place where the stack had been. Moving a clump of hay with her foot, she uncovered a hole burrowed at a slant. Armadillo. They were the great hole-makers and their abandoned birth nests were used by rabbits and rats, and even snakes.

A brass button. Its shine reflected in the morning sun. A five-cent coin. The nickel that was sure to have been missed and the loss of it was certainly mourned over.

There was a fork with bent tines...now, how could that get here?

The messed up remains of a pheasant's nest, still containing an unhatched egg. And a few broken shells. They wouldn't last long, now that they had been uncovered. They would be consumed by some animal for the calcium they contained.

A doll's dress and a pile of snail shells...and three small buttons. Pack rat. They loved to decorate their nests with anything bright or unusually shaped.

A continued circling and moving of the clumps with her shoe, she saw ruined and misplaced remnants of life at the Corners. She committed them to memory for inclusion in her next letter to Daniel. To give him a feeling of home. One that was sure to trigger a few thoughts.

Her fingers itched for the feel of the pencil, and her eyes desired the sight of paper before her. It was time. She had been gone too long but now she was back. And life went on.

It was at this time that Miss Josie put legs to her plan. Life was moving so fast at the Corners that it was hard to keep up with it. She saw her daughter moping through her days, unable to find her place in the changing parts of her life.

Josie herself had been hardly a year older when she had lived through the tragic fire that took her parents. She projected herself back to that age and her new direction, and she knew this was the time that her daughter's life must take a new direction.

"Miss Merytaten, I have a job for you." Mutt knew it was serious when her mother used her name instead of "honey" or "dear."

"I want you to set about researching everything that has happened in the Corners, from Miz Carlile on to today and every tomorrow. Take a new composition book and accumulate notes. Talk to anyone and everyone. Nothing is too good, too bad or too painful to include."

Mutt, curled into her father's most comfortable chair, listened. She looked at her mother and watched the movement of her mouth, the tilt of her head and the timber of her voice. This was indeed serious and it was something her mother had obviously been saving up to say. The girl knew her mother well.

True. Her mother had been saving this project until she, Mutt, was "ready." Ready in experience and skill level, and also with the available time. Later, her life would be complicated with everyday activity. Miss Josie had deemed this to be the time, and she seldom made mistakes in matters of this kind.

"Now, you will need to figure on including Argyle, Shady Ridge, Enterprise and possibly even Sentinel Rock. Remember the little fellow from there who was brought every day to the Academy? He had seven older brothers, and they took turns bringing him.

"Talk with adults and older people. This is a project that you are uniquely adapted to take on, and you have the ability to create an accurate account, a nugget of history, so those who come later will know how it was with us. I expect you to do well."

As the girl listened to her mother, she knew she would do it, and she knew it would be a consuming interest for the next number of years. She did not move from her curled position in the leather chair…the one ordered out from New York.

She could not move because of the racing of her mind, the grasping of ideas and the expanse of the opportunity before her. These thoughts and more were robbing her of the energy to move, or even reply. They multiplied and formed like beads on a necklace…an unending chain of thoughts. Words.

That was nothing to Miss Josie. Her mind did not create in this way. From a drawer, she removed the new Composition Book and three unsharpened pencils. Sliding these articles between her daughter's tummy and her curled up legs, she left the room, closing the door softly behind her.

It was almost an hour before the girl aroused, her legs tingling from being "asleep." She sharpened the pencils with a knife, picked up the Composition Book and left. Under the trees in the yard of the Cookie Jar, she opened the book.

She headed the first line with:

CHRONOLOGY OF CARLILE CORNERS
THE PRAIRIE ACADEMY

As Merytaten Cullen had become aware that darkness was falling around her, and that lanterns were being lighted in the cottonwood trees, Doctor Daniel Carpenter, Major, US Army, had stretched himself awake as he sensed the rising sun. Its first rays were now shining red and gold on the surface of the Seine River of France.

Housing in Rouen had become better, gradually, and the bunks were more comfortable, and for certain, no wind whistled through the walls. What had not changed, though, was the grinding sameness of the pain and agony he faced daily…of the scraps of torn flesh to be cleansed and sewed together.

Also, what had not changed was the length of the days. Doctors worked until relieved. No exception.

Seeping into Daniel's awakening mind was the memory that this week was his turn to rotate into the triage. Triage: the sorting out of whoever had the best chance to live and who must be allowed to die. Painlessly if possible. It entailed the making of a god-like decision over human life. Frightening and soul-scaring.

Clean white uniforms. The German prisoners were good at laundry. Of course, they had also been very good at war as well, or there would have been no need for the laundry.

Chaplain/Surgeon Major Carpenter was well into his morning's duty, and there was placed before him the next victim. Definitely in the third category, that of "likely not to live." Trained fingers at the pulse point of the victim's wrist. A sigh. No decision to be made…as what was left of this young man would never again feel pain.

Next action would be to collect the identity and personal effects if any. And move him toward…a gasp! His injuries had not reached his face, and Doctor Daniel Carpenter, who had first assessed the wounds of the body, found himself looking into the face of Adam Cullen, reposed in final rest.

Muscles constricted in his chest, blocking an intake of breath. The table before him tilted as his mind shut out and refused to believe what it knew was true. Both his hands holding to the edge of the board, he forced an intake of breath, squared his shoulders and looked around him.

All those in triage learned to train a "corner of the eye" watch on their fellows. Some horrors were just too heavy to bear alone. On this job, they must look out for each other.

Daniel had one of those persons. The nurse working several feet away put down her swabbing cloth and moved toward him.

The doctor forced a swallow of the lump in his throat. "Collect the identity, please and I'll be back."

"Doctor, are you...?"

Nodding. "I'll be right back." And he was.

As though there were two persons inside his body, the doctor spoke to the childhood friend within his body. "You can handle this, Daniel. Otherwise, why are you a doctor? Check his pockets. Something for Miss Josie. Let the official telegram go but write your own. Now, go back. You're needed."

He went back. The accumulated pile of identity held a started letter, "Dear Mom and Pa. They've moved me, but the address is still the same. I'm getting ready to...." And there the letter stopped.

There were a few coins, three matches, a handkerchief cut from the mottled green of army fabric. Another pocket contained four wrapped pieces of the hard candy issued as an energy boost if food was late in reaching them. A tiny file with a point on one end and a screwdriver/wedge on the other. A popular item that had many uses...such as prying open a food can if the tab broke off.

Tiny, pathetic pile of belongings left behind. The doctor gathered them into a box provided for such as these and addressed it to Merytaten Cullen. The note enclosed said, "Angel, do your ma a favor and save these things until she can accept them. Thanks."

His telegram and the army's notification came to the Corners the same day. "Sincere regrets. I bade him goodbye for the family. His bravery was great and his passing was sudden. Letter follows."

Then his table contained the next victim.

He forced his fingers to be steady as they closed wounds on someone else's friend and neighbor.

He pushed on to the next tragedy. A bullet had graced through the flesh of a jaw, exposing teeth. Tedious to gather the flesh inside his mouth and then stitch the skin of his cheek. This young man had, however, been brought in before dirt and debris had a chance to infect.

He would wear a scar forever, but he would go home to his mother, his girlfriend and his friends. Not everyone had been that lucky. Adam had not been…and no words came, but Adam's childhood friend swallowed hard in grief.

Relieved at an hour just past midnight, he stumbled to his bunk. An escape into needed sleep. Exhaustion was so great, his body seemed to be hugging itself downward against the feather pad of the bed. Eyes shut.

Eyes open! The moonlight came through a nearby window, spreading a wan light over the mottled green wool blanket. Warm wool from such sheep as those grazing behind the church at the Corners.

Eyes open and seeing:

Adam, balanced and joyfully screaming at the top of a haystack.

Adam, hooting with pleasure as he tossed a bright-colored perch from the fishing hole.

Adam, arms waving akimbo as he walked the stepping stones over the low part of the river.

And then, Adam racing across the meadow in a game of Red Rover, heading for Daniel's hold onto the hand of a smaller child. The object was to break the handhold apart and steal a player. At the very last second, Daniel would step in front of him, and the two of them would fall into a laughing tangle of arms and legs. The smaller child clapping and laughing with glee. Adam would then be retained for their side instead of Daniel being lost to the "enemy."

When his buzzer notified him that it was morning, he noted that Adam Cullen had kept him awake the entire night. "That's all right, Adam, old friend. You deserved a lot more than that."

Dear Brad and Miss Josie.

I lost a dear friend, but that is nothing compared to your loss. I have checked, and this much I know. Adam was with a contingent meant to delay an attack until help arrived, but a rocket landed with a direct hit. All I can say is that he left us while on a mission of great bravery, and his passing was instant. He was picked up within minutes of the blast and brought to the hospital. Too late.

I know that no words can help, and a white cross above him is no match for the bravery of a young man in service for his country. Aaron is still safely in England, miles west of the White Cliffs of Dover. I know that for certain.

With most sincere and painful regrets, his friend,

Daniel Carpenter

The letter went out with the next post just as a letter from Adam's sister arrived. Long and cheery. Listing the items found under a haystack. It was obvious that she didn't yet know. Blessed oblivion, but so short lived.

Doctor Carpenter knew he would never let it slip that Adam was in Europe because of a mistake in name and identity. New, young lieutenants were oriented in England. Somehow, a Captain Cullen was retained and Lieutenant Cullen was erroneously added to a strike force. It happened more times than were believable.

The often-made mistake even had a name. SNAFU: "Situation Normal All Fouled Up." Confused. Muddled. Brad and Miss Josie didn't need to know that their brave son simply followed the orders that took his life. The captain, however, had been battle hardened and ready. He could likely have survived. Just a SNAFU. One of many.

A storm came crashing in about midnight drenching the woodland and making a quagmire of the lowlands. Wounded bodies were stretched out in the soggy cold, debris-strewn battlefield. Those still standing slung their gun across their backs and began to haul out anyone in a uniform. Those calling for help were first, and if their arms were still intact they were easier to move.

One soldier, actually a limey engineer, ripped to shreds a uniform from one who would never need it, and tied branches together for a makeshift travois sled. Wounded could be lifted aboard the lattice of sticks and pulled onward by two poles. Saved a lot of strength for the rescuers who had not any strength to spare.

The impromptu equipment was so helpful, the engineer made more of them while his comrades continued working on the rescue. Mud caked, the wounded rode to the river and were placed on the board planks of the barge.

One fully loaded barge caught a rocket that took out the steering mechanism. Sideways and with one end sagging into the water, it whirled its way toward the triage station, finally lodging against a fallen tree, also adrift.

The waiting nurses watched with horror as they gazed at the barge, yards out of reach. One of them, without hesitation, stripped her heavy serge uniform over her head and plunged into the water. Others stared as she returned with a wound soldier across her back, fighting the river current as she struggled toward the shore.

Depositing him on land with no fanfare, she plunged in again, and this time returned with a thick rope line from the barge. "Tie this up tight," she ordered, "and we can bring them ashore, hand over hand."

This, of course, was a job much too hard for the nurses to do, but they did it. Eventually, when the barge was empty, they pulled their dresses back on over their sodden knickers and shivered their way into the shelter for dry clothes, then returned to finish out their shift.

Doctor Carpenter had just dozed off after a thirteen-hour day when he was roused out of his bunk. One of the triage doctors had passed out from sheer exhaustion, and a replacement must be found.

Numbly he dressed as he ate the sandwich that was handed to him, and he reported for duty. On his table was a child, a little boy of possibly six or seven. His arm was bandaged, where he should have had a hand. He had already received morphine, surely, because he was just lying on the table looking at the ceiling.

Doctor rubbed his sleep-deprived eyes and passed him on. Children seem to thrive, somehow, and someday he would likely be glad he lost only a hand.

Next, there came running toward him, a man in mismatched civilian clothing carrying a woman against his chest, her right arm hanging down straight, and her shoulders in the crook of his arm. Long, wheat-colored hair flowed down, debris-strewn and blood spattered.

The man's clothing was soaked with blood, and his screams were piercing as he dashed past those at the door and headed for Daniel's table, which had just been cleared.

Daniel, hardly awake, stared as in a trance as the distraught man placed the young woman on his table. Even with sleep-dim eyes, he could see that her left shoulder and arm were completely gone, and the blood on the man's clothing had clearly been hers. Her rib cage had been damaged, and the whiteness of splintered bones showed through the oozing blood.

Somehow, midst the trauma, the heart continued to beat, pumping blood to places that were no longer there. How...!! The man still screamed words that Daniel did not understand, except for the plea for help. He looked up to tell the man there was no use, but the frantic man grabbed Daniel's wrist and placed it on the woman's abdomen.

Struggling with the language, he managed to demand, "INFANTE!...SAVE BABE!!"

Movement under the wadded clothing. She was pregnant! While the mother lived, the baby lived, but with the imminent stopping of the heart, the baby would be.... He could not save the baby…he knew that…but the father would not listen. "CUT BABE…OUT!"

Now Daniel had read, with hardly-believable wonder, of babies being saved this way. Sometimes mothers. With thoughts racing, and trying to remember everything he knew about childbirth which was not a subject dwelt on in military training.

On either side of him stood work-weary nurses, hair straggling, concerned faces staring. One had stripped back the girl's clothing, and another put a scalpel in his hand.

"You can do it, Doctor," he thought he heard someone say.

He took the sharp, shining instrument and laid the tip against the pale skin. A red line of welling blood followed the blade, assuring him that the mother's heart still beat. Another, deeper line was incised, his hand and the knife seeming to have begun to work on their own, with himself only an observer.

The man had ceased his begging screams, and now bent expectantly over the woman, watching every movement. This layer of skin and that layer, and his child was nearer…closer. The nurses, breathless, also leaned near, one with a clean towel to receive the live newborn. Such faith!

Then a moan, and a labored gurgle as the mother passed on, just as her daughter sounded forth an indignant scream. She lay in a pool of blood and waved a small fist at the world. The grateful father burst into tears and clasped the tiny, bloody hand in his own trembling fingers.

The nurse beside him lifted the miniature body onto the clean towel held by the other nurse, and quickly tied off the cord with a piece of suture thread.

The young man took a look at the breathing child, sucked in a deep breath, and crumbled onto the floor at the feet of the three surprised medics. The nurse with the towel took charge… from here on, she was on solid ground. She knew exactly what to do live, screaming babies, and she walked away.

Two, young strong men loaded the limp and distraught man onto a stretcher and followed the baby.

Heart pounding, Doctor Carpenter stood holding the scalpel.

"Good job," someone told him, and he turned to see who they were referring to. Certainly the words were not for him. There was no way he could release a live baby from the womb of a fatally injured mother, but apparently he had. With important help from Above.

Then the bearers came and rolled her lifeless body away, moving another table before him.

There was no way a man could carry a woman in from somewhere, her torn body pressed against his chest to stanch the bleeding…but he had.

There was no way a one-hundred-forty-pound nurse could swim in rushing water, encumbered with wet clothing as she was, to rescue the injured…but she did.

There was no way the line of nurses could hold to the tow-rope from the barge, passing it under one arm and with one hand and the other arm, pass injured bodies from one to the other toward the shore. Dragging them through the icy water where they stood, barely touching river bottom with their toes… but they did.

For the next two hours the doctor worked as in a dream, until someone came to relieve him. Feet stumbling and eyes bleary, he made his way back to his bunk. Washing the blood from his hands, he crawled onto his shelf bed, wrapping the wool (from the Corners?) blanket around him. He hugged the pillow against his face, and his hand bumped against the packet of unopened letters beneath his pillow.

With a lump in his throat, he clasped the letters and held them against his chest, sobbing uncontrollably. If someone heard him, they gave it no thought. Hardly a night passed that someone did not give vent to weary, lonely agony, and they had every right to do so.

Not a soul in the room had yet experienced his twenty-fifth birthday.

Newspapers filtered into the territory speaking of talks going on. What good were words when bullets were flying? The Kaiser was weakening and willing to exchange words? Like "Armistice"?

Dictionaries were opened and fingers sought the word. "Armistice: the temporary suspension of hostilities between opponents."

What was going on here? Didn't hostilities end in a winner and a loser? What was this thing called an armistice that made the stronger party of the confrontation offer something to the weaker party? Wouldn't anyone with a head on his shoulders see that temporary meant "not permanent"?

How soon would it be before the weaker party gained strength, and the war would be on again? At the Cookie Jar, the blacksmith shop, the churchyard, and anywhere two or more met, the situation was discussed, but the talk meant nothing.

On November 11, 1918, the Armistice ended the fighting…for a time. And the men started coming home.

Last of the troops was Edward Morrison from headquarters in London and finally Doctor Daniel Carpenter was able to leave the hub hospital at Rouen, France. There had been tag ends to be fastened together and hanging paperwork to be closed but, at last, the territory boys got it done.

Aaron came home to the hugs and tears for both himself and his twin. Included in the family embraces was Marchella. He looked into her eyes and she looked into his and fireworks occurred. Neither looked away until they were married five months later. Merytaten was delighted to have her as another sister-in-law. A friend to keep handily within the family, so to speak. One never knew when they'd need a friend.

Aaron's blacksmithing skill returned as though it was just yesterday that he had worked with his dad. Father Brad watched and was grateful he was back. One son was enough to lose. If the war had lasted, he could have lost all four. Because of the Armistice… whatever that was…Aaron was back.

It was the first of December that the doctor stepped aboard the comfortable ship. Darkness was falling as his group were funneled aboard and shown immediately to their cabins. A sense of finality settled over him with the rocking of the ship in the English Channel.

Sitting on his soft, soft bed, he opened his serviceable, leather-covered Bible. A wrinkled page or two. Even an unintended smudge here and there. Marking his place of last reading was the square of stiff paper with a drawing of a book…an ancient firearm…and a sword. The new Book had very small print, which gave it a small, handy size. This one would join the other one, each of the Books having survived its own war.

He would love to have more information on his ancestor, Daniel Ledbetter. Had he been what had then passed for a chaplain? Maybe a sergeant in the infantry. Somehow he had kept the Book through whatever it was that he did, and it was obviously of great value to him. Otherwise he would not have specifically directed how it was to be passed on.

A sigh, and he stretched out on the bunk. No buzzer would wake him up to duty. No stretcher would bring him wounded soldiers. Somewhere, moving through the waves of the Atlantic Ocean, he would turn twenty-four. An even two dozen of years in his life. For what?

So many messages from his "Angel." How would she see him when he returned? How would he see her? And on that thought he went to sleep.

At the station in Kentucky he mustered out. Picked up a surprising amount of accumulated pay that he had managed no time to spend. He was given the diploma…the certificate that said he was a fully bonified doctor of medicine and a capable surgeon. It all seemed unreal, somehow.

In Oklahoma City he purchased a Model T auto. He could drive, but he had acquired very little experience. Oh well, it would be at least forty miles before he reached the Corners. Surely he could become proficient in that distance.

CHAPTER 4

The Corners. Ma and Pa at home. Angel…?

Miss Janine Cullen Wilson, wife of Jefferson Wilson (who raised Irish Conamara horses), put on her sunbonnet and strolled toward the Cookie Jar.

It was time she was checking the mail hook for a letter, and perhaps take care of another little situation. There had been an interesting conversation between herself and Miss Josie.

Ever since she had assisted Miss Josie in her first years at teaching in the Prairie Academy the two ladies had been sharers of problems. It had been Miss Josie's turn to confide and the conversation had gone somewhat like this.

"I've been thinking about a little six-horse carousel back in the New York City park when I was tiny. The circle was small, and the little wooden animals went round and round, as their poles went up and down. The horses were painted in different colors, pink, yellow, green, blue, brown and lavender. I always liked the lavender one."

With a smile, Miss Janine, who knew her friend well, responded, "I see. And was there a reason why you have been thinking of a childhood plaything in a faraway state?"

Returning the knowing smile, Miss Josie continued, "Yes, there was. I remember most children loving it, and staying on the horses as long as permitted, but occasionally someone didn't like it and screamed to get off. The thing was, once started, the circling continued until the wind-up spring ran down. The only way to rescue the frightened child was to stand on the platform and lift him off as the horse passed by."

Silence followed, and Miss Janine attended to her chamomile tea and waited, knowing there was more.

There was. "And now I see someone stuck on a merry-go-round carousel and can't get off. She might very well be crying if she wasn't almost seventeen years old, and I'm not sure that she actually hasn't shed a tear."

A quick calculation told Miss Janine that the only almost seventeen-year-old girl her friend would know that well would be her daughter. She also knew there would be more words. So she freshened her tea.

"Here she is with Marchella making wedding plans and Prissy deciding to cut in with Hats and Hankies, and she has been at loose ends. Instead of picking a direction, she has allowed herself to step onto the carousel because of her varied interests."

"And you've thought of a plan to stop the carousel?"

"No, because it can't be stopped until it runs down and by then I'm thinking there would be actual tears. The only thing I can do is lift her off. When I see her with a quiet pencil, I know her wooden pony has come around again, but before I can do anything, it has passed on by."

"How can I help?" The intuitive friend had realized there was a point to this conversation.

Relieved smile. "I have an idea. That pencil is the key. I think that is her 'lavender pony.' But she needs more. I suggested she research and set down the progress of the Corners, and she was interested, but she just can't seem to get started. Sits around with her composition book, tapping her cheek with the pencil and staring ahead."

"And you think I can get her off if you couldn't?"

"I do. She's got to get her feet on solid ground before she can go another direction. The circumstances that brought you here is typical and interesting. If you would offer to…maybe say a few words? Maybe like your mother's illness and you being forced to raise your brother from a tiny baby…."

It was Janine's turn to stare into space and hesitate. "I'm not sure…but what can it hurt to try. I'll need to mention this conversation."

"That would be fine. She's usually a self-starter, as you would know from school, but too much has happened and she's confused. There's Adam gone, and now Aaron and Daniel are back. Letters to them was an activity she took seriously, and now that's gone."

"Where is Daniel these days?"

A long and sober sigh. "I'm thinking from his mother that he is possible on a carousel of his own. He's been released from being vitally important and extremely busy in a rewarding endeavor, and now he has nothing to do and is a legitimate doctor and a licensed minister. What does not work in a situation like that, I ask you?" Without waiting for an answer, Josie continued.

"According to Carlotta, he spends hours back at the catfish pond, pouring through books he's ordered, or that he brought back with him. Mostly books on diseases. Then, sometimes he goes over to the Cookie Jar for a while. He and Mutt talk on occasion.

"Truth be told, though, I'd hate to see those two spending much time together until one or the other gets off the carousel. It seems Daniel is feeling conscious of being a little older than most of the current young people, and for certain, he's been through a lot more. John and Willie waved goodbye to their military experience, came home, and picked up their former jobs. And former lives. Daniel had no former job to pick up. Closest friends were Aaron and Adam, and now Aaron looking at marriage in a few months. Daniel is twenty-four and in the same position now as he was the age he left...fourteen."

This was going to take a while, Janine realized, so she brought a kettle of green beans to the table. Dividing the quantity with Josie, the two thought and snapped. Life goes on, and sooner or later someone would be hungry. Beans to be cooked.

Janine next. "I'm beginning to see what you mean. When Tray came home, there was the love of his life waiting with him with his first child. He even had his old job if he wanted it. It would make a difference."

Beans snapped, tea gone, sun sinking low. Miss Josie donned her bonnet and took her leave, feeling much lighter in her mind.

That was yesterday and a lot of thought had followed. Now it was today and action was on the menu.

Miss Merytaten Cullen was sitting on the bench that was attached to the table and setting under the cottonwoods planted by Digby. Before her was an opened composition book, and in her hand was a yellow pencil. The girl herself was staring at nothing and tapping her cheek with the eraser end of the pencil.

For at least a month, the pencil had been unaccustomedly quiet after the activity of letter writing to the army fellows and to the Pennsylvania paper.

Lazy pencil. The girl was getting weary of humoring it by sitting and waiting for it to begin. It had gone as far as writing:

THE CHRONOLOGY OF CARLILE CORNERS: PRAIRIE ACADEMY

To be perfectly truthful, though, it had not been the pencil's idea to write those words. The girl, herself, had shaped the letters and after that, the pencil had been no help at all. Stubbornly motionless.

She sat and thought of what she could do with her life. The best thing she could think of was the Sweet Shoppe in Argyle, and they were always looking for someone of an afternoon. Clerk help. Trouble was, she'd have to stay overnight, or someone would have to get her home. It was totally unsafe for a young lady in a buggy to travel five miles after dark.

Or maybe she could talk to Canfield Grading. Lily Gray Owl Cullen worked for a while when the fellows were gone to war, and she was even pregnant. But then....

Her far-off gaze discouraged companionship at her table, but here came someone. She focused her eyes and looked at the smiling face of Miss Janine. The friend of her mother was advancing carrying two glasses of lemonade.

"Your gaze said you were far away, and I thought it might be thirsty, way out there where you were."

The girl was very fond of Miss Janine. She had known her so long, and here she was married to her mom's cousin…. Around here, that made her family. She gratefully accepted the drink.

"Yes, I was pretty far away. Maybe working at the Sweet Shoppe in Argyle, or maybe Raymond would let me drive one of his monster horses."

Nodding, Miss Janine responded. "You could do that, but what would your pencil think? It wouldn't be appreciated at either place."

"I don't care. I'd leave it at home. It hasn't cooperated with me lately."

"Hmmm. That seems strange. As I seem to recall, your pencil has never given you trouble before."

"I know."

The lemonade had been made pink with a dash of cherry juice. The Cookie Jar owners were inventive with flavors. A lot of them were originated by Sunny or Rainy Day, and sometimes both. Some of them were really good and stayed popular. Pink lemonade! Festive!

"Well, my dear, your mother and I have been talking about you behind your back. She told me about something she really wants, and she's thinking that you may find something interesting to do before you do it for her." Not entirely true, but close enough. "You may remember that original writing was never your mother's strong trait. Numbers, puzzles, memory and planning, she is tops, but I don't think I ever saw an original paper that she wrote."

A pause, and the girl's eyes lowered to her hands. Not much reaction, but the pencil was intrigued. It quit tapping her cheek and settled itself into the crease of the composition book. A strip of yellow on the white paper. The wooden stick even turned itself over and over under her solid, square-tipped fingers.

Over and over. Stayed in the crease of the book.

Miss Janine continued, "Your mom, so surprisingly tossed out here in the Oklahoma territory as she was, has an interesting kinship with the growth of the community and the personality of its members. She thinks it would make an important addition to the history of this new country."

Time for another pause. When carving a sculpture, one mustn't force their knife too deeply, just because the wood happened to be soft.

The pencil had been listening, and crawled up into one of her hands, being held with all four fingers like a fork? a hammer? Or maybe a scepter. Yes! It was a scepter, pointing the way forward.

"I would really like your mom to have that account. It would mean a lot to her, even if it took a long time to write...like maybe years. It wouldn't take up all your time. There'll be other things you'll want to do with your friends. I remember that you used to spend some time with Francine over in Shady Ridge. That might be something you could do, but you would always know that the account would be waiting for you."

Now the pencil had come to attention. Poised upright, its point on the sheet, it twirled around within her fingers. A yellow-painted ballerina...spinning on point.

"Your mom thinks my story is interesting, and maybe it was, but the first one should be about my pa, Old Gaither, your grandfather. Now, there's someone who likes to talk, and he leaves out no details. Another thing, he can tell how he thinks and feels, and that's a hard thing for a lot of fellows to do.

"It really wouldn't matter where you started, because you could move the accounts around to suit whatever you think is best when you finally put them together. Now, Francine is another one who can tell you exactly how she thinks and feels, and she can fill you in on details about her stepdaughter, Violette. I remember you learned music from her, and you seemed to be one of her favorites. And I know Grandma Nettie would like to talk.

"Incidentally, my dear, I think your pencil wants to do it. I see it has moved up into your fingers into writing position." With a sly wink, she added, "I think there's a more than even chance that your pencil may begin without you if you don't get started right away!"

That brought a smile to the girl's face. "Do you really think Old Gaither would tell me his story? I'm only a granddaughter."

Glory be, thank You, Lord.

"My dear, he would adore it. Be sure you're ready before you ask him about it. He might give you more information than you want! And it will be such a comfort to your mom if you begin it before you start your next activity. She knows that if you start it, you will eventually finish. She knows you never leave things half done.

"And now I've got to get home. I have a kettle of beans I don't want to boil dry. They smell so bad when they burn. Bye, bye, my dear, and don't let that pencil run away with you."

With a wave she was off.

The excited pencil twirled a pirouette on its toes. The best place to find Old Gaither Cullen, actually her own talkative old Grandpa, would be over at the blacksmith shop where her pa was hammering metal.

Closing her excited pencil within the Composition Book, she returned the lemonade glasses, waved to Sunny and Rainy and crossed the street to the sound of hammer on anvil.

The trailing sprays of honeysuckle draped their fragrant blossoms from the trees that surrounded Owen's Catfish Pond, a local landscape attraction. The dark, dark green of the leaves accentuated the white and yellow of the blossoms and the flashing colors of the hummingbirds.

The tiny flying gems darted in and out, hovered, dipped and whirled, and precipitated scuffles over sipping rights into the tiny honey filled trumpets. These minor scuffles and tiffs were totally unnecessary as there were blossoms for all, and enough to spare.

Daniel Carpenter sat on a convenient flat rock and contemplated the ripples caused by catfish strikes. Set in a meadow as it was, there were grasshoppers aplenty along with bees and butterflies who had the misfortune to fly too low over the water.

The flat stone was in a perfect spot. Was it put there by nature or by accident? More likely was levered in place with a strong pry bar by Grandad Owens. It was his pond, of coarse, though anyone was invited to fish there. Fat, pond raised catfish for anyone…that was what Grandad had intended.

The young man had named the stone "The Thinking Place." It had been a recent naming ceremony, performed shortly after the Armistice (whatever that was) and his return to his home.

He had never before needed a "thinking place" as he had been busy "doing," but that was over now. Seemingly. Before him was a crossroad with neither path clear.

He had chanced to meet with Donald McGregor at the Cookie Jar. They had both been visiting the mail hooks. Donald had remembered hearing of Daniel during their stay in France.

"We heard a lot about you fellows over at the hub in Rouen. Nothing short of miraculous, the skill you fellows had. Now me, I was a medic because they needed a warm body, and we were tossed into the mix and used to fill out personnel requirements in the convalescent hospitals. Hard work and long hours, but we did not ever pretend to be doctors."

"You had occasion to hear of us?"

Wide-eyed with surprise, Donald replied, "How could we not? Our bandaged and splinted patients came from there, and we fitted them with crutches and conducted therapeutic exercises. We were the ones who sent them back into the fight, or home. We knew you all and that included a lot of actual names. I knew of you because of the Corners.

"You wouldn't remember them, of course, but other fellows from here went to Rouen first. There was the pilot who lost a foot? Raincrow from the Wichita's. He married our Linda Black Bird and they are trying to put together a school. Then there was the new fellow, Phillip Armstrong. He...."

Nodding, Daniel interrupted him. "I saw him. He was the one who drove an ambulance through the heat of battle with a compound fracture and broken fingers on both hands."

"That's him!"

"I was honored to get to write his letters home because his hands were bandaged."

A pause in the conversation. "Well, doctor, what are you doing now? Got a place to go?"

A long hesitation. "Not exactly. Still considering."

Donald again. "I could suggest something while you're considering. While I was gone, my twin sister Dorcas teamed up with Ellen Tall Tree from Westridge. Her brother, Mitch, was in the battle. Caught a bullet through his cheek and into his hairline. You fellows patched him up and he's home. He's freighting cotton and Merino wool down to Lokeba.

"Back to my sister and Ellen, those girls took a course in Oklahoma City and opened a clinic of sorts. When I came home, I started to help them, and Ellen...Now we could...."

"Wait! Cheek wound? Bullet that plowed through his scalp? He was ours? I was the one who took care of him. He was my first patient after I learned what happened to Adam...." His voice trailed off.

"Well, doctor, my sister is really glad you fixed him up. They were married a month after he got home. They're expectin' a kid!"

A hesitation as they stared at each other. Donald retrieved his voice first. "I gotta run, Doc, but I have time to say this. Occasions we could really use your skill. Accidents happen. We can handle a lot of things, like bone setting and difficult pregnancies, but we can't do a sewin' job like you did for Mitch."

Without another word, Donald turned and hurried away. The clippity clop of hooves signaled his haste. He HAD a place to go, while Daniel sat on the thinking rock. No place to go. Yet.

Which way to go? He opened the Book beside him and turned to Proverbs. He needed a few wise words. He started with Chapter 4, verse 11. "I have taught thee in the way of wisdom; I have led thee in the right paths. When thou goest, thy steps shall not be straitened; and when thou runnest, thou shalt not stumble."

Now, that would be a relief…to have one's steps straitened. Especially when he remembered that the "straitened" meant "narrowed and more clearly defined."

And where was that other place about steps. On, yes. Psalm 37: 23. "The steps of a good man are ordered by the Lord…."

That's what I need now, Lord. Where are You when I need You?

That sort of conversation is what preceded the time spent in the Thinking Place. While he watched the catfish fattening themselves on the bad luck of flying insects, the words opened out before him as on a scroll.

"Like with my friend Jeremiah, whom I knew 'when I formed him in the belly,' I have always known you. I knew of your mother's tragedy and her travail. I knew your ancestor over ninety years before your birth. I helped him contact you with the inheritance I left you.

"I placed you where you would be educated for what was ahead, and I gave your parents the means to afford the best teachers for you. I opened the way for you to learn to heal, because I knew it would be an encouragement to you.

"Who do you think placed you in position to be assistant to the professor and be sent abroad? Did you think that was merely chance…or perhaps the result of something you did?

"How did you manage to be among the first to be sent to the hospital hub? How did you so rapidly learn the stitching skill and healing knowledge you acquired?

"When you were so discouraged, who sent you letters from home? You rightly named the letters as messages from 'an angel'. That encouragement came regularly as long as you needed it. Did you think it was just something you deserved?

"Remember your seminary training on God's ways with men? How some must be forced, some can be pushed, but there are those who can be led. It should have been clear to you that you were being led. Did you think your life was guided by chance?

"Did you think it was an accident that you turned away from all offers and came back to your home? Of all the wounded, how was it that you crossed paths with those from home, and that your name was well known for your skill?

"Did you think Donald McGregor just happened to collect his mail himself rather than sending a boy as he usually did? I am well able to place my children where they should be and I have placed you in your place. My promise is that I will continue to guide those who will remember to follow."

Daniel closed the Book on his knee and set it aside. *Well, Lord, since You put it that way....*

So what was next? Many paths before him, and which to take? Still the problem remained.

No, the problem is not God, it is me. I will take a horse as go to the clinic. There maybe something to do while I wait for a clearer answer.

Miss Josie allowed herself a smile of satisfaction. What would she ever have done with her beloved sister-in-law, Janine?

A short conversation from Janine with her daughter and a change happened. There in her father's huge, comfortable leather chair sat her daughter, scribbling furiously, her face a picture of determined concentration.

Another composition book left the desk drawer. Twice she had wandered through the back of the quarter section to the sheep pasture, past the haystacks, and to the new church.

Such a wonderful piano they had been able to buy! It seemed to relax her daughter to move her fingers over the keys.

Who would have thought, when she was practically forced to learn, that the music would become a comfort to her!

Miss Josie told herself, once more, as she had so many times before, "Sometimes everything comes out all right." One did one's best, and sometimes they managed to stumble into the right path.

Miss Merytaten Cullen rested on the wide bench before the wonderful new instrument that had been purchased with the rent receipts from the sheep pasture. America Forrester Canfield, and her brother, Homer Forrester, had so generously dedicated the amount of the rent to the operation of the church. They deduced that God had been so good to them that they didn't need to keep the money.

Old Miz Armstrong, wife of the elderly minister, was the creator of music in the church, and it had been her careful choice that this more expensive instrument had been chosen. It would last a dozen lifetimes, she had said. And here it stood for Miss Merytaten to use to solace herself.

The new church had been made with an open gable, leaving exposed rafters so handy for hanging commemorative posters, and to attach the draw-curtain for program presentation.

For the girl manipulating the keys, the open gable was a sound chamber where the tone of the notes mixed the harmony and the melody together in a most interesting way. She worked her way through old familiar pieces and experimented with new ones.

There were new groups of sounds that accentuated each other. They were hidden within the keys, but by patient effort, she could find them. She had been told that by her teacher, Miss Violette, but she had thought at the time that they were just words meant to encourage her.

These new harmonious sounds intrigued and soothed her, and she was so involved that she did not hear the hesitant footsteps and the tap of the cane as Old Miz Armstrong approached. The old woman settled herself on the end of the bench and waited while the melody was finished.

Her many wrinkles moved into smile position and her bright eyes twinkled. "Darling girl, I hate to interrupt the music. It flows out so sweetly in every direction, and I think even the sheep appreciate it. I see them lifting their heads in this direction while they chew. Your melodies become more and more beautiful." She nodded in agreement with her own words.

"The reason I interrupted is, my dear, that I might forget what I needed to say to you. My old fingers have become so knotted and stiff that I can hardly move them from one note to the other. I have so enjoyed this instrument, that it is hard to let it go, but I will enjoy the melody even more when your fingers are on the keys."

Mutt felt her head jerk to attention. This was not just a social call. It was business.

The old woman continued, "So, from here on, I am requesting that you make the music for the choir. I know you are young, and there will be things for you to do that will keep you away sometimes, but when you are here, I hope you will agree to do this for me, and for the rest of the people."

In surprise, Mutt heard her voice say, "But…" and at that point, her mind kicked in. "Why, yes, Miz Armstrong. I will do what you want, and I thank you for the privilege."

The old head nodded, and her walking cane found its position on the floor. "You go right on playing, darling girl, and I will sit back and listen. I often come here, usually by myself, just to enjoy the wonderful place God has provided for His people in the Corners. So carefully He works things out for those who are in His path."

A tap, tap of her cane and she walked away, finding a seat near the center of the church and on the cushion continuously left there for her comfort.

The girl's fingers trilled through the keys bringing out the melody of "In the sweet bye and bye…." The old woman's head nodded in the rhythm of the keys, marveling at the ability of young fingers.

So now Miss Merytaten had another duty. Producing music from an organ or a piano required practice. Slowly she began to be pulled back into the community. The Hats and Hankies girls, Pat and Bridie, were always glad for company, even if it was from those who didn't pick up a needle and help.

And there was Daniel's sister, Prissy, being trained. She did extremely well, especially on the new treadle sewing machine. She remembered, now, to keep her feet still as she adjusted the fabric. Losing a small pinch of flesh in the side of her thumb helped her to remember. A lowering "presser foot" is an unforgiving piece of metal.

Most important, however, was her own research. There were times she spent two or three days at Shady Ridge with Miss Francine and Isabel, her helper. Then there was Anita Van Pelt who was a wealth of information about the later immigrants.

She could tell of the life in the Holland they had left, the difficulties in New York and the wonderful call to the territory and the land run.

There were so many to talk with. Her father, Brad, outfitted her with a pony from Uncle Jeff's corral and a single-seat buggy of her own. The small conveyance became familiar on the roads.

Doctor Daniel Carpenter again sat on the stone at the Catfish Pond. In his pocket was the letter. He did not expect it, but somehow he was not surprised. They could really use a teacher. Medical students could benefit greatly from his experiences in France, and could he see his way clear to take a position on the staff?

Kentucky. It was a long way from the Corners, but the Santa Fe knew the way. It could be the direction he should go. Then again, it could be just a place to wait for further direction. God apparently had a direction for him to go but He was being exasperatedly closed-minded about it.

Teaching medical students was a necessary thing. New discoveries were chronicled every day…many of them born of experiences learned in France and other military hospitals. It made sense, really, for him to go. It was a place where he could do a good thing. Wasn't it?

His parents weren't exactly thrilled, but they fully understood. He must do what he was trained to do. So his thoughts whirled around in his head as he stared through the windows at the darkness of the Kansas plains. The glass in the window reflected back a sober face. There would be a day and a night to ride, and he would report for the final interview. Just a formality, actually.

Doctor Carpenter spent a lifetime in the two days as he traveled east. With each mile, his doubts increased. Was he listening to the right Voice, or just taking a path that seemed open and easy to him. Was he so weary with searching for the answers he needed, that his mind was creating its own direction?

With stops and starts, Daniel was fifty hours on the train. More than two whole days, and to his best knowledge, his eyes had never allowed even a doze during that time. With burning redness, he reported to his duty station.

At his destination, he was met with serious faces and a crisp, yellow telegram.

"Son. Prissy compound fracture. Come soonest."

ABOUT YEAR 1150

The island just west of Europe was a large one. The temperate climate, however, enticed settlers from many places. It was roughly pear shaped, with the countries of Wales and England occupying the bulb-shaped southern part.

The northern 'stem end' of the pear was made up of an accumulation of rugged mountains, crystal lochs (later called lakes), a sprinkling of windswept islands peopled by a race of stubborn hardheaded survivors. They occupied the rugged northern end in a place first called Scotia.

The inhabitants at that time were an accumulation of travelers from Russia, through Germany and Denmark. There were those from the southern lands bordering the Great Sea who came through Iberia (later Spain) and France. For reasons of their own, these tough individuals chose the isolation of the rugged mountains.

Vikings came down from the north lands through the windy islands called Orkneys and settled the coasts of Scotia. These rugged persons carried their father's name, and went by Erickssofn, Swensson, Andersson and such. They brought their own words, and how did one pronounce "ss"? As they melded with the Scotia inhabitants, that extra "s" was eventually dispensed with as unnecessary.

Scotia had an influx of immigrants from across the western strait, and they were known as McGee, McConnell, McDonald, McClure and such, and that name was retained. These families stuck together and created clans. Scotia-land was hard to say, so it eventually became Scotland.

The border between England and Scotland was flexible, depending on the outcome of the last war between the two countries. One large clan from the southern border would be in England one year and in Scotland the next.

As a tribute to their preferred land of Scotland, every family in this clan, regardless of their current last name, came to be known as Scott. In this way, no matter where the Scottish boundary lay, a Scott would forever be a Scott.

It would also hold true if he were on a snake ship plying the oceans, or even on the soil another continent.

There was a legend in the old country about Scotland's hardy, stickery plant with a purple brush flower. It was said that wherever the Scotsman wandered, the national flower would follow as a protector. Maybe it did.

No one could know, at that time, that in a few centuries hence, a girl of Italian and Welsh heritage…living across a vast uncharted ocean in an as-yet uncharted prairie would write a tribute to the flower of Scotland. Neither would they know that the school children in a prairie town would be required to read the rhyming legend with the correct expression.

This would not be known, because Miss Francine Canfield had not yet been born. When that happened, she would write the following words.

THE LEGEND OF THE SCOTTISH THISTLE

Of rugged stalk and prickly leaf, the hardy Scottish thistles grow.
Seeds afloat on silken threads where gentle Scottish breezes blow.
And thistle seeds come down to rest, where only God and thistles know.

Scottish lads and lassies play 'mid the blooms beside the door.
Men blow their pipes and keep their sheep as they have done before.
Weeping women weave at home while young men go to war.

With spring the narrow snake boats of Viking Norsemen come.
Brave, young Scots with pipes and drums, rush to protect their home
Hoping they'll be home with piping, dread to ride behind the drum.

Soldiers sought a moment's rest before the marching trumpet sounds.
In darkness spread their sleeping mats, 'neath the thistles purple crowns.
Nighttime came, the sleeping sentry failed to make his watchful rounds.

Then at midnight, moonless dark, the wily Norsemen crept.
With their barefoot steps, they came, while Scottish soldiers slept.
Norsemen crept in total darkness, victory would be theirs…except….

In the darkness of the nighttime, yet six hours before the morn,
Tender Danish foot was planted on a thistle's dagger thorn.
Wounded Dane, he screamed the loudest since the day that
he was born.

Piercing screaming of the wounded woke the Scotsmen
from their bed.
Every Scotsman grabbed his long sword, while the Danish
army fled.
Not a Viking felt the long sword…never one brave Scot
was dead.

Daylight came, the Scottish laddies were all climbing hills
of home.
Sprightly marching with the bagpipes. None were riding
'aft the drums
Lassies ran to meet the laddies, thankful for the thistle's thorns.

Centuries later, Scottish laddies braved the fierce Atlantic gales.
Skillful hands of Norsemen's grandsons reached to trim the
tallship sails.
Together, on the rolling ocean, following windy, watery trails.

Wherever Scotsmen choose to wander…where the lads and
lassies play.
Surely thistles follow onward, and that is where the plant
will stay.
Scottish thistle goes with Scotsmen…it has always been that way.

Thistles came into the New World, hooked into the
Scotsman's shirt,
Or stuck inside a Danish stocking, giving him a limping hurt.
Either way, or how-some-ever, seeds took root in New
World dirt.

Everywhere the Scotsmen wander, everywhere their bairns are born.
Hills or valleys where they shelter, purple thistle blooms adorn.
Every Scotsman is protected by the thistle's dagger thorn.

Certainly the plains of the Oklahoma Territory were sprinkled with the stickery leaved plant with the purple brush-like blossoms, and it can cast its seeds to the prairie wind on gossamer threads.

BACK TO YEAR 1920

Doctor Daniel Carpenter read the telegram, and the noisy puffing of the Santa Fe brought its native son back to the Corners. Sheer exhaustion forced the doctor into deep sleep most of the way.

In Oklahoma City he took a stage to Argyle. Here he hired a horse and tried to calm his nerves on the way. No use speculating on what all was wrong with his sister, that he needed to come home in such a hurry.

At his parents' home, his pa had a pair of horses saddled and ready. They had been saddled all day, and all day yesterday.

A fast ride the two miles to the clinic.

He burst through the door and followed Donald to the room where his sister lay with one leg hanging from the ceiling in traction, and her foot swathed in bandages.

Donald was quick with the explanation. "Her leg broke in two places. No splinters and we think we have it taken care of. It's that ankle on the other foot. Not sprained, but seems to be twisted. Gives her a lot of pain."

As Daniel started to reach for her foot, Donald continued, "And there was a bit of a crack on the head, in the hairline behind her ear. We tried, but that kind of stitching…well, we felt you would want to be called."

Absolutely, he wanted to be called! The ankle could wait another hour. He propped her head and adjusted the oil lamp.

Tiny chip on the bone just behind her ear. Gash up into the hairline. They seemed to have done a good job with the stitches. But what other problems might be hidden in there?

This was a totally new area for Daniel. Cranial injury. This sort in France would have been worse, and always fatal.

"Headache?" he asked Prissy.

She swallowed hard. "All the time. Sometimes bad."

He took a deep breath. *Help me, Lord.* "First of, we're going to get rid of these pillows under your head. There might be a strain on your neck. We'll put a small one under your shoulders, and it should relieve some strain." He felt her cringe with pain as he adjusted her shoulders on the pillow and lowered her head into a different angle. Did he do the right thing? *God...are You there?*

Leaving the matter of her head temporarily with God, he turned attention to her foot and began to unwrap the immobilizing bandages. Good job of wrapping. Bad foot. Stretched tendons. Torn cartilage. How in the world could this have happened? There was swelling and fever. Small red streaks of a beginning infection. Naturally!

On the way, Pa had tried to explain about the rockslide. Rockslide? Where were there enough rocks to slide except at the back of Miss Josie's house, and those rocks were rough and flat. Nothing to slide. Actually, couldn't slide. But obviously they had.

Well, it was late and he was exhausted. As long as she had waited, another twelve hours would do no more damage, so he carefully replaced the wrapping and sat in the chair beside her bed. He'd really like to be fresh when he attacked this problem. He'd have to bring down the infection first of all.

Drawing a breath and squaring his shoulders, he asked. "How's the headache?"

"Uh...I think maybe better. I don't feel like I'm going to upchuck anymore. They told me I couldn't when I wanted to. Said they didn't want to turn me sideways if they could help it. I've been tied up like this for three days."

No more nausea. *Thank You, Lord.*

CHAPTER 5

Daniel, can I let my leg down? They said to wait for you. My foot kept getting cold, so they let it down a while."

"One more night, Sis. We'll give you a little rest right now, then up it goes again. It's getting late, and I want to see it tomorrow. You're being a very brave young lady. I going to put a cot here in the room and we'll see what we can fix up tomorrow."

Small smile. "Ma says you'll be able to fix everything…?"

He looked at her hopeful face. "Prissy, did you hear me say 'we' would see? I wasn't meaning you and me. I was referring to God and me, and if it gets fixed, you can thank Him. Together, we did things in France that I couldn't do. Just trust…Sis."

The back of his head tried to visualize the unseen damage. No mental picture came to him, as there so often had. He saw no assistance into the unknown. Like walking blind in the dark of the night. On unfamiliar territory.

She seemed more comfortable, and surprisingly, he did sleep. Perhaps it was the training in the triage center, making oneself sleep because sleep was needed. Putting worrisome thoughts into a box until tomorrow. That sort of thing. Survival.

Then a small voice in the night. He realized he was up on triage rotation and the alarm had not sounded. Or it was an attack in a village? Or a barge was on its way down river, bringing toward him mangled scraps of humanity trying to cling to life? Until they could get help. His help.

He leaped from the cot, his feet landing on the soft braided rug…not the cold, rough boards. Dim light. Leg suspended in traction.

Soft voice. "Daniel?" He readjusted his mental position from France to the clinic.

"Coming, Sis. What hurts the most?" Had he been wrong to wait until morning on that foot?

"It's not that. I think I'm dyin'. Wanted to say last words. Tell everybody I love them."

Her voice was soft, but clear. Not like a dying breath, and he should know. He'd heard plenty of them.

He was by her side. Felt her wrist...strong, even beats. "What makes you think you're dying?"

Her voice now quivered with fear. "I'm getting numb. Just a few minutes ago, I got no feeling anywhere. Except my hands. I think that must happen when a person starts to die. Will my hands die last?"

Hmmm. Well, where to start? "Head is numb?" Her forehead seemed cool and normal. He smoothed back her tangled hair.

"Yes. Well, no. Not my face, but that pain on top of my head stopped bein' there. Foot stopped achin'. Only thing it could be...seemed like. Me getting' numb, sort of."

Daniel brought the oil lamp to the bedside and sat down on the stool at her feet. Slowly, with apprehensive care, he began to remove the bandage. It seemed loose. Surely he had firmed the gauze up more than that when he re-wrapped the bandage. It would have been necessary to snug the wrapping to her ankle to avoid any further movement of displaced tissue. The fact was, however, that it was loose.

Red infection streaks not visible in the dim light. Skin cool and slightly moist. Totally normal skin. He applied light pressure below her ankle bone.

"Hurt?"

"Mmmmm, no, but I can feel it."

With his fingernails, Daniel lightly traced the sole of her foot at the arch. An instinctive jerk at her knee. A deep, relieved breath from the doctor.

"Sis, you're definitely not dying. At least, not tonight. Fever and swelling are gone." He glanced at her face and was rewarded with a pleased grin.

"Ma said whatever it was, you could fix it. I wanted to believe her and she was right!"

Daniel had never been one to lie. It was too dangerous because the truth had a way of making itself known. Sooner or later.

"You're wrong, Sis, and so is Ma. I did nothing at all. You saw me wrap your foot again until tomorrow. I had no idea of how to fix this problem and hoped I would get smarter by morning."

"Huh? But Ma...?'

"It was Ma, all right. It was her faith in my source of knowledge. What happened tonight was God showing me that He didn't, REALLY, need me. That He was humoring me and letting me think I was doing something. Head still feel numb?"

"I don't know. Something took the pain. Are you going to look?"

"No, Prissy, I guess not. God doesn't need me checking His work. You go to sleep, now, and we might have you on your feet tomorrow."

She whispered, "Good!" Likely she slept but Daniel did not.

Dawn was breaking when his mind finally put it into words. *God, I know I'm not too good at figuring out Your words, but I want to say this. I'll try to do better, and please don't send me to Kentucky and back again just teach me to understand You. You fixed my sister injuries, and it didn't take long for You to do it. I remember that You said in Your book, "Be STILL, and know that I am God" (Psa. 46: 10). You finally made me be still and back off, then You fixed the problem. You made me be present to witness Your work.*

Wide awake eyes stared at the pattern of the ceiling, and of the shadows made in the lamplight. *Just one more thing. I'm thinkin' it won't be necessary for You to give Ma pneumonia, so that*

I don't answer any more invitations to leave here. Hopefully God had a sense of humor.

The sun was well into the sky when he scrounged through the equipment and found a suitable crutch for Prissy. "Go slow, now, because of your balance. But I want you to keep walking around the clinic on that ankle. If you feel pain, even a tiny twinge, stop. Also, any nausea or dizziness…sit down. I don't expect either of those, but the doctor in me can't help giving a warning." He walked beside her across the room and back.

Her radiant smile of relief was a thing to behold.

Then the clinic door opened. Phillip Armstrong. The ambulance driver, his scar-tissued palms clinched into tight fists at his side, and breath coming rapidly.

"Doc, it's my pa…the preacher, you know. He's took down with something my ma thought was the croup, but the croup kettle isn't fixin' the trouble this time. Seems like every breath gonna be his last. Can you come?"

A glance toward Prissy, and her hand waved above the crutch handle. A smile, and she turned to clomp, step, clomp her way across the clinic floor.

Quick thinking Philip offered, "I see Owen's mare out back. Figure it's the one you're usin'. I'll get 'er ready while you get what you need."

A look at the wrinkled old man told a story. Years, concern, burdens he bore for others and many overnight vigils had taken their toll. Every breath taken in was a struggle and every breath released produced a rattle almost like that of death, itself. Bronchitis? Most certainly!

Or maybe the ague, as it was often called. There had been a lot of it caused by the mold and damp coldness off the French river. Not much could be done but treat with warm, dry air.

This seemed different. Applying the stethoscope against the bony ribs of his chest settled the question. Pneumonia, without a doubt. Bad for young, strong folks…mostly fatal for those like the preacher. Then again, he was a tough old fellow.

He'd designed and overseen the construction of the church building long after the time he should have been sitting in the shade swapping stories with a friend.

Old Miz Armstrong didn't look much better. Face sunk in with worry, chin trembling with fear. "Miz Armstrong, excuse my asking, but are you eating regular? You not takin' time to eat, you'll not be able to care for the preacher. Now, is he eating anything?"

A slight shake of her head told him the answer. "He needs liquids. Not milk, yet. Tomato juice. Garden tea, not the Chinese one. Start with peppermint. Keep up with the croup kettle. Menthol chest rub can't hurt. With pneumonia this far along, there isn't much to do but trust God. There's some evidence that juices contain something that helps combat a lung infection. Fruit juice would also be good. Maybe warm lemonade with honey."

Daniel could see the old woman taking in his words as she stood, poised for action. She'd take care of that right away. He stopped her.

"Now for you, I want you to eat an egg right now. Two if you can. Then eat another egg in three hours. Another one three hours after that. Drink warm lemonade with the preacher. Could be, Philip'd need to run over to Argyle. They carry lemons most of the time. Then you lay down and rest. Do you understand me? You gettin' yourself down won't help him in any way. I'll come back later."

The tired old eyes stared at him, and the weary head nodded.

Philip followed Daniel out as he turned to go. "I'll get on in and see if old Mac has lemons. Anything else I could do?"

At Daniel's hesitation, Philip went on, "I know, Doc. Old age and over work. Could be his time, but I hoped it'd be in his sleep on a good night and not on a sick bed. 'Course, we don't get to choose that, do we?"

With a wave, he was in the saddle and his horse's hooves were pounding the packed-dirt road.

Daniel stood in the bright sun of a fall morning on the prairie. Faint breeze, and not the gale wind that so often came. Pa's mare grumbled conversationally beside him. It was like that old question that kept coming up in the lectures. "Which comes first, tend to the health or tend to the soul?" No answer.

The adage about which came first, the chicken or the egg was easy. If the chicken had not been created on the sixth day, where would an egg have come from?

If God had not created people, there would be no ill health and dying. If there were no God, what would be the use of living? With a sigh, he patted the horse on the nose, swung into the saddle and headed toward home with the good news about Prissy. His baby sister.

She would be twenty this year, if he had his numbers right. Maybe just nineteen. She seemed just a cute toddler when he was sent off to school. He hardly knew her as a person and certainly not as well as he knew the "Angel" who kept him alive with letters from home.

Her letters were the stakes that had held down the "tent" of his existence in storm of trouble. His anchor in a raging sea. They were his tie-back to ordinary folks who did not come floating to him on a barge, their clothes and limbs torn apart. Angel was his sip of water on a parched desert. Had he ever told her what her letters had meant? Did he suddenly become shy when he saw her…face to face?

It hadn't been that way before he left. He had treated both tiny girls as special toys to be loved and cared for, and here was his sister, tall and beautiful, and requiring a full-length bed, not a crib.

And the other one. Fingers on the organ keys. Fingers with a pencil and notebook. Fingers that waved recognition when he passed by. He knew her fingers, but what about her head?… her thoughts?

She no longer had to be steadied on top of the haystack. Or humored when the pup stole her cookie. Talented and self-assured, she made her way to talk to this one and that one, taking care of her mother's assignment. Miss Josie didn't ask for much, but she intended to get what she asked for. And she had asked for…what was it…? a chronology of the tiny town…? the prairie…the new country…*hmmmm*.

Whatever it was, Merytaten, his letter-writing "Angel," could do it. Six years age difference…or was it seven? Maybe five. It had meant a lifetime at twelve, but time changes it. What was twenty-one (twenty-two?) when he was only twenty seven? Really only twenty-seven…? Seemed a hundred years. Didn't matter.

Carlotta Owens Carpenter met him at the door and followed him, "I heard! I knew you could do it?"

Holding her back at arms length, he shook his head. "No, Ma. I did nothing. It was you and God."

YEAR 1921, SCOTLAND

Old Dermot Scott was member of the huge Scott family that occupied a large tract of land on the English-Scottish border. It seemed that the English had found other things to do and had not been a bother for a generation or two.

Many of the highland wars were too far north to be a concern to him. Other than the scrappy McDonalds being an occasional nuisance, life was fairly peaceful. The Scotts were working, eating, visiting, having babies and dying, much as to be expected.

It had been several years later that old Dermot and his brother, Burnard, had discussed making the trip to the new country of America. They could just sell off, pick up their families and go. Lots of good land to be had in the middle of the country.

Then one thing and another, and the "going" did not happen. Children got older and began their own lives. Dermot's oldest son, Errol still talked of it, though, and seemed to have a hankering to go. Why not? Get one son over there, and that'd make a path for the rest. Wouldn't it?

It took the sale of some sheep (good riddance) to get his son and his son's wife over there. The two youngens. Heard the lad bought himself some land out on something that was called a prairie where one could see for a couple'a miles or more. Now just think'a that! Best way to see that far in Scotland was to look straight up.

Then came that band of marauders across the border. Scotland's men and grown boys headed out to defend the land that was bought and titled legally, and it didn't go too well. Brother Burnard came home in a wagon behind the drums, and he, Dermot, rode beside him because he had lost a foot.

His brother was put in the ground on the hilltop, closest to God, and a bucket and peg was created for himself, to let him walk without the foot. Not too bad, but that meant never going to the new country. Still and all, he had all those sheep, including those of his brother.

But there was Burnard's oldest girl, Katy. Stunning creature of sixteen and had eyes for that neighbor, Reuben, son of old Dermot's sister. Looked like a good enough match.

The surprise was when Katy came to him and said her pa had promised there'd be money to let her go to America as soon as cousin Errol got settled, and he was settled now, wasn't he?

A little thought and head-scratchin' and it was clear that more of those sheep could send that girl where she wanted to go. Then there'd be grass enough for the remaining sheep without driving them up to the high country every summer. No need for a shepherd, that way. The family was running out of strong young men who wanted to spend their summers with only bagpipes and sheep for company.

Nothing wrong there. Young men had a right to their own life, and havin' those sheep gone...that'd bring no tears from him.

The pair set the wedding bans and invited the entire clan. No gifts, please, though the Jug would be present, and any coins found within that ceremonial container would go toward the journey to America.

Nothing would go with them except the steamer trunk and two carry-on back packs. Travelin' light…no gifts please but money was appreciated.

Old Branson McDougal was hired to write the wedding song. For a small fee and all he could consume, he would compose a ditty uniquely for the bride and groom and would sing it accompanying himself on the lute. It never failed to be a winner.

The heather was in bloom and the mountaintop was alive with butterflies and a blend of aromas. Food came, every cook bringing enough for twice her family. Everyone who could stand without a cane for support wore their dancing shoes. This wedding purported to be the event of the year.

The pair was going to America, and this was their nation bidding them well. Old McDougal came in his cart pulled by pair of small ponies with a heritage from the Shetland Islands. Using his cart as a stage, he stood with his lute, and sent forth his song onto the Scottish breeze.

THE MARRIAGE OF KATY SCOTT

Miss Katy Scott, she married up, with Reuben Scott, her beau.
They knelt there on the alter cloth, so God and Clan would know
They two would be together for as long as west winds blow.

Chorus:

They danced and sang the whole night through
The way that Scottish lovers do.

They packed up bags and said goodbyes. Turned faces to the west.
Until they reached their destination, never would they rest.
Far out among the prairie trees, they planned a little nest.

Chorus again.

No one considered it a great composition, nor did they expect it. It did, however, have a wonderful beat, and who could hear the words, anyway? Certainly no one thought Dermot did not get his money's worth, and all it took was sheep. They were Burnard's sheep, at that.

The song didn't matter because several pipes had been brought and their unique sound floated over the hills and the glens. The wailing sound of courage, of marching forward to meet the foe...whatever it might be. Many dancing feet kept the time. When the bagpipes rested, it was Katy's lovely voice that filled in.

Their Katy, the singer. She would be sorely missed.

A lovelier voice was never bestowed on a Scottish lassie. Katy was a butterfly. A beautiful, loving, charming girl with the voice of angel. When she sang, even the birds kept quiet and listened. Or so it seemed.

The sailing date was four months hence, to allow Reuben time to collect the divided prize for completing his group's contract in the tin mine. What kept him sane in his underground drudgery was the thought of the wind-swept prairie air and the blazing southern sun at the end of his journey. Never again would he go below ground. Willingly.

Miss Katy spent the four months visiting friends and packing and repacking the steamer trunk.

When the pair boarded the *Angel Gabriel* out in Liverpool's harbor, she was not yet wearing her expanding garments. She also held no belief in morning sickness. She didn't have the time for such nonsense.

The good ship *Angel* moved out of the lock and dipped gracefully into the Atlantic Ocean. Arms waved until Land's End in England could no longer be seen. The *Angel* was a fast ship and she carried layers and layers of canvas. Sons of Viking seamen trimmed the sails and set them toward the west. They could expect to reach the shores of America in a mere fifty days.

Who would know that the *Angel* would have a rough flight? On day thirty-five, the depth of the Atlantic boiled up like a frantic teapot, and torrential winds came from two directions alternately. There was nothing for the seamen to do but draw in the sails and run before the wind, always a dangerous decision, but safer than the alternate.

For a "tall ship" like the *Angel*, leaving the sails to catch the gale wind was an invitation to being tipped over, and possibly turned bottom up.

The able seamen knew how to handle this situation, but it was frightening to the passengers. During that moonless, starless night, seven babies drew their first breath. One was too small to live, two had been expected momentarily, four others managed to draw breath into their somewhat underdeveloped lungs.

Small Bonnie Heather Scott was one of the last group. Well-nourished and protected for the first seven and a half months of her existence, she willing entered the world with the expected amount of indignant screaming. Her healthy mom knew what to do, and Bonnie was fed and wrapped, rocked and adored.

While the seamen fought the rudder, struggling to the keep the ship upright, the ladies below deck held to each other to stay on their feet. They did not trust the holding of a new squalling citizen of the world to just one person. One lady picked up the child as she was being steadied by another lady. Precious treasures must not be dropped.

Some of the older ladies held the new mothers onto the rocking beds as the ship wallowed and rolled. The assisting women stared wide-eyed as Reuben Scott sized up the situation with his precious Katy, then stretched his lanky frame out beside her. Miss Katy was securely locked between the ship's bulkhead and the strong arms of her "beau."

Through a night and a day, the *Angel Gabriel* fought to stay alive, then in the space of an hour, the clouds blew past, the sun shone and the waves began to calm. Another hour and the waves were such that the canvas again was drawn up on the masts and the brave ship was turned in a direction the captain deemed best.

Come a clear night with stars, and the captain could set his sextant to the heavens, and then he'd know exactly where he was. A correction, and they'd be on the way again. Hardly any crossings were uneventful, and delays such as this were figured in.

Lucky to only delay two days and also to still have a tight ship. There were many who looked up and gave their thanks.

The women made Katy stay in bed for another day, and then young Heather was handed over to her mother. The kind and helpful ladies were released and they gratefully returned to other activities, sincerely glad that it was not they who were starting the day with a newborn infant.

Having babies was strictly for the young, and preferably on land. A month later they were there.

It was two months later that all papers were signed and a suitable wagon was purchased. They were going to need one anyway, so they decided on the best. Two horses and a spare. Provisions laid in. The money in the wedding jug found places to go, and still there was a fair amount left.

There were regular caravans of eight to twenty wagons heading west, and they joined. Safety was important. There would be an escort all the way to the nearest small town to the end of their destination.

Small Bonnie was a good traveler, lulled into peacefulness by a full tummy and a continuously rocking bed. Pacified by prairie sounds, and her parents' voices as they sang and re-sang the words to their wedding song.

YEAR 1921, OKLAHOMA TERRITORY

Miss Priscilla Carpenter walked away from the Shady Corners Clinic with not a pain in either head or foot. She was quickly skillful with the crutches that she would need for at least a month.

Doctor Daniel Carpenter took his Bibles…the one left him by his ancestor, the one that comforted him through France, and the new one purchased when he arrived home.

With the three on them in his hand, he walked across the prairie grass to the Catfish Pond and settled himself on the flat stone. His Thinking Place. It was time for some serious talking with his Maker, and it might take days…or maybe weeks. He needed clearer answers, as he seemed too dense to understand his own life.

Later, he would have to ride over and check on old Rev. Armstrong. Pneumonia at his age was something to be concerned about. With all three Bibles open before him, he waited. A butterfly lit momentarily on the page of his newest book.

When the bright-winged insect lifted off and flitted away, Daniel looked quickly where it had lighted. It would be so wonderful to have the answer pointed out by the insect's feet, but it was not to be. That particular spot was a white place between two sentences that had no discernable connection to his concern. God was clearly not going to make it easy for him. Finally, he closed the Books and went back to his home.

Then at the parsonage, he met a concerned Miz Anderson. "Oh, son, so glad you're back. The Reverend is concerned for the church and says you must consider filling in until he got better. Oh, do say you will! It's keeping him so upset!"

The faded blue eyes peered out from the layers of wrinkles, intense and pleading toward him. Her eyes begged, please give the old man release by taking over his burden until he can pick it up again.

Daniel felt a catch in his breath. Answers came from the place where answers came from. At least for this instant, he knew where he should be. For the two problems currently before him, he was uniquely qualified to attend.

The old man still lingered, so God was not ready for him, yet. He needed rest, freedom from worry and pampering with the warm lemonade from the tart fruit his son had ridden ten miles to bring to him.

He was weary from the burden of the new Forrester Community Church that he had considered to be his crowning duty. He had been sent to grow the church up from the virgin grass of the prairie. He had been given the location, he created the design and arranged for every facet of its construction. He had even designed it so that it could be enlarged by fifty percent without damage to the overall design.

In addition to that, he had born the spiritual load, stopping anything to take on the duties of a rural pastor. Births to funerals, he could expect to be needed in any area by any person. So now he rested and slept...his life mate hovering protectively over him.

In the operation room at Rouen, France, Daniel had learned to look at the immediate problem and immediately do what he could do. Remembering that, he began....

"Rest assured, Miz Armstrong, I will assume his church duties. It will be my pleasure. Then about the preacher's health, it has been four days and he is no worse. That is the best sign we could expect. Continue what you are doing, and encourage soft cooked eggs for him three times a day. And certainly continue to remember yourself.

"You have escaped the pneumonia so far, and now, I would advise you to lie down beside him and sleep if you can. At least rest. If he needs you, you will be sure to hear. And when he wakes up, assure him that God is in charge and I will be here as long as needed."

Relief was visible in the wrinkled face, and she even managed a small smile.

And he rode away, the horse striking an amiable trot. He now had an answer. Maybe not the total one he sought, but it was certainly an immediate one. He would go home and pick up Bible number three. Though he had committed many portions of the Bible to memory, still it was necessary to hold the book in his hand as a conduit to a message from Above.

As he passed the Cookie Jar, the south breeze was whispering in the leaves of the cottonwood that shaded the picnic tables. He'd go home and have a snack, then bring the book back to the inviting, tree-shaded table.

But as he returned, the tables were no longer empty. At the table closer to the Cookie Jar, the young lady was bent over her composition book, her pencil moving rapidly.

Hmmmm. If he sat at her table, would it be an intrusion to her train of thought? But, if he chose the other table, would it not seem he was indifferent to her? Which…? After all, she had been the Angel who had stilled the troubled waters of his mind for those two nightmare years.

In the Cookie Jar, he ordered lemonade and popcorn. Then corrected the order, "Make it two, while you're at it."

Balancing the two glasses of the drink, and the two bowls of still-warm popcorn, he tucked the Bible under his arm and maneuvered the doorknob. Seating himself midway down the table, he set one glass and one bowl within reach of the bowed head and scribbling hand. Balancing the other glass of the drink and a bowl of fluffy grains, the Bible still under his arm, he seated himself.

"Didn't want you to starve to death amid sentence."

The writer startled and looked up. A smile, "Thanks. I was about to do that. Needed to write just one more sentence. That was two pages ago…you know how it is."

"That I do! I thought I'd sit here and we could work separately together. Such a good day."

A few more pleasantries and they both bowed to their self-assigned duties.

From the small Cookie Jar window an interested face peered. Mrs. Gwinnie McLaughlin Armstrong commented, "Well, what do you know! They're both sitting at the same table, like they might even know each other."

"Are they talking?" wondered her sister, Kristie McLaughlin Morrison.

"Nope. All I see is the tops of heads and elbows."

"Well, maybe it's a start."

YEAR 1921, AMERICA

It had been an exciting trip for Reuben and Katy Scott. There was the amazement of new sights, eagerness for destination, and evenings around the fireside with fellow travelers. It was like having a sudden family who immediately understood you.

And little Heather, with bright eyes the color of the blooms on the plant that carpeted the mountains of home…she was indeed a dream baby. Dimples when she laughed, gurgles when she was full, and smiles when she was asleep.

The group they traveled with had become like a big, happy family. Sharing food and stories, and help when needed.

There had been the excitement of the big river. The couple still had coins from the wedding jar, but the river towns begged for help. By the hour or day…or however. Reuben, being provident by nature, put pencil to paper and decided they should stop over for a month. Maybe two.

Convoys traveling westward arrived daily, and when they wanted to move on, they would just catch the next one that was going their route. Oklahoma City was a popular stopover for re-provisioning and it was one of their last points of call.

Katy found things to do, and Reuben bent his back to the stevedoring, thinking of the high-paid labor he was giving. He could smile as he thought of the fellows back home when he told them what he was being paid. Just for doing a man's natural work. Of course, there was no chance that they would believe him.

For Katy, motherhood was the fulfillment of her life. It was just the frosting on the cake of her dream marriage. Most days she was content to just straighten up the Conestoga wagon, rinse out a few diapers and hold her baby. And sing the Scottish songs of her childhood.

Reuben had chided her for using the old language because small Heather would need to hear her parents using the language of the new country.

"But she's so tiny and the songs are so pretty," Katy pled, attempting to bargain with him. Finally, they settled on one year. After that, she could not use any part of the old country language until Heather was ten.

So she sat under the shelter of the overhead canvas with her feet extended into the warm sunshine. She thought, planned, rocked and sang until it was time to prepare food. Reuben would come "home" starved as a bear just out of hibernation.

The river town had all kinds of meats, a lot of them already prepared and only needed warming up. Katy had no delusions that her life would not change radically when they reached their land, but she could enjoy this wonderful time with little Heather.

YEAR 1921, CARLILE CORNERS

Old Mrs. Armstrong was looking a lot better since the doctor had told her she must lie beside the patient and rest, so she would be ready when needed. Those eggs, too. So easy to fix. Who would have thought they might be part of the healing! The old couple could eat and rest and spend their time together.

Daniel visited regularly, and decided the tough old fellow was going to "pull through" in spite of it all. He prescribed periods of sitting up in the comfortable old chair that had somehow managed to be brought along in the cramped space of the wagon.

It now occupied a place a place of honor in the bedroom of the parsonage, right by the east window, the better to get the morning sun. He had found it a good place to do his morning reading and sermon preparation.

And when he settled himself into the padding that knew all his bulges and angles, he could almost feel himself well again. With his Book on his knees, he looked out across the yard to the sheep pasture. God's pasture.

Birds zoomed around in the bushes and trees, doing whatever it was that birds do after their family has fledged. From that window he could see the althea bush he liked to call the hollyhock tree. It was in full bloom with the coffee mug sized deep rose-colored blossoms.

The sight of that tree always made him close his eyes and offer a blessing on the young woman…girl, actually…who insisted this land her father had left his two children would be given back to God.

He could feel the tears on his cheeks to think of the way God had preserved that buried jar of coins and allowed them to be found…coins that were the accumulated tithes of her father's labors. And the way God allowed the althea bush to mark its location.

This was likely to be the old minister's last duty station, but wasn't it a grand one! It was like God wrapped together all the good things He had planned for the little town of Carlile Corners, and put them in one big package. *Thank you, Lord! You sure know how to put together the pieces of Your puzzle.*

The first Sunday of Rev. Armstrong's illness, Daniel had stepped behind the cleverly designed pulpit before the congregation. A whole new experience for him.

He had studied, outlined sermons, attended lectures and even given a few (just for practice) before he had been picked off for medical training. The Bible he knew well, and people… he was learning to know well. But nothing prepared him for the feeling of standing before a building full of benches…the benches full of people who had put aside their workday, shined their shoes and combed their hair…just to hear the music and listen to God's word. So amazing, really.

And here he was…standing between God and earth, and how could he ever have felt himself worthy, or even prepared? But he must begin.

"My friends and neighbors, we will bow…."

Miss Josie's only daughter sat alone on the front seat, ready to be close to the piano if music was needed. The morning sun shone in through the east window onto the polished floor, and a reflective glow streamed toward the pulpit. The soft light of it erased any shadows that might be on Daniel's face.

Hmmm, was that an intentional trick of the designer, Rev Armstrong? The placement of that window and the position of the sun at this time of a morning? Surely not! But maybe....

Her fingers played with the pencil in her hand. Her ears listened to the words with a parade of thoughts in the back of her head. This person had not been interviewed for the Chronology of Carlile Corners.

She had his letters. She would read them again before she talked with him…just to get the flavor of his time in France. So much of what he wrote was of the people who came to him for help. Sometimes it seemed the children upset him the most, but then, his heart bled for them all.

Do hearts really bleed? She must ask him that. She firmed her lips and sighed, and his words came, modulated and expressive…the way he was taught, no doubt. Today, his words flowed like the glue that was meant to bind people together in their faith.

So different were his letters. Looking back, and being a couple of years older now, she saw herself as being the sponge that was used to sop up the scarlet pool when his heart bled for those on his operating table.

Those letters. They were not letters to a girlfriend…or even actually a friend. They were letters to a "buddy." A buddy who would know what he meant however the words came out. Strange, that she had never thought of them that way until this very moment. Her letters were something that she wrote and sent, and his were something she received and absorbed.

Her letters. They were not letters to tell him how she felt. What would that matter to him…anyway? Hers were letters to tell how things were. What people did. Who had moved in and who had proved up and sold out. Substantial letters full of solid facts. Words that were meant to tie him to a place where there was sanity. A small life raft in his sea of horror.

Then he had come home and there were no more letters to be sent. Either going or coming. Just words of greeting in passing. A friendly wave of recognition when they passed each other on the road.

He was talking of the "invisible threads God used to keep His beloved children from falling. Threads that could not be broken, except by the stubbornness of people, or their insistence on going their own way...."

Then a pause, and her fingers knew enough to place the pencil on the bench, and the pencil knew enough to lie there and not roll off. Her feet knew to carry her quietly to the keyboard of the lovely instrument, picked out and ordered by Rev. Armstrong's life mate.

The first chords of the closing music. The voices joining the notes. "...God be with you till we meet again. Till we me...ee... et, till we me...ee...et...till we meet at Je...sus' feet. God be with you till we...."

The sounds died away and the people turned to each other with these words and those words, and in pairs and groups they left the building.

Daniel turned to his pianist with his smile. Friendly, impersonal. She smiled at him and gave a finger wave as she left the platform. Truly, she had been his life raft in his sea of horror, and she still was. This was his first actual experience before a real congregation, not critical classmates or accessing instructors, and it went so smoothly with her there. His understanding Angel.

He should say something. Should tell her so. No words came. He had been trained in words, and she was born with a head full of them. But now there were no words.

Daniel watched her leave and felt the last strains of the day's music leaving with her. Face to face, they seemed to be amiable strangers, joined in a mission that was important to them both. The conducting of a Sunday church service.

CHAPTER 6

Just like the letters that had made their way back and forth… between the normality of Corners and the hell that war had made of the lovely country of France. Could two years and a couple thousand miles make that much difference? Where were the free-flowing words?

Later, at the Catfish Pond, Daniel sat on the flat rock and watched the feeding mouths of the fish as they popped above the surface to catch a low-flying insect that was struggling to rise up on sodden wings.

Then, there were the grasshoppers. On buzzing wings they hopped and flew on to the next grassy place to feed, and it was sometimes the surface of the pond where they landed. The bulging eyes of the catfish saw them coming and knew what to do. Lunch was served. Both creatures served their purpose in life.

Daniel took a sheet from the tablet he had brought with him. It had become a habit, lately, to have paper handy. Who knew when God would decided to speak to him and he didn't want to miss a word.

A small smile on his lips as a thought crossed his mind. In Bible times, there was an occasion that the other Daniel needed a message from God, and Satan put up such a fight that the message was twenty-one days getting to him. Maybe the present-day Daniel just needed a messenger angel?

Propping the tablet on his knee, he wrote:

"Dear Angel…." Then he paused.

What in the world was he doing! Trying to write to a… an angel? But that word had seemed so natural to his hand, so appropriate to the pencil and looked so right on the paper, for hadn't he written those two words so many times before…in the dim light of the bunkhouse?

Those words and the ones that followed were often written at one thirty on a rainy morning by an exhausted hand. They were words that must be committed to paper at that instant, so they would not become a nightmare in his mind at three thirty, making him scream out in agony…as so many of them did. The words he wrote were words that would connect him to a remembered place of peace. Make him relax.

His hand kept writing.

…Today I saw a sight that I have not seen in a long time. At least, not in the last several years. I saw a person whom I would like to meet, and perhaps you can introduce me to her. I know that angels were often sent to help mortals who need them, and I fear I may never again see this person without angelic help. So I come to you.

Angel, just in case you can help me, I will give you a clue as to where to find this person. I saw her this morning sitting before me. She sat in a pool of light, and the sunshine sparkled and glowed all around her. I was so pleased by the sight of her, that when I opened God's Book the words came so easily that I knew they were not my words. They seemed to come straight from the mind of my Boss. Our Boss, actually.

Now, I know, of course, that the young lady I saw had nothing to do with my ease of speaking…or even of the sunshine that surrounded her but I thought perhaps if I wrote to you, you would be able to help me find her. It seems that I knew her once and she was able to draw me up out of myself and let me see things more clearly. I think I need that help again.

I understand, also, that it is not necessarily the mission of you heavenly beings to carry messages between mortals, but I thought it couldn't hurt to ask you. I'm certain you were there in the Forrester Community Church this morning, so you will know who I am referring to by the music that flowed so effortlessly from her fingers.

So, in closing, if you can see your way clear to help me in this matter, I would so greatly appreciate it.

But, if you see that this person is just in my imagination, or maybe someone who is not interested in being in my life, or perhaps not even intended by our Boss to be meant for me, then you could just wad up this note and toss it in the Catfish Pond.

Reverently yours, Daniel Carpenter

Living on earth by the Catfish Pond.

With a wry smile, Daniel read the words on the paper propped against his knee. How silly and stupid. What a waste of good paper and pencil lead.

With a firm chin, squared shoulders and fingers (made steady by determination and the skill required by the scalpel) he crumbled the paper into a wad and tossed it into the pond.

As the missal sailed over the edge of the water, a fat catfish made a leap with an open mouth…and missed! The fish splashed back into the water on the exact instant the paper wad hit, and the spreading ripples of its re-entry spread in every direction.

The lightness of the paper wad landed it on a ripple and rode it toward the shore, ending its ride wedged lightly between two cattail stalks. Stalks within easy reach of the preacher/doctor who was watching its progress with an amused smile.

He reached forward and plucked the somewhat soggy paper wad from the pond. He stretched it out on the warm flat rock and looked up. "Well, Heavenly Being, I guess I got the message that time."

With a sigh of relief, he propped the tablet against his knee and copied the strange note, word for word. If this was the "message" he had been needing, he did not want to risk a mistake with any part of it.

Folding the paper carefully, he returned to the house and found an envelope. Addressing it to "Angel," he headed for the Cookie Jar and its wonderful mail hooks. He was aware that the angel had her own hook, as he did, and no longer used the one belonging to her parents. He'd just clip it there and see what happened.

He hitched the small buggy to a gentle mare, the first one he located as he stepped in the corral. She was one that liked to hang around people for a possible treat from the garden. He'd drop the letter off at the Cookie Jar, and maybe have a cup of peppermint tea. Then he'd ride on over to the Clinic and see if Donald would be there.

Or maybe he wouldn't even mail the letter at all.

It was good that he had a whole mile and a quarter to re-decide that this message had Divine Guidance, and if he decided he had been mistaken, then he could just drive on.

It was a fact that the doctor/minister did not have a driving force within him. He was more of a follower of conviction and training. He was absolutely not given to impulse action. It was purely not his nature.

So…why now?

He steered the mare into the cottonwood trees around the Cookie Jar. He clearly saw who was sitting at the picnic table, tapping the eraser of the pencil against her cheek. He also saw that he could easily steer around her and get his tea. Possibly unnoticed.

He looped the reins over the hitching rail, reached down to the buggy seat and picked up the white square of paper. With firm and resolute steps, he walked toward the studious-looking figure at the table, the one who was gazing toward the treetops. Walking behind her, he tossed the white square on to the table, landing it on her open composition book.

With not a pause in his stride he walked on past, and into the Cookie Jar. Marching toward the counter, he told the girl his order…who was she? Maybe twelve years old. Maybe just eleven. Whose could she be? Didn't matter.

"I would like about four of those soft molasses cookies. Do you have any marshmallows?"

The girl shook her shiny black hair, as straight and flowing as the mane on a racehorse's neck. "We ain't got no marshmallows, but we got this." She held up a glass jar with something white inside, and continued, "We got this here marshmallow crème that we use to glue the cookies together with."

Daniel nodded. "Very good. Would you glue these four cookies and make two cookie sandwiches? And then I'd like whatever hot tea you have."

The cookie sandwiches appeared on the counter with practiced skill, and the two steaming mugs appeared beside them.

The girl. "You want I should carry these out to you and your girlfriend?"

Daniel startled at the word. But she had asked a question, and he produced an answer.

"I think that might be a good idea. I'll hold the door."

With the two hefty mugs in one strong, capable hand, she scooped the cookies into a red and white checked napkin. With a smile she turned to him and hesitated, waiting for him to start for the door.

He did. But his mind was on the strong, no-nonsense hands that could lift full water pitchers so heavy that they strained young bicep muscles, hands that gripped shears that sawed through blood-soaked clothing with absolute skill and strength, and watch amazed at the efficiency with which both of her hands could wrung out a wet towel that would have wrapped twice around her waist.

This girl couldn't possibly be as old as thirteen, but his mind could easily place her in the huge, drafty triage barn and have her knowing what to do before being told.

Finally, getting command of his feet, Daniel led her to the door and let her pass through. She walked on to the picnic table and with a flourish set the cookies and a mug before the girl, and the other mug directly across the table.

The girl looked up at him and smiled at his thanks. Then she walked with solidly placed, no nonsense feet and a relaxed stride back into the Cookie Jar and her job.

Daniel squared his shoulders and sat down at the table to await the verdict.

It seemed hours before she spoke. "You know, Daniel, I've been wonderin' where you were. Some months ago I saw a fellow come to the Corners that looked a lot like you. He caused me to think about you but I didn't want to ask him where you were. Figured he might not have known."

She blew the trail of steam from her tea. "I figured when you finally got here, and that other fellow left, we could maybe find somethin' to talk about. Was thinkin' maybe you and God had things to discuss. Could be maybe you two finally came to a meetin' of the minds. I've been there myself enough to know that it don't help to have folks buttin' on the conversation when you're not even there, and can't do nothin' about it."

Daniel nodded. "I noticed there was a bit of distance between the two of us. I did remember, though, that one time when that fellow was a long ways away, he got a box of molasses cookies glued together with marshmallows. I thought the distance between us might be so great that these cookies needed to stay fresh till they got there."

He watched her smile of remembrance of when she had ordered those exact cookies for him, for the same exact reason. But he didn't tell her he had hidden those cookies and rationed them out to himself only on the times he ABSOLUTELY NEEDED THEM.

But he did add, "I told the girl to do that, so if you don't like 'em, then your fight is with me, and not that other fellow who looks like me."

Tea and cookies gone, they climbed into the buggy, and the old mare obligingly took them up the road...headed into nowhere…and for no reason. Young people who have just met after a long absence might need a time to have no reason for doing something.

It was while they were riding, they realized words were not always necessary. In fact, they were often in the way.

Early in the next week, Daniel visited his patient and found him sitting up on the edge of his bed, his life's mate hovering over him.

She told Daniel, excitedly, "Doctor! He's been up walkin' all the way to the kitchen and back. Ain't even wheezin', neither!"

Daniel nodded. "I'm not surprised. Hard to keep a strong fellow down after he's had two weeks rest." Stethoscope read vast improvement. Seemed he wouldn't be making his final journey from his sick bed. At least not this one.

The bright old eyes met the doctor with a smile. "Yeah, doctor. I got it in my mind to come over to the church, come next Sunday. Feelin' like I been down for months…."

Here, Miz Armstrong butted in. "We was thinkin', doctor, you sayin' it was safe to be up that long, we could take his comfortable chair, the one with the high back, over to the church for 'im to sit in. We could set it right up there in front'a the first bench, and he'd be able to hear everything. We sure do enjoy the music that girl makes. Seems like she'd need an extra hand, the way she plays those notes."

Daniel listened and thought, why not? It would give the old man something to look forward to…and how could it hurt?

He and his Angel had spent a lot of the last two and a half weeks together. He had even come along on one of her interview trips.

The small town/settlement just west of Shady Ridge was called Westridge, and there were a number of families living among a sprinkling of huge boulders. Since the Armistice (whatever that was) had been signed in Europe, the fellows had come home.

There were the Fire Eagle brothers who had been among the first to volunteer. Their strength and testing indicated they would make flyers. These young native men had never seen anything but an eagle flying the way they soon would.

With a minimum of training, they were fearlessly zooming over the fields and streams of Europe delivering their lethal load of destruction. The three of them seemed to have a natural ability to evade ground fire and manage to get back to base. The English Royal Air Force begged for more like them.

Decorations and ribbons for bravery and skill were tossed into their duffle with abandon. Of course they would do well. Otherwise, why would they do this? They were discharged now, of course, but that did not mean they were at home on the ground.

They were currently on the east coast hovering over the companies creating an Air Force for America. Somebody had to test those things…didn't they?

Their military exploits were well known, as was the assignment of Miss Josie to her daughter to interview everyone. Not just the famous.

Now, there was Larry Raincrow. He was a decorated pilot, but he was grounded from his injury. A bad landing had forced him to leave a foot spread across the landing field in France.

No matter. One didn't think with his feet and thinking was Larry's strength. He designed a brace for the landing gear on the plane that crashed on his foot. He improved the earthmoving equipment for Canfield Grading while he was working there. He even improved the quality of the prosthetic foot the government made for him.

His big project, however, was in a totally different direction. He had come back from rehabilitation and laid eyes on Miss Linda Black Bird. After one look, he never looked away.

Being that his strength was using his head, he figured out that to get a girl to see you better and quicker was to figure out how to get her what she wanted. First you had to figure out what that was.

It wasn't that Linda felt herself such a good choice for a schoolteacher, it was more that she saw the need. That was the way Linda was. When she had been young, opportunities for education were practically non-existent. This problem was especially prevalent in the rocky and forested areas like Westridge. Linda thought the children there needed their own school.

When Miss Francine came to the school in Shady Ridge, Linda's age and responsibilities had kept her from attending regularly.

Her younger brother attended, however, and Linda had grilled him daily as to what he had been taught. In this way, she had learned just enough to know how much more she needed to know.

Larry, no fool that he was, did a little looking around. There were books he could order…and he did. He found a beginning school that could really use an unpaid assistant. If Linda would just marry him now, he would find a little place close to that school, and he would commute over to the Corners to his job with Canfield Grading.

Linda would. She assisted Eve Adams at Enterprize for two years and felt she was ready…at lease to start with beginners. After that, books and Larry would help her, and she would be able to take the certification test.

It had all worked. Miss Linda Black Bird Raincrow was the Miss Linda who had taught several hundreds of her settlement's children the difficult English words that let them get good jobs. She taught them to figure money, so they could start their own businesses and know if they were cheated.

Miss Linda was not an easy teacher. She had learned the hard way, and she knew of no other way to teach. Her whole town of Westridge knew her to be the last word on any disagreement. She earned a place of honor that she never would have achieved if the Christmas Eve fire in New York had not sent Miss Josephine Eleanor Wheeler to the territory.

When he could, Daniel rode with his Angel through the overgrown trails and over the sheets of lava rock that made up Linda's town. She was such a dedicated and earnest candidate for an interview. Such a pleasure to hear her dedication.

The next Sunday, Rev. Armstrong woke up early with bright and eager eyes. He lowered his feet over the bed and felt strength flow into his body and arms. Late yesterday, a pair of strong men had come and carried his chair over to the church.

October on the prairie was special time. On a clear day, the air seemed almost as blue as the sky, and the clouds were populated with geese in their favored "V" pattern, chatting conversationally among themselves.

Young animals frisked and leaped with the sheer joy of being alive. Young children hurried to make the best of the fine weather, sailing down the splintery haystacks and roaring with laughter at every spill. It was a perfect Lord's Day.

The young pianist had favored the world with her music, and the choir had raised their voices in blessing. The sunshine shown through the windows making golden squares of light on the polished floor.

The old man smiled with pleasure as the young minister took his place behind the pulpit. He could almost imagine that it was himself who was standing before the people. His people. God's people.

Daniel looked at those who had assembled themselves as they had been told by their own hearts to do. His gaze passed over the old preacher with the pleased smile on his face.

"Friends and neighbors, this is indeed a special day for Forrester Community Church. Our pastor, who was so ill with pneumonia, has miraculously managed the strength to meet with us today. We are so favored.

"We might consider the other miracle of being here today. This beautiful church is ours because of the gift of a pair of young people who were trained by a father who has gone on, to obey God's word. Also, we are blessed by a special man who was not born in this country, but carefully put aside his tenth so the money was ready when we needed it. He even planted the althea bush to mark the place where he saved it. Only God knew it was there.

"Then God sent us a minister who was able to design and construct this lovely church, and he is with us now. We are blessed.

"If you will open...."

Old Rev Armstrong accepted the praise and passed it on to his God. He leaned back in his comfortable chair, the better to enjoy a service performed by someone other than himself. A rare privilege for him.

In due time, the closing hymn was sung. The notes died away. The people began to mill about, chatting together and collecting their respective children. Miz Armstrong circulated among the ladies as was her habit, necessary for the wife of the preacher.

The old man conveniently and silently waited for the building to empty. One small boy who loved the attention the old man always gave him, rushed up the isle to shake his hand. His small feet skidded to a stop on the polished floor and he gasped.

"DAD...DY!"

Daddy came and looked at the old man who leaned comfortably against his chair back, eyes closed, a faint smile among the wrinkles of his face. The skillful, capable hands rested in his lap, and on the shiny blue serge of his Sunday suit.

It was evident that Old Rev. Armstrong had paid his dues and fought the good fight, had finished the course, and therefore a crown had been laid up for him. This was the day that had been chosen for him to receive the crown.

Philip, who had expected to assist getting him home, was called back from the visiting crowd. He stood with Daniel and looked at his father. No tears, yet. He nodded and commented, "Well, Daniel, he picked a good day for it didn't he?"

Daniel nodded, and Philip continued.

"Pa always was one to do things on schedule. First things first, and don't stop until you're through. He must have looked up at you and seen how well you fill the pulpit, and knew this job was finished and left in good hands. That now he was excused and could go to his well-deserved reward."

While he was speaking, Miz Armstrong came back down the aisle, tapping her cane for balance. Philip reached out and enclosed her shoulders with his arm. Together they looked at the man in the chair. No tears, yet.

The old woman nodded. "He did what he said he would do. I just thought he'd wait until maybe in the night, tonight. He always was strong minded...to do what he wanted to do. Didn't like to be a burden on no one, did Mr. Armstrong. I'm thinkin' he figured that God, bein' here for the service anyway, could just take him on home, and save Him the trip later."

Two strong men came, and carried him, chair and all, to the parsonage. He didn't weigh all that much anyway.

The woman looked at her son. "Did I say to you he said he would go today?"

"Yes, Ma, you did. Pa always wanted to do things on schedule."

"But, son, I thought he might just go in the night, us bein' there together on that bed. If that had happened, it'd seem to be no trouble to take me along with 'im. What am I gonna do without 'im?"

Philip sensed that she did not expect an answer, so he did not give one. He went to the kitchen and built up the fire. There was tea left over from breakfast, and he set it on the burner. There were times that a cup of tea was better conversation than words... especially those spoken just for the sake of saying something.

Daniel stepped into the kitchen with mother and son. "The men'll get busy first thing in the morning. What do you think...maybe Tuesday morning?"

Philip nodded, and raised the cup to his lips. No tears, yet.

Daniel nodded and left them alone. Not all tears were shed on the outside of the body. So many were on the protected inside, meant only for the relief of the weeper.

Most of the town of Carlile Corners gathered at Resthaven Cemetery at the back of Miss Josie's property. The name for the cemetery had been voted on by the town, but it would most often be called Miss Josie's Cemetery...possibly forever.

Words were said by Daniel. He began, "I'm thinkin' this may have been the preacher's plan. This church was the crown jewel of his career, and for an actual fact, he did not leave it. We are here to honor the remains, but he was never here today. He was never in this new wooden box. He left us the way he intended to go, waiting in God's house...."

Songs sung, and the crowd dispersed. The sound of the shovels filling in the space and leveling. A headstone would be made in a week or so. The diggers made their way back toward the blacksmith shop for coffee and talk, but before the coffee water was hot, the sky darkened with a cloud bank. By the time the men took their first sip, the rain was coming down.

One of the men took his coffee to the front of the shop and looked out at the sheets of silver drops pouring out of the skies. "Heaven's tears...maybe?"

A moment of thought, and another of the men answered, "Naw. I wouldn't think it was tears. Heaven's gonna be glad to get that fellow up there where he belongs."

A few nods. "But I'm a'thinkin' them tears oughtta be comin' down out there...they'd be for the folks that didn't get to know that old man."

Before the coffee session ended, it was decided that Brad Cullen, the owner of the blacksmith shop, should be the one to tell young Daniel that the town hoped he'd continue to fill the pulpit, at least for the present.

Philip came along with Brad to inform Daniel of the decision. "Now, preacher, that parsonage...it'll be empty by the end'a the week. Ready for you to move on in."

"Oh, no, I can just...."

"No, you can't. We have a parsonage, and we have an interim preacher. Who knows how long it'll take us to get another one...even if we want one. The preacher is expected to be in the parsonage, when a congregation is lucky enough to have one.

"As for my ma, she's comin' with me. She'll stay with Gwinnie and me until I get her a cabin built. She'll want the bed, and the old man's chair. Says she doesn't need anything else. What's left'll get you by till you decide to make a change."

Hmmmm, it was not a new thing for Daniel Carpenter. Decisions taken away from him, plans made among the men themselves, and told to him. Of course, they were right.

Like the decision that was made to give him medical training. Like placing him where his skills were used to the best advantage. Like when it was time to bring him home...to have him in place to fill what was going to be a vacancy. He nodded agreeably. What else was there to do? For a fact, he was not in charge of his own life...never had been.

Philip was a fast worker. In three weeks he had a cabin built for his mother. Twelve feet by fourteen feet, and a big east window. Plenty of room for the bed and chair and a small wardrobe closet. She would walk across the yard and eat with the family...Philip, Gwinnie and their little fellow.

She smiled with pleasure as she looked around the snug little nest built just for her. The contours of the old man's chair reminded her of him, and the bed enveloped her in accustomed comfort. She met the morning sun with a smile. No tears, yet.

Philip Armstrong's mother enjoyed her new cabin for exactly ten days. When she did not answer the bell for the evening meal, Philip went to her cabin to wake her up from her usual afternoon nap.

She was not in bed. He found her in the big chair, her small, bent body cuddled into its softness and her head resting comfortable on the high back. Her eyes were closed and she had a small smile on her lips. The curve of her smile was tucked deep within her wrinkles. A smile of pleasure.

She knew where she was going, and it was evident that she had gotten there. Also, she was certainly not disappointed. No tears. None of her tears had ever been necessary.

Philip had her placed beside his father and he walked away with his family. No tears, yet. At least none that anyone saw. He had loved his parents dearly, but he and his father were so different that they could never actually work together on anything. That was a shame, as his father's skills were with design and accounting, and his son's skills were in construction and economics.

They had, however, managed to construct the Forrester Community Church into a highly functional landmark in the small prairie town. There was one thing that he could thank his father for. That one thing was in requiring him to leave his job and come to the Corners to assist him.

If Philip had not honored his father and come when called, he would never have stopped in at the Cookie Jar. If that had not happened, he would not have had the opportunity to straighten the leaning outhouse for that establishment, and thereby allowing Gwinnie to make use of it without being frightened.

It was absolutely true that the Lord moved in mysterious ways. Actually, though, Philip thought it might more truthfully be that the Lord has to first get the attention of humans to be able to help them. Gwinnie's fear bumps at the very sight of the precariously leaning outhouse were enough to get Philip's attention. *Thank you, Lord.*

It was on that very day, the day he buried his mother, that his son took his first steps. He had been named Philip Junior, but to avoid confusions, he was called Pip. It was a shame, really, because pet childhood names often follow a fellow all the way to gray hair and a walking cane. Oh, well….

So the new minister looked around at what was now his home. At least, temporarily. Spacious kitchen, parlor with wide windows on the east, giving a restful view of the sheep pasture and the grazing long-haired, Merino woolies.

There were four bedrooms rooms, a plan practically unheard of on the prairie unless they were add-ons as the family grew. These four bedrooms were conveniently spaced to aid in their eventual purpose. There was the master bedroom, two smaller ones nearby, obviously for the children of the next pastor. The fourth room was spaced off the side, and was meant for a visiting minister, or whatever other situation presented itself.

He nodded in appreciation. Philip's pa had certainly been good at what he did. He would spend tonight in his old room, and tomorrow the bed would be brought over, and he would be here. The enormity of what was before him bowed his head in humility. *Dear Lord in heaven...Don't You ever leave me....*

Before the funeral was a necessity, he had planned to make the trip over to Sentinel Rock with Angel as part of her assignment from her mother. Miss Josie had specifically mentioned that Max Sinclair should certainly be included in the Chronology.

Merytaten had filled him in on the way. Young Max had insisted, when he was in the third grade at the Prairie Academy, that he would be a schoolteacher. He would work hard with his grades and he would take the certification test with the girls of his class. Others smiled and said nothing, because why would a boy/man lower himself to be a schoolteacher?

One interesting landmark of the little community of Sentinel Rock, was that it had a "sentinel rock." The massive gray stone pillar stood on end and could be seen for a mile away...and on a clear day, maybe more than a mile. It seemed to have been named by a previous generation, and could have been used as a geographical positioning, as in "when you reach the sentinel rock, turn south" or something like that.

Max's father was able to buy that quarter section from a homesteader desiring to "sell up." Everything looked good. It could be divided seven ways with a portion for each of his seven sons, and then here came son number eight. It seemed a good thing to send him to school, but then he said he would be a schoolteacher. Can you believe that? Of course, he was still so young, he could change his mind a dozen times.

Max, however, was made of stern stuff. He did exactly what he said he would do, and he was now in his fourth year of presiding over the Tall Rock Academy. As he had seven older brothers, his class was composed at least half by nieces and nephews, but no matter. Someone had to teach them.

Max met his old schoolmate and the new minister with pleasure. Tea was served, and the background of the interview was set.

Being the youngest of eight sons was somewhat unique, but more interesting was that the next brother older than he, was actually older by ten years. He was what is sometimes referred to as the "fall crop" but more often as a "surprise" baby. He did, however, bring particular happiness to his mother.

Seeing that when the farm would be divided seven ways to serve the sons and their growing families, there was no real place for Young Max. That was when brother number six, the one who was twelve years older, decided that Max should be the one who went to the school and he would take him there every day.

He would travel the three miles there and back each morning, and again in the afternoon to collect him. That was, indeed, a sacrifice of his brother's time, but it solved a problem.

When Max was five, the year that was considered best to start, he was taken by his brother to school every day for the next three and a half years. It was then decided, when he reached the responsible age of nine, that he could take himself. Max was joyfully in favor.

His mom made him a thick blanket to use instead of a saddle, and under the edge, she made a secret pocket for the small gun (called a snake gun) needed by anyone on the prairie. The firearm rode cozily between the saddle blanket and the horse's flank, creating not even a bulge.

His mother also made for him a protective place in the bottom of his pants pocket for the special knife he had received for Christmas. It was good for a boy to always have a knife, but there was the danger that it could be lost during play. Games of tug-war and skin-the-cat required the player to be upside down, and the knife must not accidentally fall from his pocket.

Then the really big thing happened when he was nine and a half years old, and he was on his way home riding over the three miles of prairie. He often spotted cottontail rabbits and was a good enough shot to be able to often bring home two or three for the stew pot.

As he was watching for rabbits, a band of robbers galloped across the fields, and started to pass him by, but then decided they could use his horse to replace one they had lost in a gunfight.

Part of the group wanted to shoot him immediately, so he didn't cause them any trouble, but another said they must keep him alive because he might be a help. Could be that his folks would pay money to get him back.

So Max was blindfolded with his neckerchief, and the horseless rider leaped on in front of him. Then they thundered across the hardened ground and Max had no idea which way they were going. He did know, however, that fear had made his heart pound like a blacksmith's hammer.

After what seemed to be maybe two or three hours, it was decided they would stop at a certain cave that had fresh water. They off loaded Max and put him in the cave and rolled a massive stone over the entrance. There was no way Max could move the stone, that was certain, but, if he stood on tiptoe, he could peek out around the stone. All he could see, however, was sky.

He smelled coffee, and later beans as the robbers made camp. A cup of hot beans and a spoon were handed through the crack to him. He was glad to get them and ate every speck of the food. Then it seemed they were gathered around the campfire, but he could not hear them plainly enough to know what they were saying.

It was just becoming dark when horses' hooves again pounded the packed ground, and gunfire rang out. Shouts and the whinny of horses, and then more pounding hooves, the sounds growing dimmer in the distance. After a while, the chirp of crickets and trill night birds told the nine-year-old boy he was alone on the prairie.

This cave was one of the "wet caves" having a freshwater spring within it, and it flowed out through a small tunnel off to the side. At least, Max would not die of thirst, but how long would a cup of beans last a nine-year-old boy?

He reached deep in his pocket and took his knife from its special pocket. The robbers had missed it when they searched him. Thank you, mom.

He opened out the strongest blade and poked the ground. Two inches of accumulated dirt and debris, and then solid rock. Still, he tested every inch of the cave floor until it was too dark to see. He successfully proved to himself that it would not be possible to dig under the rock.

By now he was exhausted. Pushing accumulated debris into a pile, he curled up on it and managed to sleep. For a while.

Then he thought. *There has to be a way out. Maybe I can dig around the big rock.* He also remembered where, in the Bible, an angel came and rolled away the stone for Jesus. Man, oh man… couldn't he use that strong angel right now!

The trouble was, the edge of the cave mouth was also solid rock. The boy spent the first day thinking and walking around in the dim light. He found that if he leaned over with his face near the water, he could see a spot of daylight. *Hmmmm.*

The tunnel the water passed through was about fifteen inches wide and ten inches high. It was shaped roughly like a pipe that was somewhat flattened. If he leaned over to crawl forward on his elbows, his face would be under water. The distance was so great, he could never hold his breath that long. He knew that was true because he had tried.

To his best counting, two minutes was about as long as he could manage, and there was no way he could make it all the way out in two minutes. One thing about Max, he was good at numbers. The teachers at the Academy had told him that, and his grades were very good.

The second day, all he could think of was food. He even had an idea that if a prairie rattler slipped past the rock, he would likely have him for lunch. No rattler obliged him.

By nightfall, he was becoming desperate, and wished he had paper and a pencil so that when someone found his skeleton, they could know how he died, and go tell his mother. She would want to know. The thing was, he had no paper and pencil, and his knife could not even mark a line on the rock.

In the evening of the second day, he looked up at the ceiling of rock and said, "All right, angel. Where are you? I could really use you now."

It was then that he realized that when he lay on his back, his face was about eight inches up from the floor. He was good at numbers, you remember, so he knew that. The very thought of this made his heart begin to pound.

"Angel? Did you make me think of that? If so, I could use any other good idea you might have." Then he dozed off asleep, in spite of his gnawing stomach.

He woke up early, and light was filtering in around the big rock. Max stretched himself out on the cave floor and raised his head. Nose was about eight inches from the floor. Maybe eight and a half.

He dug in his heels and elbows and firmed his rear. By squirming back and forth, he actually moved a few inches. Hmmmm, this had possibilities. How could he make himself a little bit smaller? He grinned slightly when he remembered that if he didn't get food soon, he would be a lot smaller.

Well, let's see. If he took off his jacket…well, hey, why not take off everything. Next thought…it was cold in the cave. Next thought after that…if he didn't get out, he'd be still colder.

CHAPTER 7

Well, there was room around the rock closure to stuff his clothes through. Then if he got out, they would be there, still dry. But how could he get along without clothes? *...think about it, Max. If you don't get out, you don't need any clothes!*

Off came the shoes. He could hear them clunk on the ground outside the cave. Then his socks, and one by one they were poked past the rock. Finally, all that was left was his Christmas knife. How could he possibly...? *For heaven's sake, Max! Use your head and send that knife after everything else. It hasn't helped you in here, so be brave and let it go.*

Sheer force of will made him release his clutch on the bone handle of the knife. He listened, but it must have dropped on his clothes. He heard no sound of it hitting the ground.

He stood shivering in the cave. *All right, Max*, he told himself sternly. *It's now or never.*

He stepped into the icy water. Quickly stepped out. Frigid!

"STOP IT, MAX!" He scolded himself in a loud voice that echoed into the depth of the cavern.

Stepped back in. Slowly eased into a sitting position. Shivers ran up his back and shoulders. He bravely splashed himself back full length into the water and his ears rang from his own screams.

LAY STILL, MAX!

He obeyed himself until his body had cooled enough that he could move. Elbows...heels...butt. Elbows...heels...butt. Then his head was in the tunnel. He was committed.

HUSH UP, MAX! YOU WERE ALWAYS COMMITTED. YOU JUST DIDN'T KNOW IT.

Elbow...heels...butt. He discovered that the smooth looking rocks in the stream bed were not really smooth. They began to feel like broken slivers of glass.

MAX, THOSE ROCKS ARE NOT HURTING YOUR BACK! THEY ONLY FEEL LIKE THEY ARE. SO GET ON WITH IT!

After what he thought might have been an hour, he could only see the face of the rock about three inches above his nose. If he relaxed and laid his head back, water ran over his face. If he used one hand to lift his head, it rested his neck a bit, but slowed his movement. It became clear that he would not be able to reach the end of the tunnel. Ever.

That was when the top of the tunnel began to wave before his face and seemed to be falling down on him. With both arms folded across his chest, he tried to push up.

MAX, STOP IT! IF THAT ROCK IS FALLING, YOU CAN'T STOP IT. SO SHUT UP...AND CRAWL.

Back on his painful elbows and stone-cut heels. His butt was numb, so he didn't know if it was hurting or not! Streams of hot pain shot from shoulder to shoulder as he moved his elbows.

He was so exhausted that his movements were not getting him anywhere. The same patch of moss stayed over his eyes. *Rest. Lay back and let the water run over your face, then you won't have to crawl anymore. You're not going to make it, you know. No use trying.*

He lowered his head back, and the rush of water flowed over his nose. Reflex made him jerk up his head and bump it on the ceiling of the tunnel. *Ouch!*

All right, Max, we have to decide what we want to do. I'll let you rest to the count of fifty, and then you will get us out of here. Right?

Putting both palms under his head, his nose lifted barely above the water. One...two...three...four.... He had counted to thirty and wanted to stop and crawl again, but he had promised himself fifty counts. Forty-eight...forty-nine...fifty! A deep breath, and he again stiffened his neck.

Elbows…heels…very sore butt. The patch of moss moved on past his eyes and he saw the spirals of a tiny shell that had been caught in the prehistoric lava of the stone.

Nothing hurts you, Max. Did you hear me? DID YOU HEAR ME? NOTHING IS HURTING YOU. Stop thinking and get us out of here!

Elbows…heels…very sore…. Then a crash against his eyes. The rock did, indeed, fall. He shuddered and jerked, and his eyes popped open and stared up into the golden prairie sunshine!

HE'D MADE IT! HE'D ACTUALLY MADE IT!

Relief was so great that he was paralyzed with shock. With great effort he lifted his head, and saw pink water running over his arms. Pink…?

Sitting, and then standing, he stared at the water that flowed past where he stood. Streaks of red. He felt movement on his legs. Dripping water mixed with blood. Elbows…blood. Heels a mush of cuts with oozing blood.

The sun was so warm on his naked body, he seemed to be standing in front of a stove. *Angel? Are you there? Are you the one who shouted at me when I gave up? If so, thanks!*

He looked toward the rock and saw the pile of clothes. One by one, he put them on his painful body. Carefully he pulled up the wool socks his mother had knitted. The heels of the wool socks were bloody before he got them into his shoe, but reason told him that the shoes would act like a bandage. Maybe stop the blood. Or maybe some of it.

He turned and looked in every direction. He had no idea where he was, but he noticed a hump in the trail to the east. Coming closer, he saw it was the horse he had been riding home from school, a hundred years ago. He walked toward it and felt a lump form in his throat.

There was the saddle blanket his mom had made. He felt for where the pocket was, and the small snake gun had been missed by the robbers. He picked up the blanket. He was sure to need it if it took him a while to get home. Evenings were chilly this time of the year.

Then he looked down at the horse and saw the bullet wound that had killed her. Died fast. That was good. It was so bad to suffer. He knelt down at the back of the animal and leaned forward. For the first time during the three days, the tears began to flow and there was no way to stop them.

Tears gone, finally, and he stood. Every step sent jagged pains through his heels. *IT DOESN'T HURT, MAX!*

Hungry. Very hungry, and food had to be the first thought. A wonderful thing happened when he was first experimenting with his wonderful knife. It had two blades, and where the other one was there was a thin magnifying glass. Really good for picking slivers or stickers from knees. He had also learned that the sun, shining through the glass, made a hot spot and eventually caused a burn.

There were many things that could be written about how he got home, but to go quickly with the story, it was two days that he walked. The whole time he did not know if he was going the right direction, but he couldn't just wait there. One had to do something…didn't one?

Sleeping in trees on limbs. He took the laces from his shoes to tie himself to a limb so he wouldn't go to sleep and fall out. He shot rabbits and roasted them on the fire made by his magnifier.

On the third night, he was resting on the big limb of a walnut tree, and a snarling bobcat tried to climb up. He shot once with the snake gun, then climbed to the top where the limbs were so small he could better defend himself and the cat could not leap down on him from above.

There, perched in the tiny, top limbs of the walnut tree, he waited for daylight. It was sometime in the night as he looked around, in the distance he saw a tiny light…then two lights.

Now, he knew that one light might be a trick of nature, but two lights together meant humans. He stared at the lights until it was daylight enough to see where he was going. He had to keep his eyes on the direction.

Climbing down, he could no longer see the lights, but he had sighted himself in that direction so he started walking. Less than an hour later, he heard his brother, the one who had taken him to school, shouting at his horse to get a move on.

Max drew in a deep breath and called his loudest. "HELLO! HELLO!"

Silence. Then hoof beats. The brother grabbed him and swung him onto the horse, causing all the cuts on his back to cry out with pain and start to bleed, but Max said nothing. On the way back to the house, the brother had teasingly complained that he had been sent to Argyle, five miles away, for the oil to fuel the lanterns that had been placed atop…you guessed it! SENTINEL ROCK.

Later, fed and rested, he asked his mother how long she would have left the lanterns tied to the top of Sentinel Rock. She had looked at him with a surprised expression. "Why, son, I would leave them there forever!"

So now Max Sinclair was almost twenty-one, and his school room was built in the sheep pasture near the tall pillar of stone. He did exactly what he said he would do.

The preacher and the school friend looked out the window where he pointed. There was the stone. Just one more bit of proof that the Oklahoma Territory produced strong men with a special purpose. Max Sinclair would teach children until he was gray-haired and leaning on his cane. Maybe longer!

At this moment, there was a motto written on the wall blackboard. A BOOK IS A PACKAGE OF THOUGHT. Miss Josie's daughter had to smile. That was one of the first sentences used to begin teaching phonics to older students.

Josie's only daughter and her life-long friend rode in silence as they returned toward Carlile Corners. Three miles away.

If their present relationship could be called courtship, it was indeed a strange one. They could almost imagine that they were already one person, having been sewed together by the letters crisscrossing the Atlantic. His letters giving her purpose, hers giving him strength.

His letters giving her a sight far past the territory, hers giving him a brief moment of home. Where a courting couple might converse about many things, these two had only spoke of what was currently very important. There had been no time then for frivolity that had no purpose. In this way they learned more about each other than they would have learned in a year of courtship dates.

"Angel, I'm going to need you." Daniel, in a clear and determined voice, stated his position in positive words.

She waited. It was not a question, and it did not invite comment.

"Farmers can do without a wife. Millers can do without a wife. A preacher needs a wife. There are times I will need you. There will be visits when there is no man at home. There will be problems better suited to your knowledge. There will be calls when I won't know until I get there...."

The mare plodded toward home. After a while, even the horses had an idea where they were headed. It made it handy for the driver so he could lay aside the guiding reins.

"...and you understand that it will need to be soon...."

He turned to look at his companion, her head nodding gently to the rhythm of the horse's hooves. Yes, she knew he would need her, as one hand needs the other...or else there can be no clapping. No sound.

The news was excitedly reported by Miss Josie to her mother's friend back in New York City. The one lovingly called Aunt Sharon. It was same Aunt Sharon who loved to shop for items not available on the prairie.

Return mail brought a request as to what the couple would like as a wedding present.

Miss Josie thought, and then wrote that the couple was totally unworldly and un-understandable, and what they would like was not within her power to guess.

She said Aunt Sharon should just use her imagination as Merytaten was rather much wrapped up in her music, and who knew what the new preacher would like.

Shopping was what Aunt Sharon did best. She joyfully chose two items and crated them for shipping. When the crating boards were stripped away on the prairie, there was a gift box containing, "Hymns with the Melody of Heaven."

The book contained every known hymn written with the most number of notes and tones known to a piano or organ. (That could keep her busy a while!)

And the other item in the crate was a huge church bell, clearly the size of a wash pot, with brass as golden and shiny as the morning sun. (That ought to wake up the town on a Sunday morning!)

It was a better choice than even Aunt Sharon had hoped. It became a signal. When the bell was rung at a time other than Sunday morning, the sound of it meant for the doctor/preacher to leave wherever he was and head for the clinic. It meant that something had come in that was above the skill of Donald, Dorcas and Ellen…or that there were multiple problems.

When Aunt Sharon heard about that, she was thrilled!

The couple made the trip to Oklahoma City where a friend of Daniel's performed the ceremony, but the party, the part that the Corners really liked, was saved for the town. The Prairie Academy building was the obvious place to have the wedding celebration, as there was the big play yard for the overflow.

After the wedding, a strange thing occurred. Daniel's name was changed to "Preacher" or "Reverend." It just seemed to come handy.

Miss Josie had bestowed on her daughter all the names she loved, and the child was named Merytayten after an Egyptian princess, a relative of Joseph of Egypt. Franchesca Angelique

Evangeline. Her exasperated father had reduced the name to Mutt…which she carried through childhood.

Now, though, through common consent, she became Mery. Her husband, however, had settled on Angel. Seemed to him to fit…somehow.

The big, beautiful brass bell was installed in the church yard, and the sheet music found a place in the pocket of the piano bench.

Merytaten and Daniel had lived in the parsonage for exactly one week when an incident occurred that would change their life forever.

YEAR 1922, ARGYLE, OKLHOMA TERRITORY

Reuben Scott had worked for two months on the Mississippi River as a stevedore. Being big and strong, the work was just the activity of a day, and the pay was wonderful. The thing was, though, it was meant to be temporary, and his pay was dropped into the bag with their wedding jar money.

They shopped for provisions and joined themselves to a convoy going west. They would stop over in Oklahoma City, and there would be a stage route going from there to Argyle. They would join themselves to the stage for safety on the road.

They were laughing and happy and little Bonnie Heather smiled her toothless best, ducking and dimpling in a most charming way. The parents looked at each other and nodded. Weren't they just the most lucky people in the whole world?

They reached Oklahoma City in five weeks and waited a day and a half for the next stage trip. They added their wagon just far enough behind the stage to avoid the dust, and close enough for safety.

They reached Argyle late in the afternoon and toyed with staying there overnight. They'd get an early start the next morning, and by afternoon they would be at Errol Scott's place. Reuben's cousin Errol, his absolute best friend would welcome them, and the couples would live close together. Family was so important to the Scottish.

It was early afternoon and they were packed and ready for the last leg of the journey. So early, in fact that they could travel maybe five miles yet that day and be that much closer tomorrow. They had spent many nights on the road, so another night of camping would be nothing new.

And they had started out. They had a hand drawn map that had been sent to them back before they left the old country. It was smoothed out and studied. There were the clearly identified landmarks.

They stopped by a grove of trees and made their fire. The sausages they had bought at Mac's were poked onto green sticks and toasted in the blaze until the flavorful juices dripped, sizzling, into the flames. They laughed and sang, and Katy's lovely voice floated on the mild evening breeze of the prairie evening.

Little Bonnie Heather dimpled and waved her hands about with enthusiasm.

As the fire died away, the little girl was fed and snuggled into her soft blankets, then tucked into the basket that just fit her size. Her mother commented, "Reuben, this here basket ain't gonna fit her very long."

Her father had tossed the statement away. "I'll just make her a new one."

Katy picked up the basket and stepped toward the wagon. At that moment the shot rang out, splitting the prairie air into a million harsh decibels. Then the next shot and it created a burst of flame in Reuben's shoulder.

He sucked in a terrified breath, and stage-whispered, "Take the baby and run."

She turned to him, undecided and startled. "Huh? Well I...."

He repeated urgently, "Run, I say. Go now and don't stop."

So Katy ran. Darkness had settled, and the grasses and bushes tore at her feet. She lifted the baby's basket high over the brush and ran. Heart pounding and breath ragged, she forced one foot, then the next.

Bang! A shot whizzed past her, and then another bang. A blazing flame burst forth from the calf of her leg but it still held her up, so she ran on. Darkness was falling fast, and she struggled to get out of the sight of the shooter.

Stumbling and falling forward, she protected the basket at the expense of the elbow of her other arm. Elbow scratched and painfully bruised, but not broken. A quick look around, and she decided she might already be out of sight so she squirmed closer to a low-limbed cedar tree.

A whinny of the horse. A few yells and the sound of the wagon being driven away. The baby whimpered, and Katy's hand soothed her with a few pats. The baby mustn't give away their position.

The night was two eternities as she sat on the stickery ground beneath the cedar, her wounded leg throbbing with a fiery rhythm. Night birds and crickets. Normal sounds all around her, but she knew there was nothing normal about what had happened.

Of one thing she was sure, if Reuben could, he would be looking for her. Her mind told her that only the worst could have happened. She looked about her, eyes wide and burning in the dark, heart racing madly. This could really not be happening.

With the dawn, she made her way back. She saw the cold ashes of their fire, and she saw wheel marks and scuffed grass. She spent precious minutes looking, but she knew it was useless. If Reuben could, he would be there, so obviously he couldn't. That meant she must run and take the baby, as he had instructed her with what was certainly his last breath.

Picking a direction from the position of the rising sun, she headed south. The pain in her leg was increasing and it was possible...in fact, likely...that she had the bullet still in her calf.

She didn't examine it to find out. It was either there or it wasn't and she could do nothing about it, either way.

By midmorning, the baby was awake and hungry. Katy had been expecting it from the discomfort in her breasts. She found a convenient rock and sat down to feed her. The little thing was soaked and soggy, and Katy removed the night diaper that had been doubled, as usual. Folding the flannel blanket, she used it for a diaper and wrung out the wet ones, tying them to the handle of the basket.

With luck, the diapers could be partially dry by the time they were needed again. Now fully dry and cozy, the agreeable little girl again slept, soothed by the motion of the basket carried by her mother.

Stumbling wearily and painfully upon a stream, Katy rinsed the diapers and spread them across the grass while she rested a bit. Within minutes she stood and walked again. It was difficult to rest when she felt such urgency.

Looking in all directions, she saw no signs of life or humanity. and she didn't even have the map that Reuben's cousin Errol had drawn for them. Continue south. Avoid going in circles. Something would show up. It had to.

She spent the night tucked between two boulders. She knew there was no safe place, so she chose a place where she would not be accidentally stepped on by…whatever it was…or whomever….

She traveled all day the second day, realizing she was making very bad time. Exhaustion, increasing pain in the back of her leg. Hunger, and the necessity to keep feeding the baby. As long as she could. Immediate requirements bore down on her.

She remembered how she had chuckled at the thought of anything happening as the old Granny woman at Argyle had told her. "Honey, see you put a note in that baby's basket…come chance you get separated."

She had tossed her head and said, "Ain't nothin' gonna separate us. Less'n they killed me first." Well, maybe they had.

Anyway, she had humored the old granny woman, and had written a note. She had seen it in the basket when she changed the diaper. It was only slightly dampened with a yellow stain.

With a sigh, she picked up the basket again. Bonnie would be hungry, and she could tell that what she had would not be enough to satisfy her. She'd wait as long as she could before the baby was fed with what might be her last meal.

It was night again, and there was a good woodland. It seemed safer to be among the trees than out on the open land. Tomorrow would be the day she would find someone. Or not....

The night was wakeful in spite of her exhaustion and fear. She saw the sunrise and she peered hopefully ahead of her. There was something. A wisp of smoke...from a chimney? Over there more smoke. Today would be the day. She tried to resurrect a feeling of excitement, but her leg was so painful she could hardly drag it along. She heard music.

Beautiful notes on the thin, morning air. And she saw the cross lifted high. She knew crosses. She knew music, and the cross and the music pulled at her from a depth she did not know she had.

Maybe a smoking chimney was a trifle closer, but she was pulled toward the uplifted cross. The whining of the baby tugged at her heart so she sat down by an inviting haystack. Maybe she could provide enough food to satisfy the little thing for the last... mile...?

The baby tried, but finally gave up and settled back into restless sleep. Katy lifted a sheaf of the hay and pushed the basket under the edge so the sun did not shine in her eyes. If she could just rest a minute, then she could make the last few steps, and she knew the cross would bring help.

She had done her best for her most precious possession, so she shut her eyes for just a minute.

The music was closer now while she leaned against the fragrant hay, listening and feeling muscles relax. The music seemed to fill her entire being, flowing into her hands and feet.

So relaxing. Her exhaustion, hunger, pain and fright just floated away.

She knew the cross would give her strength. She was no longer uneasy about the baby's future. Everything was as it should be. She could rest…for just a moment.

There, in the warm sunshine on the sheep pasture, she sighed her final breath and permitted herself to be pulled upward toward the voices. Pulled toward the music that was so close it seemed that it had become a part of her. She could now hear the angel voices.

So loving and enticing were those angel voices…and she looked around and saw that she was among them. They were all around her…the lovely heavenly beings. They sought for ways to comfort her. They told her they had come for her to help her go the last little way.

The small dog was sniffing bushes and grass clumps for messages from other four-footed residents of the area, and he sniffed a message he could not read. Best he call for help, so he barked. And barked and barked.

The young woman in the building heard the barking dog. The barking had seemed to last for a long time so she left the piano in her parlor…where she was practicing some of the new music from Aunt Sharon, and called the dog to the house.

"Biskit? Come on, Biskit!"

But Biskit did not come. She eventually realized she would have to go after him or listen to his yips and barks for who knew how long. Pressing a bonnet down on her hair, she walked out to the haystack.

She quickly saw the woman…girl? But before she reached her, she called back to the house, "Daniel! Come please. Looks like trouble."

It was when Biskit finally hushed and bounded toward her that she heard the baby cry. What terrible thing had happened to cause a baby to be under their haystack?

Momentarily ignoring the body of the young woman, she pushed aside the hay and was greeted with an angry red face and an open mouth. And a lot of screaming from a set of healthy lungs.

Baby...well clothed but soaking wet. Also, obviously hungry...and for how long? How did the little thing get here? It was an accepted fact that babies were sometimes found on doorsteps of homes and churches, but under a haystack...? And what had happened to the mother?

Merytaten lifted the tiny creature from the damp bed and hugged her to her chest, patting the soggy backside. The screaming quieted down to a hiccough and blinking eyes as she studied the new face. Then a few whimpers as she crammed a moist fist into her mouth.

"I'm going for food," she announced, and covered the distance with rapid steps. Maybe six months old. Strong and healthy. Has not been hungry very long. Her thoughts scoured her mind for what could be fed a baby not yet weaned.

Well...there was milk? Teaspoon at a time. She didn't think the little thing would be very fussy over the method of delivery, as she was now vigorously gnawing her fingers with a toothless mouth.

Bright eyed little thing...gazed around like she was interested in where she was. Eyes blue-violet.

The first thing was to dry her out, and Merytaten grabbed up a dishtowel from the drawer. The little girl was more interested in food than soggy moisture, and began to wail, thrashing her fists angrily.

Quickly diapered into the unwieldy-shaped item, and picked up again, she once more attacked her fist.

Milk. Oh, there was oatmeal left from breakfast. Spooning a little of the cereal into a cup with a little milk, she lifted tiny bites to the drooling mouth. It was eagerly accepted, and the mouth opened for more. Ah...she had been spoon-fed. Immediate problem solved, Merytaten thought ahead.

There were nursing bottles with nipples over at the clinic for emergency use with childbirth problems. She'd send someone…but when she opened the door she came face to face with Daniel.

"Just wanted to say I'm headed over to the clinic with Donald. They've got better facilities for this situation than we have. So I…."

She butted in. "Bring back nipple bottles when you come. We ate oatmeal, but she needs something to suck."

Slight smile, and he agreed. Who could figure women and babies…but it was a good thing. One didn't need to understand women to know they needed them.

The body of the young lady, almost just a girl, it seemed, was laid out on a table. The leg was terrible. Wide red streaks reached up from the bullet wound all the way to her hip. Infection. Poison. He blinked a couple of times and looked up…and sighed.

Donald, watching, asked, "You all right, doc?"

Swallowing, and swiping the back of his hand against his eyes, he nodded. "It just took me back a moment. So much of this happened when the injured couldn't be collected for a couple of days. They shouldn't have died. This girl shouldn't have died. Obviously healthy, but those bullets would have had to come out. There's poison in shot like this."

Donald nodded. "I thought of that, too, but I didn't see too much of it. Mostly, we were convalescent. Or dead. You know what we had because you fellows were the ones who sent us most of them."

There was not much to be done with her except plan for the funeral. The ladies would take care of dressing her and doing what they could. The box made of pine planks was being put together at this moment.

Brad Cullen at the blacksmith shop had taken to keeping a small stock of suitable planks for emergencies such as this. Seemed appropriate, as the Resthaven Cemetery was on the back of his quarter section.

Being no reason to postpone it, the funeral, such as it was, was held the following morning. Mostly ladies. Fellows were in the fields. Songs were sung, and prayers made.

Merytaten stood close by the pine box, holding the baby. Whatever happened, the little one should be attending her mother's funeral, even if she slept through it. Passing the haystack on the way back to the house, Priscilla, who was walking with her, reached under the edge of the hay and picked up the basket.

"Right pretty quilt," she commented. "She'll want it when she grows up." Swinging the basket beside her, she walked back to the parsonage with her sister-in-law.

"What'll you do with her...have you decided?"

Merytaten turned to her sister-in-law with wide eyes and startled, open mouth. "Do with her? What do you mean?"

"Well, I thought maybe since you just got married...and all...well? I just wondered." Then with a grin, "Didn't 'spect you to bite my head off!"

Return grin. "Well, I didn't. I seem to see you still have your head, and I have my baby. She came to me and she's mine."

Pricilla's turn to be open mouthed. "You mean you're going to keep her? You don't have to, you know. Fact is, I'll bet my mom would take her."

Merytaten pictured her mother-in-law. Absolutely she would take her. It wouldn't the first unfortunate thing that shouldn't have happened to her...but did...Miss Carlotta would have dealt with the problem with strength and purpose.

Firm lips and a shake of the head. "No, she was being brought to me. If you look out there from where her mother likely came, there were two houses closer and there would be smoke from the chimneys. But her mother headed this way on purpose. She brought the baby to me...or rather to the cross on the church, I'd think."

Chastened, Prissy turned her attention to the well-made carrier. "Basket in good shape. Looks new. I'll take up the wet bedding and suds it out for you. She's used to the basket, seems like, and it might be handy for you." Then with a smile, she added. "And for your baby."

Damp quilt and sheet. Soaked pad. Damp wicker on the basket bottom. Yellowed piece of paper stuck to the woven bands of the wicker. With delicate fingers, Prissy lifted the limp and soaked note and spread it onto the seat of a nearby dining chair to dry.

"Got words on here. Still can read 'em. Likely be easier when it dries out. Might tell us something."

The little girl, having consumed a cup of rich jersey milk, was fast asleep on the bed in the "children's" bedroom. Together Mery and Prissy leaned over the paper, dyed as it was in scalloped shades of yellow from several soakings. It read:

"This is my little angel. We call her name Bonnie Heather on account of the heather growing where she came from. I was with her on the ship and she was birthed in a bad storm with a rocking ship. I didn't want to write this here note, because if someone reads it, it will mean I wasn't there. Old woman made me write this, because things happen that are not good. If you are the one who takes care of my little girl, tell her that her pa and ma loved her more than anything in the world. I thank you for being good to her and feeding her or burying her if she don't make it either."

The final words were squinched together to get them all on the page. The young ladies sniffed and looked at each other. Then Prissy commented, "I wish I could'a handed her another sheet'a paper. We could use more words, like her name and the baby's last name."

Merytaten nodded, "And maybe a hint of where she was going. I've got a feeling someone not far from here was expecting her. No way of knowing who. So she's my baby."

"I think the heather would have been from Scotland. The ship would have been one that sailed when? Six months ago? Or five months or seven months?"

"Hmmm, a lot of ships and a lot of babies born on every trip. So she's my baby unless someone turns up. Now we know her name. Bonnie Heather. Beautiful flowering plant."

The scrap of paper was now dry and somewhat crinkly. Merytaten produced an envelope and slipped the paper inside. After a moment of thought, she tucked the envelope within the pages of the Bible left to Daniel by his ancestor, the other Daniel.

Little Miss Bonnie Heather quickly assembled her own fan club within the ranks of the Forrester Community Church. She attended her first services snuggly tucked into her attractive carrying basket, replete with whatever it took to fill her tiny tummy.

Any degree of restlessness while her new "mother" was occupied with the piano, was instantly attended by which ever "grandmother" could reach her first. Miss Carlotta and Miss Josie made certain to be close…just in case.

When she was seven months old, she sat up and looked around. The view was much better at that height, and she developed her own method of moving about. Scooting on her padded rear, propelled by a heel on the polished floor, she made very good time and both hands were then free to examine anything within reach.

When she was ten months old, she scooted across the parlor floor to the piano where her mother was plying the notes. She grasped one of the carved front legs of the instrument and hoisted herself to her chubby feet.

By stretching, and rising an extra inch on her pink toes, she could reach the edge of the keyboard. By extending her fingers on one hand and holding to the piano leg with the other, she could add a few notes to the upper part of the musical scale.

After a bit of experimentation and a variety of hand positions, she graduated to both hands and composed a melody of her own. Right along with her mother.

So, now, standing and looking about, she liked the scenery even better, so she proceeded rapidly across the floor on both feet…lost her balance and landed on her bottom…pulled herself upright once more. Then she took off running, and never scooted again.

The activity for the new occupants of the parsonage created changes. The preacher was not always available to travel with Merytaten on her interviews for the Chronology of Carlile Corners.

On those times it became the pleasure of her old grandfather, Gaither Cullen, to be her traveling companion. His strength and memory began to affect his ability to meet customers at his son's blacksmith shop, so his main duty became brewing the vile tasting liquid loosely called "coffee."

Actual fact was, he was no longer needed, and his son, Brad, husband of Miss Josie, took over the position. The actual work of the shop was performed by his three able and skillful sons, Aaron, James and John. They had been trained by the best…their father…and it took the trio of them to manage the increased business.

Old Gaither gained much important community status as he sat in the buggy behind the strong Conamara stallion bred by Josie's cousin, Jefferson Wilson. The attractive two-seated buggy was so often seen on the country roads, that the whole community knew about the assignment Miss Josie had laid upon her daughter. This worked out for the good, because that gave them a chance to have their own story ready…for wasn't she assigned to interview everyone? Their own interview time would surely come and they would be ready.

There was one interview Merytaten looked forward to, and this was the day for it. Miss Bonnie Heather was placed with Grandmother Josie, and they were off. Grandpa Gaither was on the reins.

The whole town knew parts of the background of the two New York children who were so suddenly sent into the territory… into the guardianship of a most unlikely recipient.

A situation existed among many of the new arrivals in America's east coast. Families often came alone...opting to leave their extended family and the country of their birth for the better opportunities in the new land.

When it worked, it worked. When something happened to a parent...or even worse, both parents...then the children were suddenly with no one. Such was what happened to twelve-year-old Benjamin and ten-year-old Beth.

They had settled comfortably in New York City, and both parents had gone to work in a factory. Benjamin had finished all the schooling that was offered, and he now had a job delivering papers. Every penny was needed.

His sister still had two years of school, but she, also, had an important job. It was her special duty to have food ready for when the two weary parents, and the growing appetite of her brother, came home.

Of her variety of duties, Beth greatly preferred that one. She had an orderly mind, and she liked blending this and that for a new flavor. She was skilled with the use of leftovers and was creative with her casseroles.

The New York apartment had a wonderful gas stove. Turn a knob, strike a match, and a blue flame appeared. Sure...it was smelly at first, but one just got used to it. Vegetables had to be bought as used, and they were very expensive. Certain ones like fresh, green peas were an expensive luxury.

Milk came in its thick bottle made of glass. First, you poured off the top cream for putting in coffee, or maybe to top a dessert. If a pudding was planned, extra milk must be ordered the day before.

It was just a matter of the rules, and Beth had no problem with them. If she could set on a food that everyone, or someone, liked, she had done her job. This was her life and she lived it, just as it was for everyone she knew. And it was a fact that many girls she knew did not have things nearly so good.

But that was before....

CHAPTER 8

The horrible news spread in the late afternoon. People came and told the children their parents had been in the factory that had exploded, and they must come along to some other place. The wide-eyed pair had no comprehension as to what was happening. They just went. As they were told.

They were taken to a place called a Shelter, but they could not stay. No room. They were taken back to the first place they went but were then sent back. They had to stay there, room or no room. At least temporarily. The authorities would try to get something done.

So they went back. Their bed was a pallet on the floor… with a lot others. Food was all right but it left them a bit hungry. There never seemed to be quite enough.

Meanwhile the authorities were attempting to find a place elsewhere for them to go. One of the neighbors had a clue. It seemed she had heard the name of someone out in the Midwest. Maybe an old relative. The man's name was Hermann Bernsteen. At least that's what the neighbor remembered.

Now, Merytaten had learned some of this story from the fellows at the blacksmith shop. It involved an old veteran from the war between the states. He was Hermann Bernsteen. All the old man wanted now was peace and quiet. He had given years of his life and a good part of a leg to his country, not to mention the loss of a few fingers. But he had learned to adapt.

He had been lucky to have been taken to a good surgeon who refused to saw off the damaged leg…as other doctors had advised him to do. It still hurt a bit, but he could walk on it, which was much better than a lot of the other soldiers could. A bucket and a peg leg worked if one made it work.

He took his military savings and headed west. There'd be a little place somewhere that his coins would purchase. It would be a place for him to stay warm and reasonably comfortable until he died. That is how he came to live in the tiny, two-roomed house on a quarter section someone had proved up and had for sale.

The old man ate this and that, never being particular. Managed to stay reasonably clean. For companionship, he ambled on his peg leg over to the blacksmith shop where there would always be other men. Fellows who remembered some of the same things he did.

The people who were in New York continued to search for placement for the orphans, of whom they had far too many. Grabbing onto the name, they sent a letter addressed to the west under the sketchy knowledge they had. It had to be the providence of the Good Lord that it even arrived.

Old Herman was amazed at the receipt of a letter. He didn't know any one...anywhere. And he didn't particularly want to know anyone...anywhere. But here it was in his hand...crisp and white and demanding attention.

He took the sheet of paper from the envelope and looked at it. From the address on the envelope, he knew it had come from the government. He had long ago made up his mind that the government had all of him that they were going to get and he would not be found. By anyone. Especially the government. He had gone as far from them as he could on the money he had, and still have enough to live on.

He read:

Mr. Hermann Bernsteen.

We are currently searching for the family of two recently orphaned children. Benjamin and Beth Thomas are with us temporarily and they are in need of guardians. We are hoping you can help us or give us a new direction to search.

Your name was given to us by a neighbor who was close to their parents, Harold and Ilene Thomas. It seemed you were mentioned as a relative who had migrated to the territory of Oklahoma.

We enclose an envelope for your reply.

New York City Services
For Orphaned Children

Old Herman read the letter again. Lifting his head, he looked around at the two-roomed log cabin built by the previous owner of the farm. Then he gazed out the window and saw the barn and the fences that had been in place when he bought the farm.

Again, he looked at the sheet of paper in his hand. Something from the outside had penetrated his security. He was discouraged and depressed.

After the horrors of the war, all he had wanted was peace and quiet, and he had found it here. He didn't ask much, so he had been content with the two small rooms of the cabin.

He was weary at the thought of being around people after the screaming hoards of the army…and the thought of two children was totally terrifying.

He looked longingly toward the potbelly stove as he wadded the sheet of paper into a ball. Being burned was good enough for something that had interrupted his quiet life, now that he had finally found it.

He tried to walk across the room to the stove, but he just couldn't make his legs work. His mind, however, was working well.

They would be Ilene's children. When he had last seen her, she was just walking good, and she still wore padded pants. She had been a friendly little thing and had smiled when he looked her way.

Still...whatever would he do with two children? There wasn't even any room for them and he must...uh...well...?

His thoughts stopped.

He was going to say they must have other family...but that was not entirely true. If there had been any kind of family left in New York, the government would not have spent the effort to find him.

And he had no idea that the children were not his responsibility. Of course they were. Family...and that sort of thing...it was.... Well, he couldn't let it go.

He smoothed the paper with his good hand and turned it over to its white back side. He wrote:

> ...These children are likely the children of my granddaughter, Ilene Fields. I've never met them, and I am not a suitable guardian. If you can do better, please do. If there is absolutely no one else, contact me at Oklahoma Territory, Argyle, in care of Carlile Corners.

Feeling very certain that his life was about to change, he sealed the note into the reply envelope and took it to be picked up by the new government mail service.

The decision made, he walked across the street to the blacksmith shop where many old men gathered. The building was noisy with iron hammer on iron anvil as horseshoes were formed and fitted to the feet of the community's most important animal, and about the only reliable means of transportation.

It was there that he delivered the most startling news the other old men had heard for years. Old Hermann was going to be given two children to raise. Great-grandchildren, yet! How could that be? Of course he must refuse.

But when he faced the men and asked them, "What would you do if you got that letter?" they had no answer. Each one decided it was time to get another cup of coffee and talk the matter over.

Now there was a special thing about the town of Carlile Corners. They loved news. They also loved children. Good news was repeated and repeated over and over. Bad news was discussed, and if anything could be done, they figured a way to do it. If anyone needed help, there was a good chance it could be found.

If old Hermann's news was startling and totally unexpected, at least it was very interesting. The day had not gone by before labor and material were scrounged up and a workday set. Skilled and unskilled labor erected two rooms, one on the other, attached to the side of the old log cabin.

The little girl could have the lower room, and someone actually had a little girl's outgrown bed that would just fit there. It would be good for a while.

The boy's room had a built-in bed that had an under-storage bin for all the things boys value. On the wall it had a special shelf and that was the one thing that old Herman had requested to be made.

He looked at the huge cast iron stove and shook his head in dismay. How would he ever produce meals for growing children? Help was going to have to come from somewhere. He cast his eyes toward the ceiling, from which he hoped came his Help.

In due time, the children were put on the Santa Fe Railway and sent west. Then the overworked New York people set their heads toward the next problem that was facing them.

The old man drove his buggy to Oklahoma City and loaded the children aboard. As he passed back through Argyle, he picked up a package Old Mac had ordered for him.

Before the wide eyes of the children, he unwrapped a shiny new 22 rifle with a beautiful wooden stock. The boy, still dumbstruck, listened to this man telling him that he would be required learn to shoot this gun because it would be his job to protect his sister.

Benjy had never actually seen a real gun. He knew what it was, but he certainly never thought of ever having one. Much less, shooting it. At first, it was a very discouraging problem for him because he compared his lack of skill to the skill of other boys who had been shooting a gun from the time their arms would reach. It was a skill required of all boys, and of most girls.

Beth, however, took one look at the huge cast iron stove and instantly fell in love. Just look at it! The magnificent contraption heated its own water! It did not make smelly fumes when it burned. It made the kitchen so cozy and it was wonderfully huge and important looking!

The biggest excitement of all was that she was given complete charge of it. If she wanted potatoes, there they were right in the ground. Milk came at her so fast, she had to think up ways to use it. Biscuits and cornbread were so much better cooked in that oven.

And look at the lovely jars of canned fruits and vegetables that were stored in the underground room! Would she get to help put the food in the jars? Maybe next year…?

The ten-year-old was so appealing by nature, that the ladies of the community took her into their kitchens and into their hearts and she was in her own special heaven.

She took great pleasure with the fuel used for her kitchen toy. Cow pats. She had never heard of such a thing. Horse poop in New York was called by a variety of names, but cow pats had a good name. It was a good and useful name.

Also, part of the fun was the collecting of them. There were enough animals belonging to the old man that the quarter section provided an overabundance of them, but they were mostly out of reach for her until her brother got good enough with his rifle to protect her.

That put considerable pressure on him. He was told by the old man that it was his JOB to learn and Benjy knew about jobs. You worked on them until they were finished. There was the pressure of doing this job for this grandpa who had taken them in, and there was the pressure of his sister and her eagerness for a greater supply of cow pats.

When he could hit the center of his target five times out six, he could take her and the sled out to where the animals rested in a grove of trees. There were piles of the precious pats out there all dried and flaky, and his sister wanted them.

And face it, she was beginning to do wonderful things with that stove she loved, and she was writing down everything her brother liked, filling up a notebook so she could cook it that way every time. He really wanted her to have the pats so this skill of hers would continue.

And finally he did it. Five out of six shots hit the bull's eye. The very next day, he hitched up the sled to the horse and they went out to the grove where the animals liked to rest. He stood on a rock and watched in every direction while she happily filled her baskets.

True, he had felt wonderfully important and efficient as he turned this way and that. It was a wonder that he even saw the well-camouflaged animals, but their silver tail-plumes, waving above the tall grass, gave them away.

Forcing his fingers to be steady, he managed to get the lead animal in his sights and he pulled the trigger. The sound made the others flee, but he had managed to get Beth up a tree to safety. He knew that if he had missed, and the animals turned to attack, he would have had time to join her. But it didn't become necessary.

Success was such a grand and glorious experience, that he smiled to himself as he savored it alone. Later, he would savor the praise of Grandpa, as well as the thankfulness of his sister. That was when he decided it would be fun to grow up to be a man in this place where personal pride was possible.

On the return trip, the sled carried the barrel of cow pats and the body of the wolf. The wolf fur was turned into a bedside rug, which was nice. His upper room was unheated in the winter and wolf fur was known to be snug and warm for bare feet on a cold morning.

They were lucky children to find their grandpa, but they may well have added ten years to the old man's life. He had something to live for. Something important. Something that needed him. And most of all, he saw where his efforts accomplished something lasting…and all of his efforts in the war had created only destruction.

Old Herman was gone, now, and the children were both grown and married. One of Benjamin's friends was very impressed by his sister's skill at the stove. Likely he would have married her anyway, but the skill with the stove certainly didn't hurt.

The young man built Beth a house on the property a few hundred feet down the road. The only item she took from the house as hers was the big iron stove. Whoever Benjamin married would just have to provide her own.

Their stories were alive with details, and Merytaten had scribbled fast. Then she asked, "How did you ever manage when you had to leave behind everything you ever knew? The loneliness must have been dreadful."

"Yes, it was. But we had each other and we were always close. When my tears came in the night, Benjy always heard and came down to my room. We would talk about everything, ending up knowing and agreeing with each other how fortunate we were that someone was willing to take us, and it even seemed that he liked us. We probably would not have stayed in New York City anyway, and just look at the wonderful place we now have to live in and grow our children!"

Then she grinned conspiratorially and added, "Then here was the grandpa we never knew we had, and he just LOVED my cooking. He let me start cooking all the meals from the second day I was here, and me only ten years old. Can you just imagine that?"

Notes complete, Merytaten took her leave.

Old Gaither was ready to go, having napped while she visited, and she rode along beside him, thinking about Beth.

Lovely lady she was, and the prairie was lucky to get the both of them. Clearly, it had been New York City's loss.

There was the day that Old Gaither was feeling a bit "under the weather" and Prissy, Daniel's sister, rode along with her. It really wasn't exactly safe to travel very far out in the country alone. One never knew when another hand would be needed to man the gun. Varmints both two-legged and four-legged could come from nowhere.

The firearm was an instrument on which all were required, by necessity, to at least become fairly proficient. Especially with the "snake gun." Most residents graduated on to a more powerful weapon, which not only covered the legless varmint problems, but also the two-legged and four-legged varmints as well.

Merytaten's father, Brad, had insisted, with force, that she acquire the skill and always be protected by her own weapon. So Prissy, with the same training, was brought along as a driver of the horse in the event a shoot-out became necessary.

And, today, the two young ladies were tooling along the road chatting about this and that, but mostly about the two new residents of the Corners that the pair of them would produce within mere months. Shortly after Merytaten had married Prissy's brother, Prissy had married Merytaten's brother, John.

At this moment, both had gone a bit past "expecting" and were "absolutely sure" of a delivery excitingly soon.

They had both reached the time of wearing clothing that was no longer meant to keep a secret, so this little trip of theirs would likely be the last for a while. Their clothing from here on would be designed to cover what was already known, rather than hiding the knowledge of what was to come. Today they hoped to interview another couple.

There had been an English couple who had settled on a tract near Sentinel Rock. When the weather permitted, they enjoyed attending Forrester Community Church.

The couple, with their four children, had purchased one of the "lock, stock, and barrel" land sales, where the original homesteaders had improved with fences and outbuildings, and for some reason, decided to sell it. And everything in it was included in the price.

That had become a rather common thing, as land values had increased so rapidly. The five years they had spent on improvements gave a per-year income that could never be earned in another way by an unskilled person. Also, the acreage had provided them a place to live, thus increasing the profit.

The Sherwoods moved in with their family of six, happily investing every cent of their savings. It was proving to be a marvelous investment, as Joseph was so handy with everything he touched, and they wanted for nothing. The Tall Rock Academy was so close the children could easily walk. Truly, an unexpected blessing.

In view of this, they had sent back to England for Joseph's brother and his bride to come on…as the living was fine on the prairie.

The young ladies from the parsonage rode along the road, discussing their various special events, along with covering the excitement of the new Sherwoods. It turned out that the brother, John, and his wife, Cecelia, were also "expecting" and had also reached the point of becoming "absolutely certain."

It was a bit of unfortunate timing, actually, but babies came when they came, and the couple had already booked their passage…waited three months for it…and they were not willing to let it go. Also, they had been promised that the trip could be made in, maybe, forty-five days. Well, maybe it could, but only with only one or two of the newest ships, and when they were lightly loaded.

Most ships that left England and everywhere else were loaded as heavily as possible to increase profits. So the Eagle Wings sailed before the wind, and the newest Sherwood's would arrive on the Eastern shore of the Colonies with about two months to spare. By their optimistic accounting.

Bolstering their confidence further, was the fact that the Santa Fe Railroad had crisscrossed the frontier, plowing its noisy and smoky way right down from Arkansas City, Kansas, through Guthrie and on to Oklahoma City. At that point they could purchase a light buggy and a pair of fast horses, and they would make it on through in one long day. It all worked out well on paper.

Sure, it was cutting the corner a bit closer than they liked, but hadn't Cecie's mother delivered seven children? And hadn't she delivered the last one at midnight and got up the next morning to cook breakfast?

Two things, however, had not entered into the plans of the younger Sherwood's. Cecie had inherited the slim bone structure of her father's family. The other thing was that Cecie's mother had delivered her children one at a time.

The traveling young ladies from the Corners were looking forward to the excitement and preparation for their new arrivals, along with making notes for the Chronology. The newcomers would be added, creating their own interest to the story.

For the younger Sherwoods, the Eagle Wings had done its part, docking only three weeks late. The Santa Fe engine roared and billowed smoke for the week that it took to get its cars to Oklahoma City.

For the three days it took for John to locate a sturdy buggy and a pair of horses for sale in this transportation-starved land, Cecie had nervously fidgeted in the rented room. She read the newspaper from beginning to end, trying to push away thoughts of the new activity within her.

Swallowing hard and trying to read fast was not very effective in halting the regularly occurring stab and slash within her lower abdomen.

The stabs were still from one hour to two hours apart, and she had heard from many good and experienced sources that a backache could be expected before any important concern was necessary. No backache. Yet.

And then late on the third day, face pale with fright, and clothes soiled and wrinkled from his activity, her husband appeared with good news. A buggy had been acquired.

Finally! At last! And with a forced cheery reassurance, he told her that it was too late to leave this late in the day, as it was not safe to be on the road at night...alone. Likely he was right on that.

They would get to bed early and be ready to leave in the morning, about an hour before daylight. That's what the livery people told him was best.

Cecie nodded, painted a smile on her face, and swallowed hard. This decision to cut the timing close had not been entirely his idea, so the blame must be shared. But she was now definitely being stabbed a regular forty-five minutes apart.

No matter. It was confirmed fact, wasn't it? First babies were always slow, and she had no backache.

She tried to lie still, but finally left the bed and settled herself in the stuffed armchair. Tossing about, the way she had been, she would keep him awake, and there was nothing he could do about the problem. Best he get a good night's sleep...and he did. Being exhausted down to a nub from worry, and facing the difficulty of finding transportation, he was about out of his mind. And he had a big day tomorrow.

She searched for something positive to think on while she stared down from her upstairs window onto the quiet Oklahoma City streets. The mercury vapor lights cast a soft glow on the locally made bricks of the sidewalk and the street.

Her thoughts finally settled on the knowledge that John knew horses. Once he got behind the team, there would be no more problems. They'd make it in a day...or two at the absolute most. He had assured her that he had located the items she had ordered, a great tin box of crackers, two pounds of rat-trap cheese, a dozen eating apples and two dozen raisin cookies. Good finger food.

That food, along with the two-gallon jug of water and their steamer trunks, had been loaded aboard. Waiting. Ready. It was all she could do to force herself to stay in the room, and not immediately plant herself among the plunder in the buggy to be quicker on the way.

A blast of the Santa Fe whistle woke John at 3:30 AM. He startled up as if he had a bee sting. He stepped into his boots and drew on his pants. He saw his wife dressed and ready, sitting quietly in the chair.

It must be said for John that he was no dummy. What should be excitement in her eyes was nearer desperation. His mind pictured the wide staircase that must be descended, and he made a sudden decision.

"You wait here while I take down the stuff from the room, and bring the buggy around. I don't want you to risk those stairs alone." With that, he ran down the staircase three steps at a time.

Cecie had nodded that she heard him…not that she planned to obey. Giving his flying footsteps time to be out of sight and hearing, she closed the door to the room and poked the key back through the slot.

At the top step, she sat herself down and extended her feet to the third step below her. Scooting on her backside, she lowered her unwieldy body down to the next step. Extended feet again, and lowering backside again, she oozed her way to the platform landing, and did not risk standing. She scooted on her rear for the six feet to reach the rest of the stair and proceeded down.

She reached the floor of the lobby and, with the help of the newel post, hoisted herself to her feet. She was just straightening her twisted skirts when John appeared at the door…eyes wildly open and hair an uncombed tangle. The sprouted half inch of unshaven whiskers on his chin added to his look of horror and desperation.

He ran across the lobby and scooped her into his arms. Backing himself out the swinging door, he placed her gently on the buggy seat and ran to the other side. Before he was even settled himself, he was yelling at the horses.

And they were off.

The stabs within Cecie were holding at about forty minutes...most of the time. Everything would be all right, now. Still no backache.

Their individual fears kept the couple quiet, except for the yells at the horses that echoed along the dark streets of the prairie town. She assembled cracker-cheese sandwiches for his breakfast and poured cups of water from the jug. She, herself, nibbled a cracker, just to keep him from knowing how badly she did NOT want to eat.

It was pitch dark when they reached the small town of Argyle. Much too late to try to follow the pencil drawn map. Stay overnight. Had to. Cecie settled her pain-wracked body into the hollow of the canvas cot. It was a moment of relief from the strain of sitting and the jounce of the buggy, but the pressure pains hung right in there.

A parting gift to her had been one of the new watches that attached to a lapel with a clamp. Cecie dozed, then a pain hit. In the dim light of the moon, she saw, with horror, that the stabs were now down to fifteen minutes...sometimes thirteen minutes. At the first rooster crow, she rolled her body toward the side of the bed, lowered her feet firmly to the floor, and pushed up with her arms.

Her arms worked well and seemed to be about the only part of her that didn't hurt. That...and the back. Still no backache so there must be time. What was it to be now...one hour more to get there? She moved her body through the door into the store that was in the lobby. John was shoveling oatmeal into his mouth and motioned toward another bowl beside him.

"I was just comin' for you. Eat quick."

She shook her head. "I'll eat crackers. You eat it." And he did, wolfing it down like a starving coyote. She met him at the door, and he carried her to the buggy…all hitched up and waiting.

He yelled at the team and the horses jerked forward and tore into the road at a full gallop.

The young ladies from the Corners had just pulled into the yard of the older set of Sherwoods, and a smiling Joseph was ready to take their animals to the corral. Fresh tea and cookies were steaming in the kitchen.

A sound of hoof beats and a scream of "Git up there!" and the pair of excited blue roans came tearing down the road… wild eyes rolling back in their heads and their shaggy manes waving about their necks like a pair of bottle brushes. The rolling cacophony of noises wheeled into the yard and the animals responded to the shout of "WHOA! WHOA, THERE!"

The man jumped out and ran around the buggy. "I need help!" he shouted, needlessly at his brother. Teamwork quickly settled the groaning figure from the buggy onto a bed. Venita, Cecie's sister-in-law, demanded, "How long apart? Tell me quick…how long?"

Quick intake of breath as a slashing stab hit. "Ten minutes, I think."

Venita's eyes popped open and her heart stopped. "All fellow out! Get out everybody, but don't leave the house. Mery, Prissy, I'll need help."

Cecie was crying uncontrollably, her breath ragged and gagging between the ripping, tearing contractions. The two childless ladies hung back for Venita to perform the first examination. They saw the sister-in-law gulp with horror.

"Girls. Bad as she's hurtin', that baby outta be showin' something. Even a foot. This ain't a'goin' right."

Merytaten stared at the terrified Venita and a sheet of paper came before her eyes. She saw, from the picture of Daniel's written words, the desperate, terrified young man bringing his dying wife to Daniel's table. She pictured him with the scalpel in his hand, and the father of the unborn child begging for something to be done. A chance for the baby, perhaps. And Daniel had been successful.

"Venita, she's gotta go to the clinic. NOW! Joseph, get on your fastest horse and head for the church. If Daniel isn't there, you ring the bell as loud as you can. Don't ask me why. Just go. GO!" The last word was shouted into his face…and he went.

"Venita, and, you're John, are you? We'll put her in the back seat of my buggy. John, saddle a horse and catch up with us on the road. Venita, you crawl back there and keep her calm as you can. Prissy, man the guns and shoot anyone who tries to stop us." Prissy collected both guns and laid them across her lap, their muzzles turned toward the outside of the buggy. Ready.

Grabbing the reins before she was hardly seated, Merytaten shouted at her team. "Git up there!" and they got. Two and a half miles were between them and help, and it meant not a minute to lose. Horses' hooves and crunching gravel were the only sounds for the whole distance.

A mile down the road, John on an unsaddled stallion, passed them, and slowed. Leading them forward in the only direction they could go, he proceeded into Carlile Corners and turned right when Merytaten shouted at him.

Daniel had been at the blacksmith shop, trying not to drink the steaming black liquid in his cup.

Like the old-time fire horses answering the bell with all senses alert, Daniel set down the coffee cup and headed for the clinic on the second peel of the church bell. He would be ready for the emergency that was sure to show up. He had just settled in, prepared a table, and washed up when a man he had never seen came up the driveway at full gallop.

Behind him came the visiting buggy with his wife at the reins. He caught his breath with the view, but realized if she was the one in trouble, she'd likely not be driving, but…. He ran to meet whatever was awaiting him.

"In labor," Merytaten informed him. "Been two days, no action."

The screaming woman (girl?) was put on the table. No pain killer until he saw what was wrong. Huge contraction... that was what was wrong! Painful, exhausting muscle effort that produced nothing. No spreading of the pelvis to make ready for the birth.

Donald stood with him, fearing to ask a question as he saw Daniel's shoulder slump forward with dismay. He could not see the picture that was stamped indelibly into Daniel's memory. Young man screaming at him to do something...girl drawing her last breaths...much too young.

He could faintly feel the encouraging hand of the older, work-worn nurse...lightly and warm against his arm. The feel of the scalpel pushed into his hand. Urging him to act.

So now it happened again. Scalpel was in his hand.

Donald clapping hand over mouth. Stopping his words of horror before they could be uttered.

"Give her morphine," Daniel commanded. If he didn't do something immediately, both mother and baby would die. He could at least save the mother. Maybe.

A sigh. A prayer.... *Please, Lord. One more time, we beg.*

The scalpel poised, its point against the contracting abdomen and blade drawn forward. Streak of red. More spoken orders.

"Get Angel for me.... Mery...get Merytaten. No one else."

Donald was quickly back. Clamps in his hands. Tying back. Doing things he knew to do. His hands worked on their own.

Merytaten appeared. Command by the doctor to his Angel. "Get ready."

She stared at him. Get ready for what? Her hands were shaking with fear and face pale with fright. She came closer. Another scalpel furrow through the skin of the abdomen. Blood. A small leg appeared...smeared red with blood. Then it disappeared.

Scalpel again. A leg was liberated along with an arm and a twisted face. A shoulder...and above the shoulder, there appeared...another leg!

Command to Angel. "Lift the baby."

Donald was ready to help. Baby, its body as slick as a fresh peeled boiled egg. Angel's hands clasp firmly at the ribs, Donald's hands behind the head. Lift...and the leg from over the baby's shoulder disappeared into the depth of the abdomen oozing blood. Merytaten felt the scenery whirl around her. She shook her head, firmly. No time to get dizzy.

Baby tied off and breathing. Screaming! Flailing arms. The sound put life into the waiting father and sister-in-law. Smiles. Eyes brightened. Baby was here! Everything was right and they were ready to see the new citizen. They headed for the door.

Prissy had no idea what was going on, only that Daniel didn't want anyone but Merytaten to come in. She pressed her body against the door like another coat of paint and gave the anxious pair a fierce stare that stopped them in their tracks.

Baby in basket. Donald was turning the next baby. Cord in position. A snip freed him.

Angel lifted the little thing and wrapped it. Her mind was numb, but her hands seemed to know what to do. She glanced at Daniel's face. Perspiration dotted his forehead. Hands steady and firm on the surgeon's knife. Then, with four hands working together, the men skillfully joined the edges of living flesh.

Daniel looked at his hands. Steady now. Trembling gone. Sutures. Joining the severed edges left by the scalpel, and the owner of the flesh still breathed. It could mean success. *Please....*

The girl on the table breathed regularly. In and out. A reassuring rise and fall. Relief flowed in trembling waves along his shoulders and down his back. Hands still steady. Clearly, a gift from Above.

Donald was cleaning away blood, making a smoother path for the joining of living flesh. This was something they both knew so well. And had done so many times…with bleary eyes in the dark of the night they had done it.

They wished they didn't know about it, but they did. It was the thing of nightmares.

Two crying voice raised themselves in impatience. Irritation at having been rudely lifted from their snug and moist cocoon, into air that must be breathed. That was quite enough to create indignant aggravation, so they screamed together…the sound seeming like an angel's song to the three in the waiting room.

They ached to go through the door, but the fierce eyes of mild-mannered Prissy kept them back.

Still breathing. Up and down. Last of the blood cleared away. Daniel sighed a breath from the bottom of his grateful soul. It was such an advantage to be young, strong and well nourished. She had a chance. *Please, God…let her have a chance.*

With her build, the twins and the rugged trip of the last months…? *Thank you, Lord. The odds had certainly pointed the other way.*

Daniel's Angel had, at last, tamed the tremors in her hands. She had attended enough births to know what to do with the finished product. Tiny, thin-skinned. Moist flannel cloths for cleaning. These little fellows couldn't possibly be full term, but they must have really needed to get out of their cramped space.

Looked perfect. The right number of ears, toes and fingers.

Already they managed to flail their fists until they accidentally reached their mouths. They looked startled when it happened. What's that mouth for, anyway? They'd never needed it before.

Behind her, the curtains were drawn around the table where lay the mother, Cecie…was that what they called her?

Daniel and Donald were talking in low tones, but she didn't bother to listen. She was looking back and forth at the two little fellows, conceived in Scotland and delivered in Oklahoma, America. Her experience told her that little fellows born in

Oklahoma usually arrived hungry, and these boys' ma wasn't going to be able to do anything about it. At least for a while

Milk. Bottles were here. She seemed to remember that midwives were in no hurry to feed the newborns. It seemed there was beneficial crying to be done.

MIDWIVES! WHERE WERE DORCAS AND ELLEN? They could have done her job better than she…but then, they had never seen this kind of birth, either.

With a grin, Donald informed her, "The girls went to the city to attend a class on unusual births. Are they ever going to wish they'd been here! Likely would'a learned a lot more."

Daniel pushed on the door, and his sister gave in and allowed him to open it. He motioned, and the apprehensive trio followed.

Gasped! Twins! Twin boys. The papa…John…buried his face in his arm and leaned against the wall. Shoulders heaving from sobs. He could have lost everything, but he didn't. Finally, with sobs sniffed away, he came to Daniel with outstretched hand.

Daniel motioned behind the curtain. She was sleeping peacefully. The horrible pain would be later, but it could be born. Fortunately, God made women tough.

John stared down at the face he adored. The sheet that covered her arose and fell. "Thank you so much, Doctor."

Daniel took his hand but shrugged away the compliment. "Wasn't me, friend. Only God can handle a job like this one was. He must have wanted you to have these fine lads and their mother." Then with a grin, he added, "Just see that you deserve them."

The young husband and father just returned the grin. They could tease and say what they would, but he not only had his beloved wife, he had a baby. Not just a baby, but a son. Not just one son…he had two! Who cared what anyone said? He knew he was the luckiest man on God's green earth. Later he would be told just how lucky he really was…so much more than he had thought.

CHAPTER 9

Daniel watched. The excited father should have his moment of joy before he was told that he was even more lucky than he had thought. Or could have imagined. There was absolutely no way that his beloved wife could have delivered those two babies in the normal way. Also, this method of delivery was so new, there was no history of the result of such an abdominal invasion. He hoped she did not have to be an unfortunate test case in future pregnancies.

As stated earlier, Bonnie Heather was seven months old, and she pulled herself up to a sitting position to look around. The view was a lot better from up there. Also she should move about and use her hands for what they were created. She could pull her padded rear across the floor by extending her leg and planting her heel as a brace and a lever.

With both hands free, she could carry toys, play patty cake and other enjoyable activities that seemed to please her parental audience.

When she was ten months old, she scooted herself to the carved front leg of the church piano while her mother practiced. With arms around the piano leg, she pulled herself to her feet and patty caked on the padded cushion. Sometimes Mama picked her up…it was worth a try.

When she was eighteen months old, little sister Sharon joined the family. Such a wonderful toy. There was now something that was even smaller than she was and it fit in the doll basket. Her doll had to sleep somewhere else.

It was when she was twenty-two months old, she performed her first duty as a member of the family. It was going to happen sooner or later, but there was a good reason for it to happen now.

Her mother was very busy. What with her duties as the preacher's wife, pianist, mother of two babies still in padded pants, and she hardly had time for interviews for the Chronology.

Of course Miss Josie had said it would likely take years, but Merytaten had times when she would like to get on with it. One didn't always get to do what one liked.

And some of it affected Daniel. There were times that the preacher was asked to help on an errand that a church member thought important. Sometimes they actually were important. After all, the preacher didn't have a regular job, did he? What else would he be doing?

So it was that Laura Ann Harrison asked if the preacher would "run here out" to her parent's far-flung farm with some food and help. Her old pa was almost blind, and her ma was down with a bad hip from accidentally stepping off the edge of the porch. The need was there, for certain.

Laura could not use the family conveyance as her husband needed it in his work, and Laura's trip was a one-way thing. She planned to stay a few days to "help out" as was her daughterly duty. That was plain to see.

That fact had already presented somewhat of a "situation," in itself. One buggy, two destinations.

Also, there was the fact that Laura was what was considered a "looker." For the preacher to be seen riding in the buggy (alone) with an attractive lady, it might seem a bit extreme. And there was that advice in the Book with the warning to "…avoid the appearance of evil…." All of these things were racing through Daniel's mind.

He could hardly ask his Angel to drop everything and go along with him as the trip was sure to be at least three hours long. At least, very nearly, considering the trip there and back, and a polite visit while he was there…which would be expected of the preacher.

He cast his eyes about the room and they lit on his daughters, giggling and squealing with pleasure as they patted each other on the face. It was a favorite game of the sisters, now that Sharon learned to control her hands…to a limited degree.

There was Bonnie Heather twenty-two months old, and it was time she was pressed into service. He noted that her dress was fairly clean, and she had been doing well in the potty department.

"Angel, I think I'll take Bonnie with me out to the Fields. It ought to be a good trip for her. Where are her shoes and socks?"

Merytaten looked a bit surprised, but relieved. "In the top drawer in her room. Her jacket and bonnet are hanging on the back of the door. Maybe you could take a couple of C-O-O-K-I-E-S along for later."

He dressed her and hitched the horse to the buggy. With Laura beside him, he left the yard with the little girl in his lap. They picked up the needed kettles and jars and headed on down State Highway.

At the blacksmith shop, he slowed and waved, letting the fellows see the little girl. She was encouraged to squeal and wave to anyone who might be close enough to notice. It was needed to be certain that the adults were not alone.

Little Bonnie was not the only preacher's child who was drafted to chaperone her father, but she may have been among the youngest. It was a duty she was to perform with enthusiasm and skill for the next several years.

It was when she was two and a half that she decided to mount the piano bench alone, as Mama was too busy to help. She stood by the bench and reached for a handhold somewhere. No help presented itself, so she backed off and studied the problem.

When the good idea occurred, she dashed to her room and returned dragging the huge stuffed bear created by Grandma Carlotta. Stepping her bare feet on the toy's round tummy, she lifted up on her toes and gained about four inches in arm reach. It wasn't much but it was enough.

By grasping a hand on each side of the padded seat, she could hoist herself up with her tummy flat on the bench. Twisting to a seating position brought the keyboard level with her nose, positioning her eyes just right to correctly place her hands where she wanted them.

With the first handful of discordant notes, her mother appeared in the doorway. She was just in time to see the chubby left hand extend down into the base notes and make what she obviously intended to be a musical "base run."

Her amazed mother sank into a nearby chair and continued to watch as her daughter pounded the notes with intense concentration. Could it be that she was musical? When could a child begin to learn? She'd always loved songs. She could sing "Mary had a Little Lamb" and "Jesus Loves Me" almost well enough to be understood. And she could attempt a few others.

Sitting on the bench and lifting the little girl to her lap, Merytaten one-fingered the tune to "Jesus Loves Me" and was rewarded by an upturned face registering the awe of recognition. She repeated the tune under the child's intense concentration. She moved her hands away from the keys down to the bench and waited.

Bonnie's extended finger pressed the correct beginning note, and the next three...then she looked up for approval. A squeezy hug and a kiss, and her mama played the tune again. This time the child managed eight notes before she stopped. What a concentration and memory for her age!

Hmmm...well, she was much too young to read notes... she could barely talk. This HAD to be the result of a good memory. Perhaps a few tunes by "ear" would challenge her, and who knew what would happen.

It was at least twenty minutes before the little girl was weary of the piano but she well on her way to attaining amazing accuracy. Merytaten was truly excited. She'd save this little discovery for a while and let her get a bit better and more confident before she showed Daniel. Little surprises were so important to parents.

She'd force herself to be patient and wait. Shouldn't take long. With these thoughts she amused herself until the evening meal.

It was after she had buckled small Sharon into her highchair, poured a cup of steaming tea for Daniel, and was preparing to call Bonnie from wherever she was, that she heard a melody. It was an unmistakable tune. "Je…sus…loves…me… this…I…know. For…the…Bi…ble…tells…." then a hesitation, followed by a very loud note. "SO…" It was almost as though she was scolding that last note for not being more easily found.

Daniel looked at Angel and she looked back. The surprise she had planned was spoiled, but this one was even better. It surprised them both!

She smiled at Daniel, shrugged and asked uselessly, "Do you think she's ready for lessons?"

Whereupon, another small duty was placed on the preacher's wife, but it would be limited in success until the child learned to read.

Growing up often comes in spurts and chunks. So it was with Bonnie Heather. It was when she was four years old and graduated into the upper Sunday School class that the next growth occurred. Young Forrest Canfield stared at her with his six-year-old intense blue eyes and she gazed adoringly at him with her lavender blue eyes. The boy scooted over on the bench and Bonnie climbed up beside him.

Young Forrest was the child of Raymond Canfield (of Canfield Grading) and Merry Forrester Canfield who was his "hired man." Merry gained fame in the territory by guarding the Canfield horses with her gun, and for being the very first person in the community…male or female…to manage to turn a stalled "tin lizzie" car into a running machine.

She was also the only person who regularly made use of the combustion engine, rather than the hay eating one, for her horsepower. Cars had a major problem at this particular period of time which greatly slowed the extent of their use in outlying areas. Some are enumerated as follows:

First: They were so new, they did not operate reliably and no one wanted to be stuck out on a country road and have to be hauled back by a team of horses.

Second: There was no place to purchase gas in the town. It had to be brought out from Argyle in five-gallon cans, five miles distant, and the gas gauges were not reliably accurate.

Third: They were rather expensive, and why should anyone have to get into such a hurry like that? If you needed to be there quicker, you just started earlier. Everyone should know that.

Fourth: They were really noisy and smelly, and they rattled abominably on the rutted roads. Besides, a tire blow-out could scare the life out of a scarecrow! Wouldn't you agree?

Fifth: No one could figure out what made the evil things stop running except Merry Canfield, and it was embarrassing to have to go ask a woman, and a very small one at that, to tell you what was wrong with your fliver, as they were often called.

There was likely a Sixth, Seventh and Eighth reason and maybe more, but it was hard for the fellows to get past number Five.

As Bonnie grew older, she begged to go to the "Horse House" as she called Canfield Grading, the home of the powerful Clydesdale horses. Merry, the caretaker of the horses, always had time for playing with children. After she had two children already through the Academy, she had Forrest, six years old, and Eva, three years old. Both of them surprise babies.

Miss Merry also had a wonderful thing called a housekeeper, so she was available to put all three children (her two youngest and Bonnie) on the broad back of Clementine and lead her around the farm. Occasionally, she handed the reins to the capable hands of Forrest and watched as he carried on...the laughing, squealing girls riding behind him.

Bonnie's mom was happy to let her play with Eva and Forrest as their mom never let them out of her sight. She was fully as careful with her children as she was with her horses, and that was saying a lot.

When the preacher's household was increased by one more, the boy was conveniently named after his proud grandfather. Ralph Carpenter, the elder, was the person who introduced the strong and enduring Clydesdale horses to the Corners, and he now operated a store called a Five and Dime. There was so much business right there in the community of nearby towns that he had no time to operate a route as he had when he was younger.

If Grandpa Ralph had his way, the younger Ralph would soon join him behind the counter and learn the profitable ways of making a living. There could be no more successful teacher and business partner than Grandpa, no matter how far they looked.

It was when Bonnie Heather was five years old that she was enrolled in the Prairie Academy. That gave her mother a slight lift in her duties. She had not one doubt that, between Miss Carmelita and Miss Rosalie, the child was not only safe, but would learn to sit still for a few minutes at a time, and she would learn with the speed of most beginners.

Also that year, Errol Scott decided to plow his east forty and put it in field peas. Those tasty, nutritious little vegetables were practically no work at all, especially if they were to be left on the vine to dry out.

That way they could be gathered when it was convenient and shelled out when one had time. It could all be done by children, or an adult while resting. When shelled, they had only to be poured into a jar with an air-tight lid…sealed…and put in the back of the cellar shelves.

They were known to last for years…even decades…and still be cooked up as tasty and nutritious as ever. Good planning.

He had intended to do that for the last three years, and now he was determined to make the time. Taking his team of mules to the chosen area, he began. He was now dealing with earth that had never seen a plow, and was so tough to get started, that he was forced to stand the plow up on its point and push with his foot to help the mules dig in.

Once the sod was punctured, the going was somewhat easier. If he had been planning a vegetable garden, or some such, he would expect to plow it several times to break up rock-hard clods laced together with a network of roots.

Field peas, however, were tough plants, and they even fertilized the soil for themselves. All he had to do was make a break in the sod, sprinkle in the pea seeds and drag with a harrow to cover them up before the crows got them.

The "harrow" was a wonderful invention for farmers. It consisted of a platform of bars about five feet square. Each of the bars had a row of "teeth" like a comb, about every four inches. These teeth were pointed and dug slightly into the sod for leveling. They were also very useful for covering any seeded area where the seed was scattered (broadcasted) rather than planted in rows.

Errol spent two full days of hard labor on the plow shares...then planted the seed. The rest was easy. The mules pulled the harrow, and they thought they'd had an easy day. Twice over and the field peas were planted.

It was when he was riding the harrow that something shiny was pulled up from the dirt. It glinted in the morning sun, and Errol yelled at the mules to "Whoa, there." They were glad to.

Errol picked up the shiny object. It looked like some kind of metal but it couldn't be. There had been no civilization on this land. Certainly not in recent history, or by anyone skilled in brass. He brushed off the clods of dirt against the leg of his overalls and looked closely.

Of course, it could not be what it looked like, but it couldn't be anything else. There in his hand lay a well-fashioned brass belt buckle with the initials "RS" clearly sculpted into the metal.

A deep throated groan of agony and a chest tightening that fairly took his breath away. Then he sat down on the toothed-harrow and bowed his sweaty face into the dusty sleeve of his shirt and sobbed. Racking, heaving sobs from the tortured depth of his soul.

So clearly he remembered the day that he and Reuben had decided to spend the money to get the belt buckles specially made. As they were obviously expensive, this was a way to show the girls that they could afford the best. Such a buckle was known to be a social asset.

When his flood of tears finally ceased, he pocketed the treasure and began searching around for more. The mules enjoyed resting for the better part of an hour before Errol found the short, sharp-pointed steel dagger his cousin always wore in a special pocket of his lace-up boot. These were locally known as a "dirks," and were of somewhat ceremonial dress.

There were three brass buttons among the clods, but he did not find the ring with the fake ruby stone. He did, however, mark the area for further searching. It was obvious that it was this spot where his cousin had breathed his last. Not even a half of a mile from his final destination!

Why, oh, why didn't he come on just a little farther? It had to be that he didn't know how close he was and had decided to wait until morning. Bad decision.

He'd be back later to look for traces of Katy and the baby, though he was doubtful of finding anything. There were those outlaws who would have kept the beautiful young Katy alive, and taken her with them. The baby…there was no knowing what could have happened to it. But one could guess.

The first pain of his grief having passed over, he set his head to the plowing. At least he could now tell the folks back in the old country as much as he knew. There had been a flood of letters back and forth trying to locate any information of their disappearance. None.

Reuben…more than a cousin! Maybe even more than a brother. Darling little Katy that Reuben had loved from the time he noticed that girls were different. The girl with a voice like an angel…or maybe even better. He had never heard an angel, but the whole heather-covered countryside had heard Katy. And would agree.

Bonnie Heather was eight years old the year of the wonderful Christmas play. Merytaten had put together a program and had advertised it for ten miles around. She had resisted the urge to make it around the nativity and styled the whole program to be around each child's strong points…or weak points as the case may be.

There were recited Bible verses…some rhymes about Christmas. There were group songs that were simple enough for the youngest participants.

There was a duet featuring two young Irish girls, their flaming red curls topping their floor-length green dresses. They appropriately sang about the Christmas tree…. "Oh! Tannanbaum." No matter that it was German.

There was "Silent Night" played by Bonnie Heather on the piano. Her fingers softly filling in around the young voices. There was a duet of Bonnie Heather and her sister, Sharon, while their mother played the music.

Errol Scott had made the supreme effort to bring his family to the program though the weather was less than pleasant. Outings such as this were scarce, but greatly looked forward to, in the winter.

He had watched the young pianist, her ash-blond hair sparkling in the light of the lamps, with colors from silver to gold to tan with highlights of a rosy red. Small smile as he told himself that someone must have had a "touch of the highlands" in his background to have produced that child. She was known to be a foundling, but she carried obvious ties to the highlands, glens and heather of Scotland.

Certainly the other girl looked enough like him that he could never have denied paternity.

But that was the way it was on the prairie…wasn't it? A bit of this and a bit of that to make a tasty dish. Someone from here and someone from there to make a complete community…?

Then when the girl sang with her sister, it was easy to tell which was the "singer" and not just that of being two years the elder.

It was a lovely program. His own children rode home singing the carols they had just enjoyed.

When Bonnie Heather was ten, he was to see her again. He had brought a couple of horses to the blacksmith shop to be re-shod, and he needed some iron braces for the shelves he planned for his wife's kitchen.

The preacher and his older daughter had made a stop at the shop with some baked goody for her great granddad, now stooped and wrinkled, and snow white of hair. Still, his trips to the shop were the highlight of his day.

Apparently, also was the girl. After a quick hug and kiss, and the wrapped goody placed on his knee, she whirled on one foot and spun her way back to her waiting father.

Gaither Cullen's gravelly voice commented on her departure. "That Bonnie Heather do make a fast git-away when her pa is a'waiting."

Errol Scott watched the departing buggy. Bonnie Heather. A most unusual name for a girl of the prairie. Scottish all the way through. "Beautiful meadow flower." And there were absolutely no heather plants growing out here on the prairie, at least not that he knew of.

Sighing at the fleeting memory of his homeland, he shrugged away the nostalgia and turned attention to his animals and the new brackets being created for him.

A while later, he paid for his purchases and made his way home. There were a lot of jobs waiting for him, as was true for all his neighbors as well. The clop of his horse's trotting feet and the jingle of the new braces in the saddle bags kept time with his thoughts as he planned. This job would be next, and then the other one, and that rainy day job could wait. Couldn't afford to waste the good weather.

It was the year Bonnie Heather was fourteen that the family came once more to the Christmas program. It had become quite clear that when the preacher's wife put together a program, time would not be wasted for those who went to see it.

He watched as the fourteen-year-old girl took over the choreography of the program. Most of the much younger children were costumed as "gifts" complete with huge bows on their heads.

These "presents" were presented before the audience one at a time...each accompanied by an older child who explained, often in verse, how this was another of the gifts given by God. Love...Faith...Generosity...Caring...and others took their turns.

"Humility" was portrayed by the preacher's second son, Samuel, who had great stage presence. Shaking his head to wobble the bow, he managed to cast it off and onto the floor.

The matter was corrected by his sister, Sharon, replacing the bow and tightening the strings so tight it just about made his eyes pop. With a meaningful stare and a stern command, she bade him to "stop jiggling his head and behave or you know what I'll do to you!"

The little fellow gave his sister a bored stare, and the instant she turned her head toward the audience to speak, he gave his head a nod and a shake and favored the congregation with a mischievous grin.

At the end of her piece, Sharon caught him forcefully by the shoulder and propelled him...not back to the group...but out into the audience and sat him firmly on the back most row of benches. Plopping herself down beside him, she left no room for further antics for the rest of the program.

Of all the heavenly graces that were honored that day, most of the viewers would remember "Humility" best of all, as portrayed by Sammy Carpenter.

Then the closing item was performed. Miss Bonnie Heather played and sang. She performed by entirely turning her shoulders so she could face the audience squarely. If her fingers missed a note or made a discordant sound, no one would ever know it.

The voice, clear as a silver bell, rang out. "Star, of the East...oh! Bethlehem's star..." and at one point she morphed into "Oh, little town of Bethlehem, how still we see thee...."

Her fingers seemed hardly to press the notes, but more like they floated into the next sounds as though the melody was being created out of air. It was as though the notes were meant to work themselves in between her spoken words with no effort on her part.

Errol gouged his wife with an elbow. "Who does that girl put you in the mind of?"

She replied with a finger over her lips. He mustn't make her miss a bit of the performance.

Chastened, he turned back to the music and stared at the ash-blond hair trailing down her back. Chiding himself, he was determined to keep this girl from stealing into his mind with... whatever it was...from his past.

The stars were bright above as the family traveled home. Errol Scott stared up at the little dipper and thought, "Star of the East, oh! Bethlehem's...."

As he pulled into the driveway, he had a seed of an idea. By the time the oil lamp was blown out and the bedroom was dark, the seed had sprouted. Sleep was erratic, giving the seed a chance to grow, and by morning it was in full blown flower.

He wrestled for a week and finally lost the fight. "Honey," he told his wife. "Get on your coat and bonnet, we're going for a trip."

"Right now?"

"Of course right now! If it was after while I would have said get your coat on after while." He tempered the teasing with a smile, and explained, "I have an itch that needs scratching, and I think it will be of interest to you as well."

It was a sunshiny winter day, as so often happens in Oklahoma. The crunch of gravel under the wheels…the jingle of the harness and the raucous calls of the winter crows. Lovely day for a ride. Mostly they rode along in silence. A good marriage does not need chattering entertainment. Just being side by side and pleasing each other was enough.

She was relaxed…it had been a nice break in the day. If he had an itch, and if this little trip would scratch it, it was fine with her. Times like this were stacked up and accounted in her favor, against the time she needed something from him. After all, "Giving" had been one of the gifts that had been in the Christmas program.

Most of the town's people, including the Scott's, were aware that Bonnie Heather had been a "foundling" child. In this dangerous time, that was not so very usual. Errol had raked and sifted the dirt out in the east forty, and, other than a small chain, a key and two more buttons, he had found nothing. Absolutely not a trace of Katy. He had bowed his head in sadness for what was surely her fate.

The parsonage had not expected them, but that was not unusual. The serious-faced couple was taken into his "office" at the church, and Errol had requested Merytaten to be present. The quartette gathered into the small room with grim faces. This had to be serious….

"Preacher Daniel, please don't think hard of me, but I need to be put out of my misery. That oldest girl of yours…do you know anything at all about her? Like maybe…where she could have come from…or…." His voice trailed off, at loss for words to continue.

Daniel and Merytaten watched his expression, searching for a clue. Then Daniel turned to his Angel and nodded his head. She smiled and left the room. Minutes later she was back. In her hand was the wrinkled and yellow stained note that was taken from the basket under the haystack.

Without another word, she handed it to the couple, and they read it…then read it again.

Errol raised his head and looked at Daniel. His face began to crumble with emotion. He leaned forward onto the table before him and buried his face in his arms. The shoulders of the two hundred and fifty pound man shook like cottonwood leaves in the wind. Sobs wracked his body in agonized waves. His wife and helpmate reached into her bag for a handkerchief, then wrapped an arm around his shoulders, eyes searching helplessly toward Daniel and Merytaten.

There was nothing to be done except to wait until the internal fury passed. From his pocket Errol took an envelope and handed it to Merytaten. It was postmarked at Oklahoma City… exactly fourteen years ago.

It was just a short note:

"…Reuben and me, we got the purtiest basket for our little girl. Reuben has the wagon all ready, and we are on the way. I'll bet we beat this note, but I just wanted to tell you we were close.

"Our baby is so beautiful, I look at her and it makes me want to cry. When I sing to her, she smiles and her eyes look almost like the heather blossoms…."

With a ragged breath, she put the note on the table and bowed her head soberly. What change would this make in their lives? It was patently evident that the child was their relative… their own flesh and blood…. Cousin, once-removed to Errol.

When the sniffles had passed, and the moisture was almost dried on his sun-wrinkled face, Errol explained. "Oh, Preacher, you don't know how happy this makes me. Everything fits together, and this girl is certain to be the child of my cousin. He and I were closer'n brothers, and I just couldn't stand to think he left this earth without leavin' a trace.

"And you've done such a good job with her. I know that he and Katy would both be grateful, the way I am. We would have loved to have had her ourselves, but we had no way of knowing... if she.... But that was not meant to be.

"If you think it would not upset the girl, we have a packet of letters from her mother, all the way back to the highlands. We would like for her to have them sometime, but if you think this is not the time, we can wait. We don't want to cause her or you any concern."

Merytaten swallowed deeply from intense relief and took a cleansing breath. The danger was averted. They would not be trying to take her away from them. *Oh, thank You, Lord.*

Daniel nodded in response to Errol's offer. "Let's let some time pass and give it some thought. We know you must become part of her life, and we need to plan the best way. She knows, of course, that she was a foundling and she keeps her basket in her room with the quilt and blanket and the diapers she was wearing. Let's give this some thought as to the best time...."

"How about a cup of tea?"

Tea. The universal accompaniment of joy or sadness, sickness or robust health. To lift spirits. To allow thought before speech. A kindness to offer guests in your house. It would, of course, have been offered when they first arrived, but the seriousness of the itch took all other thoughts from their minds.

Then Daniel. "What, exactly made you put all this together?"

A nod and a deep sigh. "Well, it was first seeing her in the programs. That hair they used to call ash-blond. Some English word, I think. Somehow she didn't quite match the rest of the family, though I was aware of her background and that isn't too unusual out here. I began to have the itch when she sang with her sister a couple of years ago. Then when she turned toward us and sang, I looked in her face and saw the little Scottish girl I watched grow up. The one who considered my cousin her beau from the time she knew the word. I had listened to that voice as it rang out over the glens and the meadows of the old country. Even in small gatherings folks begged her to sing."

He paused and sipped the convenient tea. "I thought… her being found and all…that she might want to know more about where she came from, if you folks didn't mind. I was thinking I might need to just watch her and wait until she was older. But the thing was, I really wanted to know if it could be true. So that I didn't get my hopin' up for nothin'." A thoughtful gaze out the window, "'Speck we'll never know the whole of it… how it happened, and all."

Then Merytaten, "The one thing I know is that her mother, in such pain as she had to be having, passed two houses that were closer and headed toward the parsonage. I had thought… the cross and all…."

"That'd be Katy, all right. She was brung up to know where God is."

EPILOGUE

*(Researched and written by historian
Merytaten Franchesca Angelique Evangeline Cullen Carpenter)*

There is an interesting thing about a chronology. Being that it is an accounting of the passage of a period of time, there is so much before and after it that make it merely a snapshot of current activities. There are little box "cameras" now that enable anyone with the money to take pictures without calling a photographer. That would describe a chronology.

The camera pictures record forever the style of the hats and dresses of the ladies, and of the moustaches and sideburns of the men. Also, sometimes their hats especially if they were farmers. It tells very little about how they had looked five years ago, or about how they would look five years hence.

So was a chronology, even though Miss Josie insisted on as much detail as possible.

By this time, her daughter had passed out of the childhood name given her by her father. It would have been difficult to call the wife of the preacher by the name of "Mutt." By the same token, very few…actually, no one, could bring themselves to call her "Angel" or even "Angelique." So Merytaten it became, though a lot of the older folks referred to her as "Miss Josie's girl." None of this was of concern to her, and she answered to whatever she was called.

One of her favorite names was "Mama," the old-country form of what the majority of the prairie used. Or just "Ma."

Back to the chronology. It seemed a lot easier to start than to stop. There was such an obvious and unassailable beginning. The Christmas Eve fire in New York City that had tossed Miss Josie and her expensive education into the rolling plains of the prairie was the obvious beginning.

Looking back, one could convince himself that the Hand of the Almighty had a part in it, though it seemed cruel to believe it at the time. The eastern city of New York had many lovely young ladies who could fit into the life where they were born. Just as Miss Josephine Wheeler would have. They would rear beautiful daughters who would follow them.

The actual outcome of Josie's tragedy took a different path because of Josie herself. After two reproductive failures, her parents had produced a girl with a strong mind and a true sense of values. It seemed she would be the only child of her father, who was well able to provide the best, and he made use of his daughter's mind and values.

He did, of course, have no reason to believe that life would not go on as before and that she would not live and finally pass on still living in the city of her birth.

If that had happened, one of the best parts of what made up Miss Josephine Eleanor Wheeler would have been unused.

The seventeen-year-old Josephine could well have blamed God for the misfortune and could have taken the easy route. Her father's legacy would have seen her through a life of ease and plenty. Her inherited position would place her high on the social ladder.

Her wise father, however, had chosen another route for the "Plan B" of her life. His wife's hard-working sister and brave brother-in-law seemed best to finish the duty of caring for his children if he could not.

So Miss Josie came to the prairie with her strength of mind, her expensive education (certainly good enough for a son) and her acceptance of what life (God) had prepared her for.

The Territory of Oklahoma had settled so quickly and the central part of it had been peopled in one day (that eventful day of 22 April 1889), that no special thought had been planned for the education of the territory's children. Anyone who could read and count fairly well inherited the duty of training one or more children. It did not work well.

Educated parents did their best, but life and a mere existence was so demanding that meaningful efforts toward their children were sporadic.

Certainly, that was the educational picture of the settlement of Carlile Corners in 1895, six years after the famous "Run." The fledgling Department of Education was begging for teachers and would even drop the age down into the low teens to find them and pay them what the territory could afford.

Miss Josephine knew that she was not a teacher, in the finest sense of the word. She did not have the dedication to love the job and be intrigued by its possibilities. Or be challenged by its heights.

She saw it as a job to be done and depended on the strength God gave her to get it done. That was all God needed. He had teachers in abundance just waiting for her, though they were still, at that moment, playing with their dolls. And patty-caking in their cribs.

Now, almost thirty-five years later, it was easy to count the teachers she trained, and those trained by them, and reach past two dozen of these private schools. All of them were taught by teachers who knew they were teachers, and the stern and thorough education of Miss Josie had made them even better teachers. And it gave them the confidence to know who and what they were.

Now, as the great lady had passed age fifty, she could look back and be satisfied that she had made use of the talent God had entrusted with her and had increased it many times over.

Back to the Chronology.

When part of Bonnie's background was known, it scratched an itch in Daniel and Merytaten as well. Small things she would do had made them wonder, is it just her or could it be from her parent's people?

Well, one thing was certain. Her music had come with her, and the training she was given only made it more pronounced.

Merytaten could sing but not like Bonnie. Merytaten had studied piano and could play well enough to bring tears to the eyes. That is, if she had the total and complete sheet music notes.

Bonnie could play anything she could hear, and with fingers that seemed boneless as they created their liquid sound. That was seen to be true when she was just a child of fourteen. With a keyboard, she had complete and effortless control of its function.

A new Steinway piano was moved into the church, setting across from the organ. It almost seemed that the keys of ivory and ebony were contesting with themselves for ways to please her. Interesting to imagine what she would become?

Just where, and in how many ways, does one go with a Chronology? Avenues range out in all directions like the spreading web of a spider. It seems unfair to leave things hanging, but one cannot extend into every direction. Also, one cannot go on forever. All things must close. Maybe just a little way further, though.

Miss Josie's daughter ended up with four children, three from the marital union and one from under the haystack. She never failed to thank her God for the nosy pup who had found her first daughter. That had been Biskit's most important discovery.

Young Miss Bonnie took her life seriously and made many pastoral trips with her father to be certain his name was never disgraced. She did not know until she was grown that there was a purpose to it, but she received a very good knowledge of the neighborhood while it happened.

Though she was less than two years older than her sister, Sharon, she protected her and cared for her as though it was her responsibility. She even went so far as to "tattle" on her when she thought the younger girl could have done better in her lessons. At this point, Mery explained that Sharon really didn't need two mothers. And that she, her real mother, didn't need to know absolutely everything her younger daughter did.

This stern attention did not bother Sharon. She loved her big sister dearly and promptly forgave her bossiness. The girls spent a lot of time at the Horse House, about a mile up the road. Steady, reliable Forrest Canfield managed to put up with the younger girls...Bonnie, his sister Eva and finally, Sharon. He never seemed to act as though they were a bother to him.

Being his mother's son, Forrest became proficient with the horses at a very young age and the four children seemed to consider the mammoth animals as so much playground equipment in their vast play yard.

There were other times that they played in the sheep pasture by the church. In late summer the haystacks were piled high to dry quickly in the sun and preserve their nutrients for winter animal feed.

While the stacks waited, they were climbed up, slid down and circled around. They were the center of games, many made up in the moment and never played again. From the window, Merytaten could see the boy holding the hands of the younger girls so they could climb to the topmost straw of the stack.

Then a playful shove sent them laughing and squealing their way down. Heels over head! Lace on bloomer legs in full view! A fleeting image passed through her mind of Daniel guiding herself and his sister to the top of the stack. Summer fun. Sunny days, when tucked away in memory, can last a lifetime.

When Forrest turned thirteen, and had completed his years at the Academy, he was given a car. Not a new one, and that was best. This was to be a car for him to play with and learn on, and he did just that.

One sunny afternoon, Daniel motioned his Angel to the window. There, in the yard, was Forrest's "tin lizzie" with its bonnet flaps folded up to display the wonders inside. Exposed were the pipes, tubes and wires that produced such magic.

Over one fender leaned the young man, balanced on his stomach with both hands down into the machine's inter-workings. On the opposite front fender was perched their oldest daughter, cross-legged on a fender and leaning into the same inter-workings. Conversation was low and friendly.

The motor, containing the oily and dusty guts of his "lizzie," was just another place where the two children had a close and intriguing meeting of the minds.

When he was fifteen and Bonnie was thirteen, the chug-chug-put-put of the engine turned its rubber tires into the parsonage driveway with Miss Bonnie Heather behind the wheel. Her parents held their breaths as the car advanced rapidly toward the front porch, but released it, as a screech of the brakes happened just in time. Not even one of the petunias in the flower bed was damaged.

After that, the "lizzie" became their most time-consuming toy while the younger girls found other playthings. One time when Merytaten stepped out the front door, just to check, what she saw was a pair of girl's Mary Jane shoes and a boy's high-topped, lace up brogans side by side on the "grease quilt."

Their four hands worked as a team, tightening nuts and cleaning away the constant accumulation of oily road dust. Parts that had been removed now lay in a row on a convenient board, and there was no doubt that they would be back into the lizzie before the day was gone.

Dear Lord, is this a sign of the future for my daughter? If so, thank You very much. Then Merytaten added in her heart, *I'm not surprised, Lord, that You are watching out for her. You were there in the haystack when she needed You.*

Still, the interviews for the Chronology must be continued to its logical end. There was one interesting thing that seems to fit here. It had to do with the young couple on a tract about two and a half miles to the east. Located well within the area that Miss Josie wanted canvassed.

Even more interesting than the couple, themselves, was the way they had arrived. It started back in medieval England through some historic practice of turning the whole of the family estate over to the oldest son. That practice began to be necessary when it was noticed that a man with, say, five or six sons proceeded to chop up his estate and divide it equally. After a few generations of chopping, there was hardly enough land for each to build a house…let alone make a living.

So it seemed better to practice primogeniture. And the Earl of Grantville did just that, and turned his estate, Hemphill Castle, over to his oldest son, practically at birth. Then the second son was born, and it was always good to have an assistant living in the castle to bear some of the burden of running it.

Then came the third son, who was clearly the "insurance" son, and he was placed in the position of "estate manager" to ensure that he stay close. After two daughters, who would naturally not figure into the inheritance, though they had a lifetime right to live in the castle (there was always a need for "spinsters") their existence did not affect the plan.

Then along came the fourth son whom they named Wellington Grantville, and they scratched their heads as to what to do with him. Of course, there should be someone to supervise the gamekeepers. (By telling them which deer to shoot for the castle table?) But what was an earl to do?

Wellington liked the job…actually. He became best friends with the grown son of one of the caretakers. They were very close from early teenage on to early twenties. As time went on, the friend's sister became much closer to Wellington than her brother was. Care was taken that this fact did not attract the attention of the earl.

The less the earl didn't notice his son…the more the son noticed the daughter of the caretaker. The more Wellington thought about his own future, the more he knew he must make radical and far-reaching plans to avoid what he saw coming. And the plans must include Miranda.

It took a lot of thinking, and Miranda was a good help when it came to that. "How about that…place? The…colonies…? We could go there and hide."

"Hmmmm. Hey, why not?" So when the "where" became clear, the next questions were the "how" and the "when." The "when" was easy. The sooner the better.

The "how" took a little longer. Now, as the earl's son… no matter the number of his birth…Wellington had access to funds. Money to spend. And having to hide to see Miranda, there was no place to spend his allowance so the coins accumulated. It was the brother who finally set his friend and sister on the right path.

"Well…you dummy…just give Miranda the money for passage and let her arrange for the trip. I'll even help. Then when you're in the colonies, you can tell the earl where you are…or not."

"But how can I leave without being seen? Everyone knows me."

"Not everyone. Besides, who says you have to be seen? I can find a trunk big enough for you, and I'll even wheel you aboard. Sis would have to buy passage for the huge trunk, anyway, and before anyone knew about you, you would be days out to sea. If there was a question of fare, just hand over the money right then. The captain could keep the money for himself, and that would keep him from telling anyone about who you are."

The other two looked at each other and nodded at the simplicity of it all. Passage was booked for the lady and her huge steamer chest and the excited couple waited anxiously for the five weeks before the ship would sail.

Coins were stitched into the hem of Miranda's cloak, just on the chance they got separated somewhere and she had to go on alone. Just a safety thing that her brother insisted on. He sincerely wanted her to get safely across the ocean because he had every intention of following. Being a caretaker on the earl's estate just was not in the future he had planned for himself.

The looked-for day arrived. The young lady, obviously an important lady from the way she was dressed, made herself a right aggravating nuisance, including the spillage of a drink on her expensive dress, and the necessity of being quickly shown her expensive first-class cabin so she could change. RIGHT NOW!

The four wheeled dollie bearing the steamer trunk was taken to her cabin and the door closed and locked, to the relief of everyone…both inside and out of the box.

The brother saw to the liberation of the captive, who had made it in fine shape, then he took his leave.

The girl stayed behind locked doors when possible, and otherwise the earl's fourth son stayed in the trunk. The good ship *Conqueror* cleared the southern end of England, and past Land's End, formerly thought to be the last piece of earth in the world before ships would sail off into nothingness.

Four days out to sea, Wellington Grantville went to the captain behind closed doors and handed him the gold coins to buy his secrecy. The pleased captain was happy not to admit he had been tricked, and gladly married Tony Grant to Miranda Smith, and the ship's manifest was adjusted to accommodate the new circumstance.

In due time, the *Conqueror* conquered the Atlantic and pulled into port at Jamestown, Virginia. The couple headed inland with haste and landed in a spot on the windswept prairie called Oklahoma City. From there it was easy to find someone who was "selling up" and heading back east.

So, at the time that Mery and Prissy visited the "Grants," the brother had arrived, with wife, and the four of them were doing well on their quarter section. Somewhere between the brains of the brother and the money gladly sent by the earl, who was pleased to pay blackmail to make certain the problem was taken care of, life went on.

Naturally, the earl would just as soon not have it known to the world that his son had married the gamekeeper's daughter.

The fellows easily became the "Grant brothers" and their land happily produced sheep and wool for the market.

Tony's son, young Charles Grant had just finished at the Prairie Academy, and decisions were being made as to whether he needed more education or not. Likely not! His sisters, Isabel and Lavinia, were enrolled in classes along with cousins, Robert and Sawyer.

The adults related their stories with embellishment and chuckles at how wonderfully they pulled it off and how much fun it was to live in a tiny town where everyone was equal in social status. Never could have happened if Wellington had been the second or third son...to say nothing of being the first son who had absolutely no choice as to what he would do with his life.

In the small town of Carlile Corners, things rocked along as they often do in rural life. If nothing unusual happens, nothing much gets changed. There was, however, a change coming.

It had been an interesting fact that most of the young men coming from military service, arrived home in one of the new tin lizzies. After the first burst of excitement over the new toy, most of them reverted to the comfortable horse who did not run out of gas, puncture a horseshoe on a thorn or have a spring or screw come loose inside its hide.

In addition to that, what was the hurry? If you didn't want to be late, you just started sooner. Simple as that.

Even Daniel, the chaplain/surgeon, came home in a brand new four wheeled motor carriage, and it now sat parked under a shed in his father's yard. Somehow, the need for it never seemed to present itself. Until....

There were two incidents and they were very close together in time. One was the epidemic of diphtheria and the other was that of Forrest Canfield coming of age.

There was the talk of the throat and lung disease in Oklahoma City and it was spoken of in hushed tones. It seemed to come upon its victims like the spring tornados came upon the prairies. It could not be turned away, you either weathered it or you didn't, and when it passed there was destruction in its wake.

The first case in Argyle was a two-year-old child, and he was laid to rest before the week was out. Children were kept out of school for fear of "spreading."

The shiny lizzie came out from under the shed and Doctor Daniel made a quick trip to Oklahoma City to see what could be done. Well, maybe there was something. A substance called vaccine was gaining some notoriety, though there were those who insisted that getting the disease was bad enough without inviting it into one's innards on the end of a needle.

Daniel, however, ordered a supply of the substance. Tried or untried, the people deserved to have a choice. There seemed to be good reports of it from the east coast.

The lizzie was gassed up fully on the way back through Argyle, as he had no way of knowing if there would be a need for speed in one or the other of his professional capacities.

Another death in South Bend, down by the river. Did damp air have something to do with it? Not much was known about diphtheria.

Windows were kept closed and bolted. Shady Ridge had a case, but the sturdy eight-year-old boy had lived for a week, already, and the prognosis was considered good.

Families watched their children closely, and any sniffle required that child to be quarantine in a separate room. The small clinic located between Shady Ridge and the Corners that had been such a blessing to the community would never be able to cope with an epidemic. Something had to be done.

It seemed to affect mostly the children, so it seemed better to take away the well children who could be more easily be handled as a group and let the parents care for their sick ones.

The Prairie Academy was closed down and notice was posted in the Cookie Jar that the well children could come to the school and please bring whatever food could be spared. Also a change of underwear. Miss Carmelita and Miss Rosalie acted as overseers and the mothers took turns at preparing the cereal for breakfast and soup for other meals. Neighbors brought biscuits and cornbread as needed.

The overhead room under the pointed roof was pressed into a dormitory for the girls, with pallets spread wall to wall. For them, it seemed to be a two week long slumber party.

Babies and toddlers were brought to the parsonage, and their activity often spilled over into the church building. Parents took turns at their duty stations and prepared for the long haul.

When the vaccine came in, Daniel again headed the lizzie toward the big city to bring it back. The time savings of gasoline horsepower was appreciated.

Notice was posted that the vaccine was available and was dispensed at the clinic to all who were interested. It was amazing, actually, how many brave persons availed themselves of the service. Also, amazing to be said, not one vaccinated child succumbed to the gagging, choking disease.

The final tally of losses were four from Sandy Ridge, mostly on outlying farms. And three from the Corners. Those who had accepted the vaccination felt vindicated when they all survived, but who would ever know the truth of it?

Possibly, as bad as the deaths were, among the survivors, there were a number of cases of deafness where the infection had spread inward and damaged the eardrum.

Deaf? Couldn't hear? How utterly terrible, and one might as well be dead! Why, those children couldn't even go to school. What was the use if they couldn't tell what was said?

And their voices became different. Not being able to hear their own voices, they could not remember the sounds of the words. Dear Lord in Heaven, what was to be done?

That was when Miss Prissy Carpenter Cullen, sister to Daniel and wife of John, Merytaten's brother, came into her own. After a sleepless night or two, and a feeling that she was not doing her part, the idea came. She would argue until her dying day that it was brought by an angel, but what did that matter? And who was there who was qualified to argue?

She marched herself to the Horse House where Forrest Canfield lived and announced that she wanted a trip to Oklahoma City to look for something terribly important. What was it? She couldn't tell them. If she knew what it was, then she wouldn't need his help. Now, would she?

So, as they were tooling down the road to Oklahoma City, Bonnie Heather curled up in the front seat beside him, Forrest whistling as though he owned the world, or at least the best part of it. Possibly he did.

Miss Priscilla sat in the back and raked her brain. Medical department? No. That was Daniel's area. Library? What could she find there?

Maybe…the bookstore? She had heard that a new one had opened, and it had at least five hundred books and maybe more. That would be the first stop. Forrest would be able to find it easily or the "angel" who brought the message to her would not have told her to go to Forrest for help.

Well, certainly, Forrest told her. He'd just go down Main Street and circle back on the next street south. If it wasn't there, he'd make a run back up the street to the north. Nothing to it.

Miss Prissy leaned back in the bouncy little car and turned that part of the job over to him. Bonnie Heather leaned back and wondered if they would get home in time for her to help Forrest's mother see that Queenie's baby made it safely out of its mother and whether its name be Dennie or Dorita.

The girl had bonded firmly with America Forrester Canfield in the matter of the Clydesdales. It was nothing to see her sitting practically under one of the beasts holding a foot to remove a burr, or stroking the long, beautiful face of another beast while Merry took the piece of chaff from its eye.

Forrest seemed to think it was a normal thing for girls to do, and he was busy with his car, and other thoughts.

The bookstore was right there where God had put it. The lizzie chugged and rumbled to a stop and the pair in the front seat remained seated as Miss Priscilla gathered her bag and left.

A few minutes later, Forrest looked over at his seatmate, cuddled in the corner with her knees pulled up under her skirts in a most unladylike position. What if something happened with the car and she had to jump out? She'd never get her feet untangled from her pettislips.

Young Forrest saw none of that, however. It was normal for girls to sit in a wad if they wanted to, but if you were six foot tall going on another three or four inches, you just didn't fit that way. It was just the way life was.

"Bonnie?"

"Huh?"

"You know what I'm going to do?"

"Not until you tell me."

"I'm going to have a store back in the Corners."

"Store like Ralph Carpenter's Rollin Five and Dime?"

"Yep. Only I'll have things for a car."

"What things?"

"I haven't thought it all out, yet. But the first thing will be gas for cars."

"Where'll you put it?'

"In the ground."

"Won't it get muddy there?"

"Not if it's in a barrel. Or maybe six or eight barrels. I'll need a pump so it can be pulled up into the gas can."

"Hmmm."

"'Course, that'll only be for now. I saw a picture of a metal pillar that had a glass case on top. Gas could be pumped up in the glass case, and it would run down into the gas tank of the car."

"Hmmm. That ought to work."

"Sure it'll work. You can't fight gravity."

"Who'd want to?"

"Not me. And you know what else?"

"There's more?"

"You bet. We'll have tires and tubes and air pumps. Hoses and belts and floor mats."

"What if something breaks and has to be fixed?"

"We'll fix it."

"We…? You got a frog in your pocket, or something?"

"No, but I've got a helper right here beside me, and we've fixed this one a lot of times. How different can the other cars be?"

"What if it's something we don't know about?"

"No problem. We'll just ask my ma."

So then Bonnie was free to go back to thinking of Queenie. All of Forrest's answers made sense, and it was sure to happen just like he said. But right now, Queenie was the next concern.

Miss Prissy Cullen accosted the salesclerk, who replied, "Yes, we have something that might interest you. I've sold six of them already and have only two left."

Prissy flipped quickly through the pages. Small drawings of hands with multiple finger positions decorating the page. Words or phrases were printed below. SIGN LANGUAGE! Say…that angel knew exactly what he was talking about.

Finger positions that meant words and hand movements that could mean a complete sentence. Those who were deaf would talk! They could have their own language, and it could be learned by anyone, no matter how well they could hear. Then they could converse with those who didn't.

"I'll take both books. No, wait. Someone else might come in. I'll take one and ask you to order me six more. I'll pay for them now, and you can send them out to Argyle."

"Oh! Out where Doctor Carpenter is?"

With a nod, "He's my brother."

"Sure! And he sent you in."

Prissy did not think that observation needed an answer. She sorted out the coins, picked up the book and marched back to the lizzie parked on the street.

"Alright, youngens. We're going to buy a sandwich or something and head on back. I've got work to do."

"Ice cream…" Bonnie decided.

"Ice cream, it is."

From Forrest. "You must have found what you wanted."

"Sure did. When an angel wakes you up in the middle of the night with a command, it's up to him to show the way. We just followed along."

Fed and on the way again, Miss Prissy tried to look at her book. Couldn't. The road was too jouncy and rutted. Oh, well, she now had the answer.

"Forrest?"

"Yes, ma'am?"

"When is your pa going to get the gravel spread on this road so it don't beat a person's brains out?"

"It'll be another six months. He's put in a bid for the job."

"Sure he'll get it?"

"Don't he always?"

Couldn't argue with that. So she closed the book and leaned back. Might as well rest a bit. She had no clear idea of what she would do with the book in her lap, but that was not her problem. She had laid it squarely on the broad back of the angel, right where it belonged.

With a bump and a crunch of gravel, the lizzie pulled into the driveway of Canfield Grading. Bonnie untangled her feet from her skirts and jumped out.

"Aunt Prissy, tell Papa or someone I have to stay and help with Queenie."

Her aunt nodded, and the lizzie made a wide circle and then putt-putted down the road to the parsonage. After that, it would be just a path through the sheep pasture to her house.

While she walked, she ticked off in her mind what she would do with the other six books. There was Francine at Sandy Ridge, Eve Adams at Enterprise, Neecie Forrester at Midway and Max Sinclair at Sentinel Rock. Then the other two would go to Prairie Academy with one to use and one to loan out where needed.

The seventh would be for her to study and decide how best to teach it, and then she would demand time during lesson hours to get the classes started. If she just started teaching the sign language, it was sure to take off by itself as the students would be intrigued with this new way of speaking.

It happened just as Prissy had thought, and why not? When one had an angel in charge, wasn't success guaranteed?

It was a month later that a plot of land was measured off in the Canfield Grading quarter section. Two weeks after that, the drag lines and the dirt slip were peeling off layer after layer of the virgin prairie soil for the burying of an underground gasoline storage tank. The barrels Forrest had thought of were not practical, Papa Raymond decided. If his son was bound to do it, it should be done right.

Forrest and Bonnie sat in the grass and watched the machinery carve out their future. Small starter house appeared. A thing called a "fill up" station arose out of the ground and became a FILLING STATION. Whatever that was.

A sign was carefully drawn and painted by the pair, and the words stated that the building was FORREST FIXIT for Auto Repair. A truck with a large tank on the back came and emptied gasoline straight into the underground tank. No more need to bring it out from Argyle in five-gallon cans.

A pump was installed. It was a pillar with a glass globe built on it. Pump handles on the side would bring up enough gas to fill the globe, and little marks on the side of the glass globe would show how much was put into the tin lizzies.

That was a day to be remembered. The communal brain of the group of communities instantly knew there would be gas, and therefore there would be no necessity for the five-gallon cans.

They also knew that young Canfield would fix up broken cars with new parts. He would...because he said he would. Everyone knew that if he ran into something he couldn't fix, he could just ask his mom. America Canfield was the fount of all knowledge that pertained to auto mechanics in that community. She would continue to be...for years to come.

Bonnie Heather eventually married Forrest. For the young couple, work came first, and then came marriage, though everyone knew it was just a matter of time. The wedding party provided by the parents of the couple was a thing to be remembered. The happy couple stayed for most of it but had to leave a bit early.... as there were two disabled cars back at the station, both needing minor attention and work came before play.

That was all right. The community of Carlile Corners did not necessarily need the presence of the bride and groom to enjoy a wedding reception.

As noted before, a chronology is an unwieldy thing. Where to start? And then...where to stop...? A line must be drawn somewhere, and for Merytaten it seemed practical to make it with the wedding of her first daughter, Bonnie Heather. If there was to be a continuation, it would be done by another.

There was, however, one other little addition.

Out back of Canfield Grading was a quarter section of land that had, as yet, no road cut out for it. A pair of narrow tracks marked where a cart had been used to transport necessities to the tiny, two-roomed cabin setting by itself, flanked on either side by a privy and a cow shed. That made up the three items of absolute necessity, and that was all that Uncle Ezra needed.

Didn't need no more. There was room enough for his two goats, a flock of chickens and a cat. Otis. Who could ever need more than that?

It seemed, however, that his cat needed more. The huge orange striped feline took care of the homestead in fine shape, but no bigger that it was, he had time to roam around and see how other humans lived.

He knew no fear, and went where he pleased, but never, to anyone's memory, caused any trouble. He was just curious… it seemed.

After a period of time, he arrived at the Cookie Jar operated by the McLaughlin sisters, now married with families. Gwinnie and Kristie started the business as thirteen- and fourteen-year-old girls and it had quickly grown into the unofficial meeting place for everyone.

Inside at the table with the chairs that looked fragile… but weren't, or at the solid wooden picnic tables under the cottonwood trees when the weather was nice. Either way it was a place where people met.

Then was the time the cat came by as an observer and stayed to take in the excitement. It was a time that Miss Francine, teacher at Shady Ridge School, was at the Cookie Jar for a cup of tea…or something…that the cat slipped through the door around a pair of convenient feet belonging to any customer who could open the door for him.

Hanging from the cat's mouth was a fresh-killed gopher. He headed for Gwinnie full of intent and purpose and laid the dead rodent at her feet. Then with a quick turn and a leap, and he was on the counter. He daintily helped himself to a fried pie, leaped down, and headed for the corner to curl himself up under a chair and enjoy his reward.

A comment on the cat's antics, brought Miss Francine the whole of the story. It had been back a year or so before, that Gwinnie had set out to catch a particular rat that was quite trap-wise. The thieving varmint was skillful and adept at tripping the trap and then stealing the tasty morsel meant as bait.

The girl had attacked the rodent with the broom, hot water, noise, and about everything she could think of and still he pestered her with nighttime gnawing and foot scrambling, along with leaping to the counter and leaving trails of poop pellets.

That was before Uncle Ezra's cat had come. Looking back, it seemed likely that it was the aroma that attracted the cat in the first place, and he had likely been planning how he could get one of those spicy pies. That was when the tyrant rat made an appearance.

Without ado or hesitation, the feline leaped into the air and flung himself toward the rodent, landing onto its back and sinking stiletto teeth into its neck. One piercing squeak, and the small fur-bearer squeaked no more.

Instead of doing as was expected, and finding a place to consume his catch, the cat placed the carcass at Gwinnie's startled feet, and leaped to the counter. He politely took the fried pie that was nearest him, clamped it firmly in his teeth and then leaped to the floor. Heading to the corner, he proceeded to eat the pastry, clean his face and paws and leave with the next pair of feet that would open the door.

Gwinnie had thankfully disposed of the rat's body and told herself that cat could freely have whatever he wanted, whenever he wanted it. But the cat had different ideas.

It was discussed that he had observed humans and had seen the exchange of something and receipt of something, so it could have been that the wonderfully tasty treats required something in trade. His clever brain had decided a dead rodent was acceptable currency.

Miss Francine, the rhyme maker, put pencil to paper and wrote "Uncle Ezra's Cat." It still hung in the Cookie Jar, having been copied a few times when the paper yellowed past reading.

Merytaten decided that the event needed to be recorded as part of the chronology, especially in view of what happened years later.

A message was given to her that Old Ezra wished to see her when it was convenient to come. And, no, the message was not for the preacher. He was very specific. He had said he needed to see the preacher's "angel." So the historian took her paper and pencil and helped Grandpa Gaither Cullen into the buggy with her.

The narrow trail to his house had been scraped into the resemblance of a road. The county was not interested in making a road for one old man, himself obviously not long for this world. So Raymond Canfield had instructed his grading crew, when they had time, to begin cutting a path. As he had the time, he would make a road at his own expense.

Merytaten headed her team up the marked-out roadbed, wondering what she would find. Old Uncle Ezra was sitting in the yard under a cottonwood tree as she approached and stood up as she and Old Gaither descended from the buggy.

Well, she noted with relief. He was obviously not on his death bed, though he appeared as though it could happen any minute. He struggled, along with her help, to serve the obligatory tea to company. Then he got down to business.

He had been told in a dream that he would need an angel to help him with what he wanted to do, and the only angel he knew of was the one belonging to the preacher. That was why he had sent for her.

He would not be living very long, he told her, and he had no relatives or even close friends to inherit the valuable piece of land beneath their feet. What he wanted to do, he told her, was to find a young couple with children to receive the gift of the land.

They should be deserving and hardworking, as the old cabin and shed were leaning precariously and the fences were in sad state of repair. It should be a couple who would promise faithfully that their children would be taken to school at Prairie Academy every day.

And now, here was what the dream told him to do. He would ask the "angel" to advertise in the Oklahoma City paper for applicants. She must collect them for a month, and then go through them and pick out the most deserving couple. It must be her choice.

Nodding her understanding, she assured him that it would be no trouble to bring the applications to his house and let him pick, but he shook his tottering head. That was not the way the dream went. The angel would know the right choice.

Then the old man's head leaned back and his eyes closed with weariness. Assuring herself that he was still alive, she and Gaither climbed back in the buggy and made a silent trip home.

That would take a trip to Oklahoma City to place the advertisement, and her son-in-law, Forrest was happy to take her.

During the month of the advertisement, there were twenty-seven applicants who tried for the free land, and Merytaten went over them and over them. There must certainly be a "right" one and it was up to her to find it.

By ruling out and resorting the lot, she came down to the last one.

Couple…twenty-five and thirty-one. Three small children under six. He was currently working on a farm as a sharecropper, and a co-worker had spotted the add. Not being interested himself, he had handed it to Duncan McGee.

The letter had stated that there was no school close enough for his children, and his wife had so greatly wanted to be able to have her own garden and be part of a community. She had attended church as a child, but there was none available where they were.

This couple sounded so interesting that she had Forrest drive her to see them. Within minutes she knew they were the right choice. When Old Ezra heard that the decision had been made, he brightened up with new life. They could come anytime, he insisted. That way they could have the fields ready for spring planting.

The wagon with its canvas covering pulled into the yard, and tears streamed down the wrinkles of the old man's face. He struggled to his feet and tottered a bit, but before he could fall, Sophia McGee was at his side, her strong arm around him. He muttered that he would like to serve tea…but….

205

And Sophie shook her head. He must stay in the chair and she would serve him. She had a very good kind of tea right there in the wagon. It was made of a blend of the kinds she had grown herself.

The children wandered around the yard staring with fascination at what would be their new home. Duncan squatted by the old man's chair and told him what a wonderful thing he had done, and it would be their greatest pleasure to take care of him in every way. For the rest of what they hoped was a long life.

Old Ezra insisted on seeing the "paper" and Duncan handed it to him. He handed it back to the young man who held the contract steady while the old man applied his mark. It was done. Totally legal.

Duncan said his Sophia was a wonderful cook, and the children were accustomed to helping with anything they could. And…oh, didn't he have such a beautiful cat! The children just loved a cat. That was evident as they had gathered around and three pairs of hands stroked the orange striped feline. Wonder of wonders, he allowed it.

Forrest and Bonnie were leaning against their car, watching with interest. Merytaten walked away unnoticed and stepped into the car, smiling. Sometimes things just worked out right, and the little car putt-putted away down the marked-out road.

As Forrest dodged the worst of a pothole, he commented, "Pa'll get this road fixed now."

It was a pleasant and busy week as the space was marked out for a cabin big enough for the family. The men from the Corners would give a workday and that would put the building well on its way to being habitable.

Ten days later, old Ezra sat in his yard chair and held the orange cat in his lap, the animal lounging across his bony knees. He stroked the thick fur with a trembling hand and muttered soft words to the animal that it seemed to understand. The sun was warm and the cat purred as Ezra leaned his grizzled head back against the high back of the yard chair and quietly went home to his Maker.

The cat draped himself more comfortably across the old knees and the hand stopped stroking his fur, though the bony fingers still lay heavily across his back. He leaned his whiskered face against Ezra's overalls and decided he'd had a good life and it would be up to another feline to clean away Miss Gwinnie's disgusting rodents.

When the evening meal was ready, Sophia came for old Ezra, but he had already gone on without her. The last small present he left her was a faint smile of peace tucked within his many wrinkles.

He was taken to the Resthaven Cemetery, placed for his last rest in the aromatic wood of the new pine box. The orange striped cat was placed beside him and words were spoken. Duncan and Sophia and the three McGee children stood by the grave, hands clasp in the attitude of prayer.

Merytaten, the preacher's angel, stood and watched, thoughts crowding into her mind. If there could be a more fitting end to the Chronology of Carlile Corners she couldn't imagine what it would be. The town had just witnessed the passing on of a parcel of its land to another who would own it for a while… then pass it on again.

But while the earth stood open to accept the pine box, there was no one to give the final farewell. No family stood by to signal acceptance of the passing. There was no hesitant and grieving hand to put the first soil onto the top of the box.

Silence. Birds sang and crickets chirped, but the pervading sound was the silence. Then the air was pierced by a high-pitched wail of keening…the sound of agonized pain pulled from the depth of a soul experiencing deep loss.

Sofia McGee had stepped forward, away from her family, and she again wailed in her agony. Reaching forward, she scooped up a handful of the prairie soil and lifted it high…staring toward the sky while sobbing her anguished farewell. The dust of the soil filtered through her fingers onto the lid of the new box.

Then she turned and collapsed against the chest of Duncan's clean overalls and his white, starched Sunday shirt. He caught her and pressed her within his protecting arms. The three children clustered around, arms extended to enclose their weeping parents, torn into emotional shreds from the greatness of the gift and the painful loss of the giver.

It was clear to all that old Ezra who had lived a quiet and lonely life received a proper farewell and an abundant thanks for the gift he left them.

It was then that the clarion voice of Bonnie Heather sounded out above the keening of the woman who was mourning her loss. The bright and talented Star of the Prairie and The Scottish Highlands, lifted her voice in song… "In the sweeeet, bye and byyyyye, we shall meet on that beautiful shore…."

On the second and third words, she was joined by the gathering of town's folk and the sound of their voices covered over the scrape, clunk and rattle of the shovels and the falling clods of dirt that filled the hole.

The music continued until the last of the filling was completed and the grave was leveled.

The preacher's angel stood by watching and wondering… knowing within herself that a MOMENT had happened. The inspiration and drive to complete the chronology…the fierce urgency and energy that had lasted with her for almost twenty years…had begun to fade. The force, sometimes more pressing and other times taking a back seat to necessary events in her life, had existed strongly, and now it was taking its leave. It had served out its time.

It had been an integral part of her, but now she knew the inspiration was going…oozing away from her as surely and as unstoppably as a cloud that darkens the sun. Within her, there developed the mixture of relief that a duty had been done and an assignment had been completed…and coming toward her was the feeling of emptiness that she knew it would leave behind.

She knew what would happen, because she had been there before. It was possibly true that every writer has been there at sometime. A literary equivalent of a post-partum depression…a signal that delivery had been completed.

Conception, maturation, and ultimate delivery. Finished…completed.

The inspiration for the chronicle was gone. Not even an echo remained of its passing.

When the inspiration fades, there are no more words to be said. Carlile Corners would go on as usual, but there would be no more words for the Chronicle after the passing of old Ezra and his golden striped cat. She had known there would be, at some point, a last word and a final period. Then it would be taken out of her life.

And it happened now. She was no longer Miss Josie's only daughter with an assignment, or Merytaten, armed with her composition book and charged with a purpose.

A future chronology of the Corners might continue. There were grumblings in Europe. Germany was restless…France was apprehensive…and England was still war-weary, but that would not matter. So what! That there had been an Armistice (whatever that was) was of no consequence. The matter had not been settled, only kicked forward as a small boy kicks a stone down the road. The war would continue and another group of young men would attempt to settle it.

Carlile Corner's sons would step up to the plate and do their best…and some would rest under a white cross many miles from home. A flag and a letter of sympathy would take their place. Which of their children would that be?

But for me, Miss Josie's daughter, the MOMENT has happened. The writer has gone, and the wife, mother and friend now remain.

That person is me. While I stand here...empty...my oldest daughter, my bright star of happiness and joy, works her way toward me and with the half-smile of a shared secret, she slips a note into my hand. Knowing it to be of importance, I glance at the words written in a familiar hand then at the figure moving away from me through the crowd.

The note said, "How would you like to be a grandma?"

A sigh escapes my lips. Such a completion this day has been. An old life passes but not before it was carefully connected to a new family, grateful for the chance to carry on.

A brand-new life is tucked within the body of my bright and shining daughter...the one who can adjust the timing on a Stutz Bearcat...replace the pistons in a Model T Ford...or bolt a fender back on the old rattly Chevy. The daughter who could reach a strong arm into the contracting womb of a pregnant mare to assist the birth of a live foal and then pull the stickery "goathead" burr from the side of a stallion's tongue.

Anything she does not know, her mother-in-law can teach her. America Forrester Canfield, my friend, whose unselfish wish gave the Corners their beautiful church, she will teach. America is a magnet that holds a community together, and she will pass her talents on to my oldest daughter. Truly, God bless America!

Any future chronicle, however, will not be written with the talented hand of Bonnie Heather Canfield. I now know this for certain.

While I stand with the others who are preparing to leave the cemetery and return to their every-present work, I glance toward my second daughter, my lovely, long-burning candle of a girl...my solid and unshakable lady who quietly and steadily becomes important in the lives of others. Sharon is my rock and she senses my thoughts as no one else has.

Her soft and delicate fingers withdraw the note from my hand. She reads it in a glance, smiles and tucks it away. The next time I see it, it is within the pages of the Bible left to her father as an inheritance.

Along with it is the note taken from the woven basket. The note that was yellowed from contact with the sodden diaper of her beloved older sister...the screaming scrap of humanity hidden under the edge of the haystack.

One part of the first note was directed especially to me by the lady who gave her birth. "...Thank you for feeding my baby or burying her...."

The second note was printed on a scrap of paper. "...I just wanted you to know that I love my Scottish family, but I'm glad the angels told Katy that you and Papa were my real parents."

The third note said..., "How would you like to be a grandma?"

On the next page of the Bible is the tiny white feather that was placed on the forehead of her father as a new-born infant. A white feather of peace, and it has been truly prophetic. Her father was trained in weaponry only enough to save his own life if the hospital was over-run. Truly a man of peace and healing.

With a knowing smile from my lovely second daughter, we returned to the parsonage where she has spent her life.

If there is to be an addition to the chronology, it will be written by her. Already, her hand knows the feel of a pencil. It is she who straightened out and arranged the order of the many composition books that cover the last thirty years of our community.

There will be changes in Sharon. Naturally. She receives a lot of special attention, and it seems she may have settled her own eyes toward a special young man. If he turns out to be the one, we could not be happier with her choice.

Young John David Raincrow is the only son of Larry Raincrow, the pilot who left his right foot on the landing strip in France in WW1, and Linda Black Bird Raincrow who had a burning desire to bring book education to the children of her community. If he is the one, it will have been her choice.

Her choice may not be John David, but whoever it will be is up to her to decide. She may not write a future chronicle but whatever she does, it will be something of quiet importance.

I think of my community and feel the satisfaction of my mother. A tragic fire in New York City brought her to the prairie, and I thank her God for that...every moment of my life.

She bravely did what was given her to do with never a complaint. She passed the torch, and then it became my turn. I picked up the flame and did the best I could.

I have given the prairie a bright and shiny star...a shimmering curtain of northern lights...and also I have given it a long-burning steady candle to illuminate the family supper table...a lantern to light the way to the barn for the early milking or a lamp beside the bedside of a sick child.

Two girls I have given to Carlile Corners. The prairie needs both kinds of girls, and I was the fortunate one chosen to provide them.

Thank you, God.

-BONUS EXCERPT-

BURNT TREE JUNCTION

THE ACCLAIMED HISTORICAL FICTION SERIES

- VOLUME 1 -

ROADSIDE STAND
& BROTHER
PHIL'S ANGEL

JOANN KLUSMEYER

EARLY 1900s - RURAL ARKANSAS - FAMILY FRIENDLY

ROADSIDE STAND

HANGING TREE

Burley Collins trudged along Ridge Road, his eyes peeled for the sight of the huge oak tree and the storm-tumbled roadside stand that he remembered so well. It wasn't much of a place to stop and rest for the day, but it was better than nothing.

Also, it was a designated point and a place to look forward to reaching when the feet were weary. There was a tree for shade.

His first sight of the limb that extended toward the road included the body of a man… gently swinging from the taut rope slung over the limb. Burley rubbed his eyes… blinked… and looked again. What he thought he saw just couldn't be.

But the body still swung, twisting slightly this way and that, and Burley knew there was no need to rush to the victim's defense. That time had passed some minutes or hours ago.

Below the hanging body was the scuffed hoof prints of a horse, having been slapped on the rump to hurry him forward.

Though he knew what he'd find, Burley touched the limp hand hanging from the sleeve of the plaid, flannel shirt. Still slightly warm.

He bent over the hoof prints. Sharp edges. Relatively new shoes on the animal. That knowledge might be important. He looked up to the limb and noted that he could reach it from his saddle. Bringing his chestnut mare under the limb, he loosened the tension and lowered the body gently.

Hepsebah, or Heppie, stood blinking her eyes as any good pack donkey would be trained to do. She blinked slowly and wisely. Who knew the ways of humans?

For her, no day held a surprise. Go… stop… get fed… walk. Graze… sleep… live through this day and wake up tomorrow.

So… there was a human, hanging from a limb just for the thing of it. She did not know or care what the other human did now… or any time in the future. She waited; she moved when told.

So she just stood by. Strapped to her back were the packed bags containing the worldly goods of the human who gave the orders. And furnished the food. She waited, eying a clump of grass and deciding whether the dusty blades were worth the effort of stepping forward.

Nearby, the chestnut animal, generally referred to as 'Brownie,' watched with interest as the man examined the victim of the hanging. Strange, actually. But who knew the way of humans…? Still, one must admit they were interesting. Sometimes.

Burley checked the pockets. Knife, matches, a few coins and a key chain with one key. He put them aside. Something would have to be done with the body, and any person with legal authority to make a decision in this circumstance was a fresh horse and several miles away. And Brownie was as weary as Burley himself. Best the body be buried, if only temporarily.

He looked around. The crumbled roadside stand leaned drunkenly against an oak. A mallow vine had seemingly attempted to hide the miserable pile of splintered boards and rotting shingles. Burley remembered the old codger, Hake Simms, who ran the stand long after he should have gone to St. Peter or wherever it was that decent people went.

The man had spent the last days of his life tending the stand, offering for sale anything the Simms family could spare. Made a few pennies… asked for very little. Burley sighed and nodded… it was a life and a fellow could do worse. A lotta fellows had.

The fallen stand was located on a bluff where the road made a wide turn. Huge rocks overhung the valley and a small stream of water flowed from around the rocks and made a sparkling descent into a small lake a short distance into the valley. He could take the body down the rocky bluff, but that would be laborious and would accomplish nothing. Rather, he could step into the grove of trees and find a spot of soft soil. He made a mental picture of this young man so he could notify... someone...?

The victim's shoes were new... hardly even scratched on the soles, so Burley removed them. Why waste a valuable item when it did the wearer no good? They would fit someone. His neckerchief, wadded as it was within the noose of the rope, was also new and of an unusual pattern. Should be good for identifying him. Maybe.

He wearily dug the best he could among the tree roots and carefully laid the body straight. Standing and staring down at him, Burley shook his head sadly... what a waste! Young, strong... and gone forever.

Hesitated. Sighed long and dismally. Scoop after scoop with the small shovel from Heppie's back, and eventually the unfortunate victim was covered over. Not good, but the best he could do.

Walking back to the animals, he slouched wearily. He hated waste, and this was one of the worst. The sun was slipping down toward the valley and was settling past the bluff when his supper of beans began to bubble and the coffee in his percolator settled down to issuing fragrant steam.

He had loosed the animals and hobbled their feet to keep them close and had spread his sleeping bag inside the crumbled remains of the roadside stand, when a sound attracted his attention. There in the road, in the direction from which he had come, someone was walking. Strange. No one walked on the ridge road this late in the day unless there had been trouble.

He watched and waited. A young woman and a small boy approached, the boy stumbling, but the woman did not pick him up. She couldn't have. She was already carrying the heaviness of her next child under her light weight clothing, and her own feet wearily stumbled almost as much as those of the child.

Bad trouble. Had to be. Burley watched, scooping a few bites into his mouth and washing them down with coffee. It had been a long time since breakfast. The woman and child reached him and she called out to him.

"Mister...? Was you here very long? Would you have seen a fellow on a spotted horse come by?"

How should he answer this? Trouble it was... for certain. "Well, ma'am, I just..."

"Please try to remember. My man... he was just goin' down the road to see if there'd be any help for me. We camped back down the road a piece, me knowin' my time was close. We'd wait there and if help was close, it'd be good help for me." She looked into his face, her eyes pleading. "He couldn't been gone long, but I was gettin' worried. Wouldn't'a been like Sonny to leave me too long."

Burley finally found his tongue. "Ma'am, could you come over here and rest a minute. There's bad news, I'm afraid, and in your... condition...? Well, I think...."

She approached, hopefully, but when she saw the pair of new shoes setting on the crooked counter of the stand, with the neckerchief laying across them, she burst upon Burley with the fury of a crazed wild cat. "DID YOU KILL MY MAN! WHY... YOU... YOU...!" In her anger, words failed her. She came at him with pounding fists held out in front of her protruding abdomen. The child, a small boy, screamed in fright and hid behind a tree.

Burley stood and caught the small fists in his large hands and tried to calm her. "Ma'am, it was me that found him. See yonder rope? It was done by someone that took his horse, I'm thinkin'."

"You didn't... ? But he's... ? Where is he? Those are his shoes and his handkerchief. Where is he?"

Amid her sobs and angry screams, he was able to tell her what he knew... which was precious little. He led her to the fresh earth. He did not scoop away the heaps of dried leaves as it would have been cruelty to the little boy to have the mental picture of his dead father. Better for him to wonder than to know and have that certain image in his head for the rest of his life.

Leading her back to the fire, her anger melting down into sniffs and sobs, he began to take charge. Night was fast coming on. Something had to be done for her and the boy, now blinking sleepily in front of the fire.

"You said you had a camp? How far away?"

"Just past them trees is a lane. Our wagon's there, but no horse."

Burley scratched the top of his head and tousled the black curls… hoping he could scratch up an idea or two. "Wagon…? Well, I got… Ma'am, if I hurry now, I might find it and bring your wagon on up here. You ain't in no shape to make the trip and you'll be needin' your strength, so you'll just have to trust me. Lay the little fella on my bed roll, and hide yourself in there with him. I'll try to hurry."

She sniffed and nodded.

In minutes, Brownie was thundering back down the road where she had just come. There was still enough light to see the almost hidden lane and the beginning of a camp site just beyond. There was the wagon. Burley, working mainly by feel in the dim light, hitched Brownie to the shafts and led her back to the road.

What a wagon it was! It had been built onto and now it looked like a small house riding along on the wagon bed. Windows and a door. Shingled roof. Heavy for one horse to pull, but they had obviously planned on short days and slow travel.

The last rays of sun slid away as Brownie pulled the tiny house into the campsite while Heppie, her mouth working on a wad of grass, watched with vague interest. There was no knowing what humans might do and this clearly did not involve her.

Brownie was unhitched and again hobbled for the night.

The wagon had been pulled behind the wreckage of the stand and Burley trudged wearily back to the young woman, now hunched pathetically over her abdomen. She looked up, her face a strain of agony. "Mister… there's more bad news. I'm wishin' Sonny could'a brought help, but I can do it alone."

She stood on shaky feet, holding to a loose board of the old stand. She paused, grimaced and groaned slightly as another pain passed.

Staring into his eyes, she began, "I gotta ask something else of you… and us bein' such a trouble already." She paused as another of the sharp-edged daggers of contraction attacked her body.

Burley just stared, not knowing what to say or do. She continued.

"If you was to help me into the wagon and stay away with my little boy, I'd consider it a blessin'. I know what to do, and you mustn't mind for my yellin'. Charlie, there, sleeps like a rock, so he'll not hear… him bein' so tired."

Burley swallowed hard. "But you…"

"Mister, ain't nothin' gonna happen as ain't happened before. Just help me up into the wagon, and if you hear a sound," she paused and waited for the passage of a stabbing pain, "If you hear anything, it'll likely be the nightwind in the trees. And that's what you can tell Charlie if he wakes up."

Burley held steadily to her arm as she negotiated the steps, her feet amazingly strong and determined. She stepped over the endgate and through the door. "I'm thankin' you again, Mister. It sure weren't our intention to put this onto a stranger, and you've been more'n kind." Shutting the door firmly behind her, she was gone.

Burley stood staring… wondering… and then a swathe of soft glow appeared from the tiny glass window. Candle. Had to be. Then he turned and retraced his steps to the bed roll and the sleeping child. He took one of his packed bags carried by Heppie, leaned it against the tree and sighed once again.

What else could he have done that he had not…? And he could think of nothing.

As the stars popped out into the inky blackness overhead, he tried to doze and maybe he did, but it seemed a long time until morning. It was an endless, silent time except for the call of a bobcat from down toward the lake, and the screech of an owl across Ridge Road. The boy slept soundly and at last it was morning.

THE MORNING AFTER

The twenty two year old mother of two crept softly through the trees, clutching a flannel wrapped bundle close to her chest. Somehow, she had to say goodbye to the person to whom she had given her heart.

Burley Collins's sharp ears pulled him from his dozing state to a place of total alert. Someone... oh, it was just the young woman. Sadness for her squeezed uncomfortably at his chest restricting his breathing. What was there for her to do now... no man... no horse... and nowhere to go? The sound of her murmur and her sobs carried faintly toward him on the still, mountain air. What... actually... was ahead for her? And he didn't yet even know her name.

Though more importantly, what was it that he... Burley Collins... was to do? What was meant to be an overnight rest-pause under the spreading oak took on the troubles of a lifetime... or so it seemed. He must somehow notify some authority of the death and hasty burial and that would mean at least fifteen miles and two days. He could surely not leave her alone, but what was there to do with her? Did she have sufficient food in the little house, and could she manage an active two year old and a newborn until he brought help? Somehow it had become Burley's problem and he momentarily wished to go back to sleep.

Through slitted eyes he glanced at the boy, still asleep on the bedroll. His own soft comfortable bedroll. Burley had spent a restless night leaning against his pack saddle propped against the oak tree. The hanging limb branched innocently beside him.

A slight movement attracted his attention and there by the boy he saw the wolf, resting on his haunches staring at the sleeping child, clearly silhouetted against the streaks of light in the east. Then a slight wag of the bushy tail. Burley's muscles tensed like knotted ropes. His right hand crept, quiet as a breeze, to the ground by the gnarled root of the tree. His Colt 45 was there, cocked and ready of course, and he could get a clear aim and it would be a sure shot.

But the animal made a slight movement in the dry leaves and the boy's eyes flew open. Like the spring in a jack-in-the-box the boy was up and throwing his arms around the animal.

"Jumper! You found us!" And the boy and the dog spent a joyous moment entangled with their affection. "You brought rabbits! You couldn't find Papa, so you brought them to me!"

The rising sun shoved away the morning gloom and Burley saw the two cottontail rabbits lying stretched out on a rock. The dog, with wise eyes and a wagging tail, began to investigate the camp. Burley had not a moment's doubt that the dog knew exactly where Papa was, and was searching for what he should do about it.

Burley could see the leather collar around the dog's neck, and the short length of leather strap. Tooth marks on the end. In the dimness of the evening, he had missed seeing the dog when he got the wagon.

What a trained dog, indeed! Most dogs would have barked or at least whined at the approach of a strange human, but this one had waited silently to see what to do next. He had likely scouted the camp, then caught the rabbits, assuming his puzzle would be clearer in the daylight. It had to be.

Well, the presence of the two rabbits erased the concern as to what was for breakfast. Burley heaved his more-than-forty-year-old self to his feet and checked Heppie's backpack, also leaning against the tree, for the huge iron skillet and his jar of frying grease.

He pulled together some scrappy dead limbs and a handful of leaves and built a fire where scores… maybe hundreds… of fires had preceded it. The iron grate left by someone was resting on three solid rocks.

A spring of water flowing from under a rock nearby furnished the water for coffee and it perked merrily in his percolator…

his one luxury. Perked coffee instead of boiled... it made a big difference in taste.

Aroma of coffee in the air. Things looked better with the fragrance of the coffee bean. Next problem. While he skinned the rabbits and while the boy played with the dog, he scraped his brain for an idea about the authorities. They had to be notified, and now he could tell them the young man's name as soon as he spoke to Constable Ike. What to do for the widow?

And there she came through the trees, stepping carefully among the accumulated dead leaves.

Sound of wheels on the gravel. Burley's spirits lightened. Someone was coming, and possibly he could share some of his sudden load of responsibilities. Maybe a neighbor who could put her up for a while.

But no, it was Frenchie McFey, the route man for the Watkins Products. He was the man everyone wanted to see as his van carried everything from pepper to Pepto-Bismol, and from matches to Macanaw coats. He called on as many stops as he could, but had to tear himself away from most of them. He was better than a newspaper for spreading information, and closer than a gossiping neighbor across the fence.

Today Frenchie... actually Bertrand, but he preferred Frenchie... had left his camp long before daylight to make the trip along Ridge Road where there were few customers. If he could make it to the Big Oak, he'd cook his breakfast on the grill by the crumbled roadside stand. The way so many other travelers did... and be on his journey. But it was not to be.

It was now light enough for Burley to see the red and black letters on the bright yellow van pulled by the matched paint ponies. Good-looking rig... its black wheels shining with fresh paint. Black letters announcing simply FRENCHIE. No one along the Ridge Road needed any further identification.

The route man sniffed his appreciation at the aroma of coffee, and coffee was always shared. Rules of the road. And he saw the boy. Now would be the time to share a bag of cookies, and maybe leave a candy stick. Sweets helped to spread good will. In addition to that was the sack of peanuts roasted in their shell that he planned to have as a major part of his own breakfast. Fried rabbit would be better.

Then he saw Burley. Frenchie knew everyone and that included the wanderer who seemed to find business to be on the road a lot.

"Hey, man!'"

"Hey, yourself. You're the fellow I need to see. Are you headed back to the warehouse?"

"Sure am. Somethin' you need?"

"Sure thing. Have to get a message to Ike over at the station." The station being the log cabin within spitting distance from the Watkins Products warehouse if the wind was right. Frenchie nodded his attention. The law was to be notified.

"Had a hangin' here at this tree yesterday. Young fellow, seems to'a been robbed and hung, and they his horse took." He glanced toward the boy. "His kid over there don't know it yet. I had to bury him outta sight till I got help, and then here you come. Good timing. Camp wagon back there has the kid's ma and a new baby that come in the night. I been needin' to go two directions, and not bein' able to leave her here, with not even a horse."

Frenchie was quick thinking. A few more sentences explained that Burley was set on tracking down the murderers. Shouldn't be too hard if his other problems could be taken care of.

Frenchie nodded. "Tell you what. I'll swap you this sack of cookies for a leg off that rabbit, and then I'll head on out. Got fresh horses and it's downhill a lot of the way. Should be there in an hour and I'll send 'im back. He can take care of the lady, maybe. Then I'll be back up by here later today. If she's still here, I'll take over till you get word back."

Burley nodded. He'd have expected nothing less from Frenchie or most any local farmer. Folks on the ridge looked after each other.

So, with a steaming, browned rabbit haunch, Frenchie clicked to his horses and was gone, raising a small trail of dust behind the wheels.

Zennia had crept up as the men were talking. *Good*, thought Burley. So he wouldn't have to repeat it. Opening the sack of sugar cookies, he set them and the skillet of rabbit pieces on a loose board. He smiled to assure the silent woman... actually almost a girl for looking so young and scared. Still dry-eyed. Tears and agony would come, but she had wisely put it off in view of the circumstance.

"Don't you be worryin', ma'am. I'm gonna busy myself with the boards for a while. I aim be here a short piece then I have an errand. Seems I got ideas about what to do with this here piece of land."

She nodded. Young Charlie knew what to do with the food, and the dog stood ready for the remains.

The first thing Burley did was put the two rabbit skins together and wrap them tightly, circling them with a scrap of paper from a farm sale... or something. Rabbit fur had uses, and being bound together would keep them soft until he had time to do the job right. Cut in four pieces each, he had cleaning rags that were highly washable and dried soft. A body never had too many of them.

He sorted the pieces of old lumber. Not enough, but some of what was there was usable. His pliers pulled the nails and he set them aside. Couldn't risk them being hidden in the dirt and being stepped on. All the while his hands busied themselves, his mind was on its own journey.

There'd be more than one killer. They'd have a hide-out cave, and his mind sorted through the few he knew of. It was going to be a frustrating search to find the right one in this rough country.

Hooves sounded on the road gravel. The boy squealed happily, "Ma! There's Dapple!" Then he noted with disappointment, "But Pa ain't with 'im!"

Zennia caught her breath in an agonized hiccough. "No, son. It's not..." And that moment Jumper's ears cocked and he ran at the horse who reared and turned into the brush. Charlie was puzzled, looking from his ma to the strange man. Why would Jumper be running at Dapple? They liked each other.

Burley looked at Zennia, who sadly shook her head. "Son, the horse looks like Dapple but he isn't. Jumper knows that."

Burley's mind snapped to attention. "He ain't your horse? Then we'll get 'im and hold 'im till the law gets here." And he proceeded to do just that, with Jumper's help as soon as the dog recognized what the man was going to do. Smart dog... that!

Constable Isaac (Ike) Cordell arrived and was quick to size up a situation. Bringing a deputy to stay with the young lady, he headed down the path to the north toward the nearest cave that he knew of.

By now, Burley was hot and thirsty, and surely the lady was the same. He was not accustomed to caring for a lady in distress, but that was no excuse. There was a first time for everything. Taking his water jug from his pack, he headed down the path to where he knew a spring of water jutted over a rock on its way to a lake some distance down the valley. Cool and good-tasting, as he remembered the water. This was a well known camping site for local travelers.

Jumper had cocked his ears and watched Burley, then came trotting after. *Why not*, the man thought. He might be thirsty too... but there was more. He had hardly gone under the overhanging lip of the bluff until he heard a voice. Sounded young. Couldn't make out the words with the echoes bouncing back and forth. The dog, however, thought he could.

Water. He'd get it and take it back to the lady, and then he'd follow the dog. Needed his gun, anyway. It did not occur to Burley that the deputy might be the best one to check out the noise.

JUMPER IN ACTION

The terrain of an Arkansas mountain was not strange to Burley as he climbed over dead trees felled across the paths, huge rocks, twisting vines and sprouting bushes knitting the hillsides together. The dog stayed about 20 feet ahead of him, leading him on with tail-wagging assurance. Burley watched and nodded, plodding onward. Dog like that deserved to be followed.

Then he could hear the words. "HELP," the voice (young?) pled. Jumper dived into the underbrush and disappeared in that direction. It was only a minute before he was barking 'treed' as if he had a coon or a possum up a tree. Snarling and yelping, he circled the foot of a bois d'arc tree. He would have climbed it if he could have. Obviously there was a reason for the animal to be vicious.

Burley raced toward the ruckus as fast as he could plow through the undergrowth. Jumper was snarling and showing a fine set of fangs. Front paws pounded against the trunk of the tree as he lunged at the feet of the human in the limbs. What was wrong with that dog? He had been so friendly…?

Wedged into the limbs was a boy? Young man? Totally frightened out of his wits. Sizing him up quickly, he seemed to be about 16… maybe 17. Could be only 15. Good clothes, solid shoes and a recent haircut. One hand held to a limb above him and the other hand held a gun.

"Son, drop the gun."

"You gotta help me. This dog's gonna eat me up!"

"First you drop the gun."

"I can't. I brung the gun to prove who I am and what I gotta tell someone."

Remaining safely out of range, Burley reasoned, "In that case, I'm the best you're going to get to listen ya'. I can stand here longer than you can stand there, and I may be able to calm the dog if you tell me who you are."

The young man listened. Made sense. "Mister, I stole this here gun to show I'm who I say I am but when they see it's gone, it's me that they'll come after."

"Who is 'they'?"

"My brother and three other fellows. They made me come along so I wouldn't tell where they went, and they stole a horse and hung a fellow from a tree back up on the road. They thought that horse was stole from them, but then they saw it wasn't and they didn't care. I'm scared and I gotta run away somewhere. I can't go home."

The kid had a point. "First thing, drop the gun or I leave you there all night. Then we'll see about the dog."

A slight pause, and the gun slid down though the bushy limbs of the bois d'arc tree. The snarling dog turned from the boy to gun that landed in the grass. He nipped at the weapon, flipping it over with his nose. Then he came toward Burley, lowering his head as though trying to say something.

Burley, no stranger to strange dogs, reached a friendly hand forward to the dog who sniffed and tail-wagged, and looked back at boy in the tree, apparently satisfied. "Good boy, Jumper. You did good." He picked up the gun and extended it toward the gray-brown canine, who sniffed again and snarled, a growl deep in his throat.

Huh, well, they'd see. "Son, start down the tree slowly and be prepared to climb back up if he runs at you."

The boy didn't want to, but what choice was there? The dog watched from beside the man who held the offending gun.

With both feet on the ground, his eyes were wide with fright. "Mister, I gotta get outta here and off the ridge. My brother said he'd kill me if I didn't do what he said and I believed him."

"Good enough. You can come along and tell your story. I'll try to find help." What he had really hadn't needed was another person who needed help, but, at least, now they knew who did the murder.

There wasn't much to the story. The four others had been stealing animals and vandalizing property (well known to everyone on the ridge). James had overheard the plans, and had been forced to come along. Then he sneaked the gun away while they were sleeping, and tried to reach the ridge. Would have made it if it hadn't been for the dog.

Back at the camp, Deputy Darrell Jones attempted to interrogate James, who pursed his lips and held tight. He had handed over the gun to prove his purpose, but he had a more important lever than that. He wanted safety... and he wanted it NOW. He above all others knew what his brother's gang was capable of.

"You take me away now and hide me, and someone go whisper in my ma's ear where I am, and then I'll tell you where their supplies are hid."

That would be an important lever, for certain. The 'gang' had been going up and down the ridge spreading theft, arson and anger. They committed mayhem, though up to this point, had stopped at murder. That was past. It was speculated on who the perpetrators were, but not all of them or where was their headquarters.

The boy demanded to be taken under cover to a hiding place and provided for until he could leave the state... or at least the county. The deputy looked at Burley, who returned his own puzzled stare. Remaining under cover, and speed would be required... then what? These were the catch.

A sound of gravel crunching on the road turned their heads. Frenchie! The answer for certain. Clear as if handed down from heaven. Maybe it was.

James was not a large boy, and a bit of shuffling of Frenchie's wares provided a hiding place behind a lower shelf. Deputy Jones with the gun rode along, just for safety first.

Burley ran the words through his mind to be able to update Ike, who would soon be showing up. The constable had not actually been prepared to go cave hunting. That would take a posse… fanned out in the directions of the most notable hideaways.

While he waited, his head spinning with the activities of the last two days, he set aside the usable boards and rebuilt, within his mind, the old roadside stand, only better. It would eventually be what he would do with his life. He had not known for the last few decades what it would be, but now he had a twinge of excitement and an eagerness to see this through. Clear as a bell, it was, what he would now do.

He had known about this strip of land that had the 'hanging tree,' the stand, and the spring with its waterfall, as well as the roomy cave behind the waterfall. He also knew that the landowners on both sides had opted to carve that strip of land from their tracts as being untillable due to its rough terrain, therefore not deserving of the 25 cents per year taxes. Burley didn't know, however, if someone else had seen the possibilities and purchased it. He also needed nails which meant a trip one way or the other, and Berryville was closer than Eureka Springs.

But then there was the lady, the new mother, who must not be left alone. How was he going to manage that? Actually, it seemed that it should be Ike's problem as well. So he'd just work with this mess of scraps and lumber and watch out for the little Charlie.

The kid was scuffling with the wolf-shaped dog, rolling and tumbling, with the dog nipping at the air beside the boy's chubby arms and legs, making him giggle and crow with laughter. It was obvious this was a much-played game. No one could have guessed the snarl and growl and the exposed long fangs of the animal, or more surprising, how he had seemed to discern that the gun, not the boy in the tree, was the problem.

- END OF EXCERPT -

ADDITIONAL BOOK SERIES BY JOANN KLUSMEYER

The Great I Am Bible Story Series for Kids
6 books

The Young Pioneers Adventure Series for Kids
5 books

The Wentworth Triplets Mystery Series for Young Teens
3 books

Footsteps in the Canyon Adventure Series for Young Teens
4 books

Burnt Tree Junction Historical Fiction Series for Adults
6 books

Ozark Mountains Historical Fiction Series for Adults
7 books

Taming the Wilderness Historical Fiction Series for Adults
4 books

The Sheltering Stones Historical Fiction Series for Adults
5 books

The Trilogy of Wishbone Hollow Historicial Fiction Series for Adults
3 books